FELLOW
TRAVELERS

FELLOW TRAVELERS

Alex Beam

ST. MARTIN'S PRESS / *New York*

Design by Janet Tingey

Library of Congress Cataloging-in-Publication Data

Beam, Alex.
    Fellow travelers.

    "A Thomas Dunne Book"
    I. Title.
PS3552.E145F4   1987   87-16423
ISBN 0-312-00001-4

First Edition

10 9 8 7 6 5 4 3 2 1

To MVK and KOL, with love

FELLOW
TRAVELERS

1 / *Fear of Flying*

I am a nervous flyer, and this particular Aeroflot jetliner didn't bolster my confidence. The wings seemed swept too far back, like on one of those Beast or Bear bombers the Russians are always sending over Alaska to terrorize the Eskimos. The hairline cracks running through the cabin walls were no advertisement for the USSR's internal aircraft manufacturing monopoly, nor did the sporadic gestures of service on the part of the bullish *styuardessy* assuage me. Just after we inched upward off the runway in Frankfurt, I asked a flight attendant for a copy of our magazine, which has several European editions.

"Repeat the name, please."

I recited the title slowly.

"Is bourgeois or democratic press?" Though far from pretty—she had twirled her tinted brown hair into two buns that stuck to her ears like muddy doughnuts—this woman must have scored high on the political reliability index.

"American magazine. News. Photo-camera." I wiggled my index finger over an imaginary shutter release. Doughnut Ears disappeared and returned with a soggy copy of *Soviet Friendship*, a magazine "devoted to improving understanding between peoples," according to the contents page. The lead article, on Soviet-Indian cooperation in copper smelting, sent me right off to sleep.

When I awoke, Russia—a harvest green, late summer Russia—was rising up precipitously to meet me.

From five thousand feet, the country didn't look so bad. Lots of open pastures and sallow fields cut up into little squares like shredded wheat. At the corner of each field stood a tumbledown hutch—where the peasants lived, I supposed. Apart from the stomach-churning descent, there was no indication that we were approaching a city, much less Moscow. That is, until the tape recording began.

"Good afternoon, ladies and gentlemen, . . ." a schoolmarmish voice, speaking English as a third or fourth language, bristled across the scratchy intercom. "We will be landing shortly in the hero city of Moscow, capital of the first in the world peasants' and workers' state." Disturbed by the idea of landing "shortly"—an infelicitous translation for a fearful flyer—I missed the subsequent description of the "epochal October revolution led by V. I. Lenin" blah, blah, blah.

As my crash fantasies abated, I heard the voice describing the various government "organs" headquartered in Moscow—"the State Committee for Peace, the State Committee for Atheist and Antireligious Activities, the State Committee for Combating Zionism . . ." and then blowing a hurricane of meaningless statistics through the tinny loudspeakers: "Just now, Moscow has five hundred forty-six kindergartens, ninety-eight technovocational schools . . ." and so on. After repeating that worrisome phrase about "landing shortly," our invisible tour guide bade us adieu, and reminded us that "picture-taking is strictly forbidden at the Sheremetyevo Aerodrome."

To reinforce this last point, my favorite stewardess

lumbered down the aisle to my seat. "Nichts photo-camera." She waggled her finger sternly. "Verboten."

"Amerikaner," I replied feebly, pointing at myself.

"Nyet photo," she warned grimly, and trudged back to her lair.

Just as she turned away, the plane slammed down on the runway with a heart-stopping crunch. The fuselage started shaking like a Mixmaster as the reverse thrusters tore the jet to a screeching halt a few yards short of a wheat field. In the midst of the whole hor-rifying episode, the stewardess strode calmly to the front of the plane, unperturbed. She was an old hand at landing shortly.

As we taxied past the outlying hangars, I saw why picture-taking might be discouraged. Far from the cen-tral terminal, near the end of an auxiliary runway, Aeroflot was trying to hide the elephants' graveyard of aviation. Airplane parts—not just nuts and bolts, but giant chunks of wing, hideously twisted propellers, slabs of cabin wall that might have been bitten off by a giant metal-eating monster—had been junked willy-nilly inside a hangar, and spilled out over the asphalt perimeter. Two mechanics in black overalls were tour-ing the wreckage, occasionally stopping to kick at a wheel or peer under an engine cowling.

I stroked the shuddering plastic of my airplane cabin with new fondness. There but for the grace of God go we.

As our plane nudged forward to the terminal gate, green-capped border troops cradling tommy guns took up stations alongside the wings. They looked about six-teen years old, and frowned up at us outlanders with the exaggerated seriousness of adolescence. Inside the terminal, more troops, armed with small pistols, led us to a passport control booth where another child in uni-form—the youngest clone of this genetic strain—examined my passport and visa for five full minutes before speaking.

"What is your name?"

"Perkins. It's written on my passport."

As if seeing the document for the first time, the guard pored over my passport for several more minutes and nodded his head. "Da." Then he corrected my pronunciation. "*Pair*kins."

A few moments later, he tossed my papers across the counter and yanked aside a metal gate leading me to the baggage claim area. The Iron Curtain had parted. I had officially landed in Moscow.

After claiming my luggage, I found myself eyeball to eyeball with a gray-suited customs agent who hungrily eyed my bright red Samsonite bags. Rubbing her Ruritanian silver badge like a genie's lamp, she mumbled some perfunctory questions about currencies, then plunged into my flight bag. By chance, she happened upon the latest issue of the magazine.

"Any anti-Soviet material here?" She flipped through the pages quickly, stopping only to ogle the Marlboro Man.

"Nyet."

"You speak Russian?"

"A little."

She put down the magazine and fumbled through the bag for my address book. "Have any friends in Moscow?" She read every page, checking for herself.

"No."

"That is good. Friendships can often lead to unpleasantness." She plopped my address book back in my bag and waved me through to the arrival lounge.

Fuck this, I thought as I plunged into a press of gray-suited East European tourists. I want to go home.

4

2 / New York, New York

The morning I was assigned to Moscow, Sharon woke up first. Sunshine didn't wake her, because no sunshine ever reached the bedroom, which faced onto the brick wall of an abandoned garment factory. It wasn't the car alarms; for the first time in a month, the night had passed peacefully. I could tell—it was anxiety.

"I *hate* the Village! It's so *cramped!*"

She banged her fist on the pillow and jiggled into the bathroom. Was it the Village, or was it me? We both harbored our suspicions.

"Together" only six months, we had already established a morning routine, though of course we wouldn't have called it that. I poured the 100 percent natural cereal; Sharon pushed the oranges through the molded plastic juicer. She milled the Jamaican Blue Mountain; I put Mr. Coffee through his paces. She read the *Times*, I read the *News*. At eight-fifteen, we switched.

We watched "Good Morning America" on even-numbered days, except when David Hartman was sick or on vacation. Then we switched full-time to odd-numbered Jane Pauley until David returned healthy, or with a tan. We never turned on the sound.

"Her hair's just like mine." Sharon pointed her spoon at Miss Teenage America, whose dark bangs parted in the middle of her forehead like a stage curtain.

"You can be Miss Subways," I grunted.

"Jesus, you're hostile." Sharon opened up the real estate advertisements, and stage-whispered co-op prices in Hoboken. I was being encouraged to move, because Sharon hated the Village.

This is how people end up married, I thought. First come the rules about sex (nothing from behind), then rules about the dishwasher (long-stemmed glasses on the lower rack). Next thing you find yourself in a co-op with impossible maintenance payments, betrothed by the Invisible Hand. Gotta have kids—we need the deductions. What awful reasons to be married.

Who set this universe in spin? I did, at an early springtime party on Central Park West. Sharon later admitted she was looking, and I was looking, too. She was wearing a Kermit the Frog for President button. I commented, she commented; we talked. I was a journalist, she worked in publishing. She looked enough like my last girlfriend to send us shooting down Tenth Avenue in a taxicab, kissing hard on the torn vinyl seat. Outside my apartment is where we should have stopped, yellow with passion under the Houston Street sulfur lights, still kissing and rich in expectations.

But of course we didn't stop. Who ever does? We wanted someone. So, as my prudishly promiscuous peers might say, we started "seeing" each other, and, inexorably, The Wheel accelerated at each turn. First dinner and lovemaking twice a week, with Friday and Saturday combined. Around Stanley Cup time the pace quickened. I couldn't leave the television, and Sharon kept me company, reading a book on my lap. By the end of the final series, the Islanders had launched their dynasty, and Sharon needed closet space for her clothes. As she pointed out: "I'm practically *living* here!"

Just after the digital clock in the lower corner of the "Good Morning America" screen registered 8:15, David Hartman started interviewing Julio Iglesias, suspended like a smiling, burnished angel on a television monitor above the studio floor. Behind him, the sun was shining, and the palm trees were swaying, as they always do for Julio. Sharon and I exchanged papers.

"Nothing good."

"Nothing good here, either."

"You're going to miss Grace Slick."

"Where?"

"With David Hartman."

"Again?"

Strange as it may sound, we were doing three things at once: watching television, skimming the papers, and advancing our relationship. That was Sharon's term—she wanted us to "progress." I enjoyed the sex; the threat of intimacy was something else again. I defended, sometimes vehemently, the status quo.

In the past month, we had added a new morning ritual: Sharon's 8:45 phone call to her mother in Lake Success. One morning I had overslept, and discovered Sharon chatting away on my kitchen phone, making herself at home and me uncomfortable.

"It's just my mother," she whispered, cradling the receiver as she filed her nails. "She wants to know where I am."

From that innocent beginning, an agonizing routine was born. If on any morning Sharon forgot to call, Mrs. Sherwin dialed us at 8:50 to ask what was wrong. The third or fourth week after the calls started, Mrs.

Sherwin finally got what she wanted—me on the other end of the line.

"You must be Mr. Perkins."

No, I thought, I'm one of Mr. Perkins's white slave clients. He leases your daughter to me three nights a week. . . .

"Yes, I am. Sharon went into work early this morning, Mrs. Sherwin. I think you can reach her there."

"No, that's fine. I'm glad to have the chance to chat with you."

"I'd love to, but I have to get to work myself. We publish today, and—"

"Oh, yes, your magazine. Sharon has told me. I'm afraid I don't read it." To soften the offense, she quickly added, "But I do see it at the hairdresser's. Lots of pictures. Very snazzy."

"We like to think of it as readable, Mrs. Sherwin."

"Yes, I'm sure it is. But tell me, Mr. Perkins, how are you and my daughter getting along?"

"I think we're getting along fine, Mrs. Sherwin."

"You know she's a wonderful, wonderful girl, Mr. Perkins. Very sensitive, too."

The silence became embarrassingly long. "Yes, I agree, Mrs. Sherwin, she is."

Another pause.

"Well, do you think you're making some progress?"

So this is where it was coming from.

"Progress toward what, Mrs. Sherwin?"

"You know, toward a more substantive relationship, something beyond mere cohabitation." She talked slowly, coughing up each syllable as if trying to explain a complicated idea to a child. "Perhaps toward engagement, and ultimately marriage."

Mercifully, the microwave oven began to beep, telling me yesterday's coffee was now warm enough to drink. I jammed the phone receiver up against the oven and shouted into the pulsating din. "Mrs. Sher-win! I can hardly hear you! The smoke detector's gone off! I'm going to evacuate the apartment now!" Slamming the receiver into the wall mount, I fled to the subway.

In the long run, of course, there was to be no escape. Sharon continued providing her mother with "progress reports" on our relationship. There was some flattery in it for me; I heard myself described as "charming," "talented," and "caring." But always at a price: the necessity to "progress," as if we were a pair of chimpanzees with higher evolutionary expectations.

Just a few days ago, Sharon had returned from her weekly visit to her mother, who firmly planted the seed of the engagement idea in the fertile soil of her daughter's mind. Now Sharon had begun pressing me for a date.

I turned up the volume dial on the TV. Julio was flashing those phosphorescent choppers and rhapsodizing about his good friend Weelee Nell-son.

"Ni-i-i-ck! Don't do that!"

"But we agreed not to talk about marriage for a while."

"Nick, we'd only be engaged."

"But it's engaged to be married. People would expect us to set a wedding date."

"No they wouldn't."

"This is your mother's idea, isn't it?"

Sharon's eyes flickered guiltily. "Nick, please don't be upset. She just wants us to advance our relationship."

"I want to stand still for a while."

Sharon stroked my arm across the kitchen table. "You're so prickly. You refuse to imagine any future for us."

"I can imagine a very unhappy future if we rush into something like marriage."

After a lengthy silence, Sharon reached over and shut off the TV. "You haven't forgotten the other thing, have you?"

Just the night before, we had quarreled over use of the television. I wanted to watch the All-Star game—after all, Linda Ronstadt was singing the national anthem—but between innings, sometimes even between pitches, Sharon insisted on flipping the channel back to a molasses-paced BBC "drama" on public television. In the end, no one was satisfied. While Sharon ogled the snot-nosed Edwardians, I missed the game-winning double steal. Cowering from my holocaust of anger, Sharon missed the purported "climax" of her program. Then she began to rant and insisted I buy a second television, or a Betamax, to prevent a rerun of the evening's histrionics. Having stonewalled the engagement, I had agreed to buy the Betamax, which would squander only my entire savings, and not my entire life.

This morning, I had already forgotten my promise.

"The Betamax, you loon. Come here and give me a kiss."

She kissed beautifully, wrapping her arms around my head, then pulling me to her breasts. And I loved the straight drop of her black hair behind her head, which I was allowed to caress only very gently after she had brushed it through.

I stroked the back of her head. When could I tell her I was unhappy? What could I tell her I was unhappy with? It would have to wait.

Journalism has its nooks and crannies, and I was filling one of them. My job title was "staff writer;" I wrote the sections of the magazine that most people thought came out of a machine. I had prided myself on my flair for writing captions and headlines until Sharon expressed amazement that human beings performed such work. "I thought they came *with* the story . . ." she confessed to me one evening.

For two years I had also excelled at obituaries, those fifteen-line blurbs we placed inside the back cover if some ad salesman failed to meet his quota. Now, for the third consecutive month, I was "editing" the Letters section. Each morning in my windowless office, some goblin from the mail room poured an avalanche of envelopes across my desk, leaving me to ferret out the messages from the handful of readers who hadn't forgotten how to write English.

To expedite my task, I had devised a system of culling postmarks. First off, I threw away all the California mail. Judging from the letters, their schools had phased out English courses in the early 1960s. And I had memorized the illiterate ZIP codes of New York, where derelicts must have brought the magazine home at the end of a day's housebreaking in the East Village. Our obsession with "personality" journalism angered the slum dwellers, or else provoked their sense of injustice. One letter writer from Flatbush mockingly inquired what *he* would have to do to merit a write-up in our pages. I was tempted to suggest some surefire publicity stunts, like seizing power in a small African country, marrying Mia Farrow, or squeezing a continuous line of spermicidal jelly from the Yukon to Punta del Este. Happily, judgment triumphed over impulse, and I threw his letter away.

On top of this morning's pile, a new twist: a letter *from* the editor, scrawled on his personalized memo paper—"See me."

Strolling down the corridor to Jonas's office, I riffled through my file of expectations. Gaffes, foul-ups? Not since I had jumbled some caption materials late one Friday night, and credited Venezuela's new president with the lowest ERA of any rookie pitcher in National League history. That incident was ancient history. A staff cutback? Quite the contrary—we had just been acquired by a deep-pocketed conglomerate determined to transform us into a "hard news" magazine, or bust our budgets trying. Like children in a candy store, we were indulging the kind of journalistic excess that had long been the preserve of our broadcast colleagues. Fact-checkers were flying first class to war zones to confirm body counts; instead of scarfing cream cheese sandwiches at their desks, editors were feasting on hundred-dollar lunches at The Four Seasons and Le Cirque. Suddenly anything seemed possible. On a whim, I had even applied for a foreign correspondent's job.

Why did Jonas want to see me?

I loitered outside his door until he looked up from his papers and motioned me in. "Ah! Perkins! Come in, come in."

Jonas was a friendly, decent man—an unlikely choice to be editor of a national magazine. At one of his foreign postings, he had acquired an English accent, half-frame glasses, and a Sherlock Holmes pipe that drooped like the elbow joint of a wash basin. With his spectacles, his musty halo of aromatic tobacco, and his unthreatening demeanor, he had floated to the top of the editorial masthead like a hot air balloon.

We chatted. He knew me, sort of. I was one of the drones down the hall who ran copy through his office for approval, broke an occasional story, goofed an occasional caption. There were a lot of us, packed into dimly-lit cubicles half a football field away from the plush-carpeted tranquility of the top editors' offices. Around Christmastime, we were called "the life-blood of the magazine." Jonas had my personnel file open in front of him, with my memo mentioning an overseas assignment on the top. He patted it tenderly.

"I've been looking at your record. You've been coming along nicely. Salary OK, I hope?"

I nodded.

"No problems down there in the engine room?"

"Not really."

"Good, good." He slid his half-frames up his nose. He ran his fingers around the edge of my memorandum. "Like to go abroad, I see?"

On his anglicized palate, my ambition sounded paltry. "Yes," I replied, fidgeting a little. "I mean, as a kind of career goal with the magazine."

"Did you have any place in mind?"

I glanced up at the map of the world hanging behind his desk. Jonas had placed red-topped stick pins in the few countries where we had correspondents in place. There was plenty of territory left. "I don't know, Europe, the Far East . . . maybe the Mediterranean. I understand how OPEC works." I had just paid my Con Ed bill.

"Single?"

"Absolutely."

"Plans in that direction?"

I thought of Mrs. Sherwin. "Oh, no."

Jonas shifted in his chair, and shuffled some papers in my file. "We may have something interesting for you." The way he said it, "interesting" sounded like a girl from MIT with two heads and bottle glasses.

"Know any languages?"

"French. I spent my junior year of college in Paris. Studying, sort of."

Jonas lifted his eyebrows just slightly, as if to say,

I know what college boys do in Paris. "Like to go back?"

I practically lunged across the desk at him. "Sure!" That sounded overeager, unprofessional. "I mean, yes, certainly."

"Hmmm. Maybe we can work something out down the line." I got the message: That's the carrot. Here's the stick.

Jonas leaned back in his chair. "According to your resumé, you know Russian."

"Well, we were taught it in the army. For spying, electronic eavesdropping type stuff. I never really learned it."

"How is your Russian?"

This conversation had just banked sharply to the north. I tried to head back toward the equator. "Not as good as my Spanish." Which I was learning from subway advertisements each morning.

"Can you speak it? Russian, I mean."

I remembered the cheer from last year's Soviet-Canadian hockey clash. *"Da, da, Ca-na-da! Nyet, nyet, Sov-i-yet!"*

"Sounds very professional."

Maybe I had been watching too many "Late Show"s after Sharon fell asleep. We have a light plane waiting on a small airstrip along the Finnish border. Black parachutes, of course. And you'll want these capsules in the event of capture. Remember to bite down hard.

Jonas tapped his pipe against the side of his wastebasket. He was starting in on the Pipe Trick, not a good sign for me. Jonas had a penchant for delivering bad news while pretending to focus his attention on filling and relighting his pipe. Diffident by nature, he reserved this nonchalant pose for potentially tense conversations. By the time the pipe was lit, you were either fired, promoted, or reassigned.

14

"Nick, let me explain. As well as anyone, you can see the changes going on around here. Our new owners"— to my surprise, Jonas pointed to a freshly hung photo of the new chief executives on his wall—"want to broaden the magazine's coverage. Raise the tone. No more 'Charlie's Angels' covers, if you see what I mean." Step one: He began packing little pinches of tobacco into the pipe bowl, glancing at me as an afterthought.

"They find us too . . . fluffy. Not enough policy analysis, not enough international stuff." Step two: Jonas snapped open his gas lighter and trained his eyes on the bubbling flame in the pipe bowl. "Hmm. Norwegian tobacco. Smoke doesn't bother you?"

I shook my head: no.

"Mmmm. Good. So we've decided to open a Moscow bureau, and we think you might be the fellow for the job." Step three: Jonas snapped shut the silver pipe cap and looked me straight in the eye for the first time. "What do you think?"

This conversation definitely had a compass problem. In another few minutes, I'd be offered the North Pole.

"Wait a minute! Ten minutes ago you hardly even knew who I was!"

"Yes, but just from this brief meeting, I can see that you have the right qualifications."

"Like what?"

Now he was fidgeting, shifting the pipe from hand to hand. Like the guillotine, the Pipe Trick usually cut its victims cleanly. I was expected to pick up my head and go home. Clearly, the new owners wanted to push one of those red-tipped pins into Moscow, and they couldn't care less who went.

"Well, your language seems impressive."

"Begging your pardon!—how the hell would you know?"

Jonas ignored my taunt. "We're prepared to be very

15

generous. Foreign travel budgets, living allowances, expense accounts. . . . If you agree to go for a year, we could try to get you that Paris assignment afterward. . . ." He narrowed his gaze, searching for a response. I glowered.

Unfazed, Jonas leaned across his desk, whispering conspiratorially. "Look, we can crib all the goddam news from the wire services. Just send us the occasional feature, some crap with on-scener feel, you know—Our Man in the Bread Lines—Jesus, my dog could write that stuff! You can screw up all the captions you like. Except for the guy with the eyebrows, Bunthorne, or whatever his name is—"

"Brezhnev."

"Right, except for him, we don't have any idea who counts for what over there."

Catching himself, he sat up straight and regained his composure. "You'll be very popular with our new owners if you accept. And thirteen months from now you'll be walking down the Champs-Elysées, clapped up like a cockatoo and happy as a clam. With plenty of this—" he rolled some imaginary bills in the plan of his hand "—burning a hole in your pocket. How about it?"

"I absolutely refuse. I'd go to Newark first." I hoisted myself out of my chair. "Call me when the owners want to start printing news from a civilized country. I'm heading back to the engine room."

Jonas hopped out from behind his desk to escort me out the door. "Don't make up your mind immediately. Give it some thought." He squeezed my elbow hopefully. "I'm in the phone book, on the Upper East Side. Call me at home if you change your mind."

"No way."

We shook hands.

He mumbled his parting shot: "It would be a lovely escape."

* * *

I spent my lunch hour in Bryant Park, warming my crotch with a hot pastrami sandwich, watching the bums on parade. Daydreaming, I conjured up Russia:

The Bear. The Cossacks. The knout. The Moscow Circus. The Bolshoi Ballet. Give me your poor Baryshnikovs, your tired Nureyevs, yearning to dance Balanchine. I vant to defect.

From my childhood, I remembered Khrushchev visiting Castro at the Hotel Theresa in Harlem, staring out from a sea of black faces as if he had taken the wrong subway. Shoe leather on the podium: Vee vill bury you. Bleep. Bleep. Welcome to the Age of Sputnik. More than ever, they shoved those quadratic equations down our throats. After all, young Ivan's studying his. . . .

Walrus women, chesty generals, military parades, factories with numbers instead of names. Food lines, corruption, special stores. Fat cars for the fat cats, shoes from Poland for the proles. No sausage today, comrades. Meat-processing Kombinat Number Three in the name of K. Y. Voroshilov has failed to achieve Plan. But take heart—fraternal Vietnam has sent us a wagonload of mango skins.

I recalled a Bob Newhart joke about Russia's two-party system: the Communist Party and the Farewell Party. Stalin, the Gulag, the death camps. First thing we do, let's kill all the writers. One gets away. Aleksandr Solzhenitsyn, preaching Holy Russia to Harvard men. Beware: The icepick cometh.

The arts. "Song of the Volga Boatmen"—what a beautiful tune! Ugh-ookh-nyem. Ugh-ookh-nyem. Sung by the Red Army Choir on their smash double album "Christmastime in Kabul." Tchaikovsky, Rimsky-Korsakov, Scriabin and his psychogenic light show. Freak out. Give me your roly-poly Rostropoviches, your second-generation Shostakoviches, longing

17

to play "The Star-Spangled Banner" on the Fourth of July. I luff America. I vant to defect.

Tolstoy, Dostoyevsky, the Soul Brothers. Dead Souls. Doctor Zhivago, *the movie. Spain never looked so soulful. Lara in Siberia, Lara in the streetcar, Lara at the hydroelectric station, a worn-out cog in the socialist machine. But Lara is Julie Christie—she's one of ours.*

Revolution! I loved it in college. First thing we do, let's kill all the opposition. What appealing logic, to an eighteen-year-old. One Party, one paper, one people. Workers' solidarity. Loudspeakers on the beach, microphones in the walls. A stadium full of Olympic Misha bears, chanting in unison: "Or-vell! Or-vell!" The sad man with the pipe, consummately one of ours.

Army Intelligence was where I came closest to the Bear. In anticipation of a European land war, the Signal Intercept Corps was preparing fifteen of us college-educated Vietnam dodgers to monitor radio chatter between Soviet tank commanders and battlefield headquarters. For twelve months, inside a windowless gray box at Bradley Barracks, we studied tape recordings of radio intercepts from Soviet troops parked in East Germany:

> IGOR (from headquarters): See the fucking hockey last night?
> BORIS (from inside a tank): I was on duty all night. Who were we playing?
> IGOR: Fucking Czechs.
> BORIS: How'd we do?
> IGOR: Fucking lost.
> BORIS: To the fucking Czechs?
> IGOR: Fucking believe it.
> BORIS: I'd like to blow their fucking heads off.

We had no idea what they'd be saying in battle. During maneuvers, they turned their radios off.

*　　*　　*

A bedraggled victim of the monopoly capitalists was approaching me for bourgeois charity. What can he expect from the state, the handservant of the exploiting classes?

"You got some change, mister?"

"Yeah, sure."

I parted with two quarters. Don't we know anything *good* about Russia?

Each Wednesday before Sharon's weekly visit to her mother in Lake Success, she and I met for drinks at the Steak 'n Brew in Penn Station. Tonight, Sharon was anxious, molding her fingers around the ashtray, and twirling the matchbooks on the table top. Like some hideous python, the idea of our becoming engaged was wrapping itself around her, coil by slimy coil, reinforced just this afternoon by an hour-long "phone date" with her mother.

"Nick, we've got to grow up. We've got to show some confidence in our relationship."

During the intervening silence, I swallowed half my scotch and water while Sharon nursed a pink gin fizz. The daytime Sharon, neatly tailored in a dark suit with angled collars, was as beautiful as the night version. She looked like an advertisement for women's briefcases—cool, self-confident, and professional. She didn't look like my future wife.

"What should I tell my mother, Nick?"

"About what?"

"About us. What should I tell her?"

"Tell her we're mixed up kids. Tell her I'm gay. Just don't tell her we're getting married."

"Engaged."

"Don't tell her anything."

"She's going to ask why not."

19

"Because I'm not ready."

Sharon squeezed my hands across the tiny table. "Nick, how do you know? We're happy, aren't we?"

I waved for a second scotch.

I stared into her eyes. "Of course we're happy. But I can't go any further right now." I pounced on the scotch the moment it alighted. "I'm not a very emotional person, Sharon. It takes me a long time to feel deeply about something, or someone. I just can't get too close to anyone too quickly." There was some truth in all this.

I can't remember why I blurted out the next sentence. In a trial, I would have pleaded temporary insanity. "Maybe it would be better if we spent some time apart."

Was Jonas looking over my shoulder? How did he know this would happen?

Sharon withdrew her hands. "Do you want me to move out?"

"No, no. Maybe I should leave for a while. Just to give us a little breathing room. Some time to think things through."

"Think what through?"

"You know, this engagement idea."

In my attempt to defend the status quo, I had unwittingly gone on the offensive. Sharon recoiled in her chair and raised her eyebrows suspiciously. "What are you talking about?"

"I don't know. There's a chance I might be going overseas."

"Did you get that foreign assignment?"

"Not really. Well, sort of. I haven't accepted it."

"To where?"

Now I was fidgeting, and I didn't even have any scotch to swish around in my glass.

"I don't think you'll believe me if I tell you."

"Try me."

I swallowed hard. "Moscow."

"Russia?" Sharon whistled softly. "You must have messed up a lot of captions." She ran her index finger around the circumference of her glass. "You're joking, right?"

"No, I'm serious. It's some scheme to suck up to the magazine's new owners. They pulled resumés and saw that I knew Russian. I would only have to stay a year. Jonas is offering me a raise and a job in Paris if I survive."

"What are you going to do?"

"I don't know. I wanted to talk to you."

"Why me?"

Because weren't we lovers, friends even, just a few days ago, before we got bogged down in these ridiculous contract negotiations? "Because I care what you think."

"If you went, what would happen to us?"

I resisted the temptation to crunch the remaining ice cubes between my molars. "I don't know about us."

Sharon stared at me, her eyes glistening, as if she already missed me. In her mind, the curtain had descended on our affair. For no reason she could understand, our relationship had died, and she was sad.

"Oh." She stood up, straightened her clothes, and shouldered her overnight bag. I walked her down to the train platform. We didn't speak. She let her hair swing forward so I couldn't see her crying. Head bent, she darted into the coach. "At least I'll have something to tell my mother."

Just as I was falling asleep, the phone rang. Still drowsy, I shambled into the kitchen. Mrs. Sherwin's voice screeched down the line like a wire-guided missile. I woke up fast.

"Is that you?"

I had exhausted my supply of sarcastic comments. "It's me, Mrs. Sherwin." Guilty as charged.

"Sharon went to bed half an hour ago, Mr. Perkins, and I can still hear her crying. Listen—" For a few moments, there was no sound from the receiver. Then across a bedroom wall and all the way from Long Island I heard Sharon's muffled wailing, and her gasping for breath.

"How does that make you feel, Mr. Perkins?"

"Very sad, and very tired, Mrs. Sherwin. I'm not worth all this. I want to go to bed."

"You feel no regret, no anguish?"

Oh, God. To think this woman might have been my mother-in-law.

"I feel very sorry all this is happening, Mrs. Sherwin."

"Why aren't you crying."

"I don't cry."

That was not the answer she expected. After several seconds of silence, she came back on the line.

"Maybe you should do some rethinking, Mr. Perkins. I think it's time you looked deep inside yourself. You seem like a very cruel and indifferent young man."

Clack. She rang off.

I was rethinking, very, very hard. After five minutes I dialed Jonas at home, and told him to sign me up for Moscow.

Why don't I cry? At an early age, I was instructed not to. My father was an airline pilot, at home three days a week and routing around the country for the other four. His schedule always varied. Some nights I would wake up unexpectedly, to find him standing alone above me, gazing down at my bed with a dreamy, forlorn look, holding a small suitcase in his hand. On other evenings he would push through the front door at dinnertime, just like a real father coming home from work, except that he always carried the suitcase, and brought home gifts like a toy San Francisco cable car, or a plastic St. Louis arch, as symbols of his perpetual farawayness.

As a young boy, I cried every time he left. Starting around age three, my mother slapped my face to stop my tears. "Never, *never* cry," she insisted, voicing the words like a nursery rhyme I would never forget. "Never, *never* cry."

And after the age of about four, I never cried again.

When I was twelve, I never cried during the three months when my father failed to return from one of his assignments. I didn't cry when my mother sat me and my brother down at the dinner table and solemnly informed us that daddy had been in an accident and wouldn't be coming home any more. My little brother burst into tears. My mother gazed straight into my eyes, and I nodded affirmation of our secret pact: never, never cry.

Ever since my younger brother graduated from college, my mother had been living in a high-rise apartment building in Anacostia, Virginia, across the river from the Lincoln Memorial. During the past two years, she had begun sampling the religious doctrines of her neighbors, many of whom were older widows like herself. She once confessed to me that she was hoping to "reach" my father, who had been reported missing in a single-engine training plane, and was never found.

Most recently, she had been "checking out" the Baha'i faith, prodded by the widow of an army colonel. The word "immanence" had crept into her vocabulary, as a synonym for "inherent." Ronald Reagan, she told

23

me, was "immanently" stupid. Sharon's longing for marriage was "immanently" within her. For several months, my mother had been reporting "feelings" from my father's "shadow" in the Other World.

Over the phone, she sounded intrigued by the idea of my traveling to Moscow.

"My son the foreign correspondent! Sounds great!" Bless her soul, she remained indiscriminately loyal. If Jonas had me writing obituaries, my mother read every line, and secretly hoped that more world-class personalities would "pass on," to showcase my talents. If I was editing letters, she memorized excerpts and quoted them to me over the phone. I told her I wouldn't be able to fly down to Washington before I left—I was calling to say goodbye.

She sighed. "Well, all right. I'll miss you, sweetheart. Don't forget to have fun."

"Mom, I'm going to Russia, not Miami Beach. It's a form of punishment. It was either this or get married."

"Don't be silly, that nice Sharon will be waiting for you when you get back. And I'm sure you'll have a good time over there."

"It'll only last a year, at least."

"Nick, you'll do fine. Besides, Russia's a very interesting place." I heard her rustling through some magazines. "In fact, maybe you could look into something for me."

I feared the worst. There was no intellectual cul-de-sac my mother had left unexplored. Kennedy assassination theories, Mormon supremacy theories, Martian control of the FM band theories—she reveled in all of them. She probably had some "information" as to the whereabouts of the lost princess Anastasia.

"You remember the flashing white bugs John Glenn saw outside his space capsule?"

"Mom, I was only ten years old."

I heard more paper shuffling. My mother was rooting through her trove of oddball periodicals. "Yes, here it is. Illuminophosphorescence. That's what the Russians call it. They think it might be alive." The line went silent for a few moments. "It might be intelligent life, Nick."

I tapped my shoe against a kitchen cabinet. "Someone's knocking at the door, Mom, I'm going to have to go."

"Well, all right. Stay in touch. Make us proud of you."

"Is there someone in the room with you?"

My mother started humming softly. "I think your father's nearby." She paused. "Yes, he is."

"Mother, I have to go now."

"Well, say hello to Sharon. Do be careful. Remember what they did to Gary Powers." She squeezed a kiss into the receiver, and hung up before I could ask what they did to Gary Powers.

The Moscow logistics were moving forward more quickly than planned. Our accreditation, which Jonas had requested long before he had a body to fill the job, was approved. A lengthy telex from the press department of the USSR Ministry of Foreign Affairs explained that I could assume my duties immediately, and take over the office and apartment of another American reporter who had just been expelled, "at the request of local citizens' groups."

"Who says they don't have a democracy?" Jonas mused. He handed me the telex, pointing to the bottom of the page. "There you go. New address and all. They're even giving you a translator, a citizen Nikolayev. Probably some KGB dolly."

He raised his eyebrows suggestively.

The magazine gave me a week off, and a few hundred dollars in expenses, to brush up my Russian. I bought some language cassettes and listened to them on my

Walkman while lounging in Central Park. Pyotr and Nikolai complaining about the luncheon menu ("What the devil! Fish soup and buckwheat groats again!") didn't sound much like my friends in the tanks, but my ear was still good. If I took the lengthy vacations Jonas was promising, I might last out the year.

My last two weeks with Sharon had more in common with our six months of protracted emotional haggling than with our thirty seconds of genuine feeling at the Steak 'n Brew. Each day we took a step toward striking the set, dismantling our tenuous relationship drawerful by drawerful. Sharon's effects, and finally Sharon herself, migrated back to her apartment uptown. We still lived together, but not every night.

I proposed that she come visit me on her next vacation, and assembled some travel brochures with excursions that seemed reasonably priced. Sharon feigned interest, in the desultory spirit of her abandonment. Maybe, maybe.

Several evenings before my departure, she left me during a party to spend an hour dancing with an "old college friend." As they parted, I saw him jot down her phone number and kiss her on the cheek. Now I was sad.

Walking home, she acted happy for the first time since I had announced my departure.

"What a coincidence, bumping into Jimmy!"

"The timing couldn't be any better."

"Now look who's hurt." She squeezed my hand. Sharon was going to be fine. *I* was going to be lonely.

3 / *First Things*

Standing alone in the Sheremetyevo arrival lounge, I felt like a jet-lagged periwinkle, washed over by successive waves of gray-suited Eastern Bloc tourists. One glance at the schedule board convinced me that I had been red-pinned into the wrong hemisphere. All the flights departing Moscow were heading for places one could spend a lifetime avoiding: Tripoli, Poznan, Grodz. A hand squeezing my elbow rescued me from my snowballing sense of self-pity. Turning around, I found a tall young man dressed in a blue suit, smiling at me through a line of teeth frequently interrupted by silver.

"Mr. Pairkins?"

"Perkins."

"Yes. I am Boris Nikolayev, your translator."

"Ah, yes." The KGB dolly. We shook hands.

"How did you recognize me?"

He picked up one of my bags, and bulled us through the clumps of tourists clogging the lounge. "I have seen your picture. In your magazine." I didn't recall my picture ever being in the magazine.

Crossing the parking lot, Boris explained that he worked for the press department of the Ministry of Foreign Affairs, even though he was nominally in my employ. His job was to "facilitate me" in my work as a correspondent. He mumbled a vague sort of thumbnail biography: After graduating from "foreign language academy"—his English was halting and archaic—he had spent several years pursuing "practical work," the nature of which he never divulged. Maybe he had been listening to tapes of GIs bitching about their favorite baseball teams. He casually mentioned that he had worked for my "predecessor," the correspondent who had just been expelled.

"A very bad man," he muttered.

"How so?" I had switched into Russian.

"His work featured only the dark side of Soviet reality."

I wondered if he had ever written about Aeroflot. Where would one look to find the bright side? "Oh, really. Why was he expelled?"

"Local citizens demanded it. The foreign ministry had no choice in the matter." Boris rested my bag on the ground for a moment. "You speak Russian quite well. Where did you study?"

"I learned it while doing practical work." I saw a quick grin flash across his face. "Maybe I won't need a translator."

Boris shook his head fiercely. "All correspondents need translators," he insisted. "It's the law."

We dropped the bags next to a car resembling a squared-off version of the old Ford Fairlane. Before prying open the trunk, Boris petted the fender. "A Soviet Volga. Original design. Our office car." Inside, he had screwed a polished leather Alfa Romeo knob onto the gearshift. "Drives like an Alfa," he explained, chugging out of the parking lot.

The ride into town picked up where the plane flight left off. We were still in the country, surrounded by uncut fields of wheat and barley, with occasional one-story peasant houses scattered along the roadside. After a few miles, we met the first sentries of the Soviet state—huge agitational billboards, larger than any pro-motion-mad capitalist would dare erect. The messages were admittedly wacky: "Comecon—Mutual Economic Achievement for Peace," or "Peoples of Africa! A Res-olute No! to Imperialist Meddling!" After a few more miles, the countryside ended, and we plunged into a thicket of twenty-story lookalike housing develop-ments.

The view was Village Modern. The homogeneous apartment blocks provided the ideal backdrop for the planned society, but the extras hadn't seen the script. In a parking lot between two high-rises, a man and a woman were scuffling next to a beer stall. The lot was empty because a truck had dumped a load of melons across the entrance. While a line of cars honked madly, an old grandmother in a gray apron was calmly selling off the stack of melons to a long line of customers. Consumerism, Soviet style.

A fifty-foot-tall statue of a Red Army soldier "wel-comed" us to the city proper. The mood sobered. The highway became a tree-lined avenue thick with shop-pers and urban wanderers. Suddenly stores appeared, labeled with childishly generic signs: Bread, Household Goods, Spirits. Some stores were empty, while others spilled out lines halfway down the block.

Disguised as a city, the village was thinly veiled: Huge crowds swarmed against red lights, hauling knapsacks full of canned goods and produce past po-licemen red in the face from whistle-blowing. In front of a shoe store, a blonde toddler dressed in a sailor suit was being passed back and forth above the heads of a crowd locked outside the door. Finally the child plum-meted into the arms of a woman, presumably its mother. A people ruled but unruly.

"Gorky Street," Boris announced proudly. "Like your Broadway."

"Have you seen Broadway?"

"I've seen pictures. In your magazine." He allowed himself an ironical smile. As we drove, Boris began reciting his own version of the Aeroflot welcome-to-Moscow recording, highlighting local government "organs"—the Moscow City Soviet, the State Committee on Tourism, etc. Suddenly, the boulevard plunged downhill, and he pointed through the windshield. "The Kremlin."

Indeed, there they were, the thick red brick towers with the pointy tops, screening the view of the swirling soft-ice-cream domes at St. Basil's Cathedral. The Statue of Liberty with horns and cleft feet. I had arrived.

Boris jerked the car right on to Fiftieth Anniversary Square ("anniversary of the first in the world workers' and peasants' revolution," he reminded me) and headed up an avenue lined with glass and steel skyscrapers, which I later learned was the only modern-looking boulevard in the city, Kalinin Prospect. "Now I'll take you home."

We crossed over the Moscow river, and passed a hideous wedding-cake skyscraper, the Hotel Ukraine. Across Kutuzov Prospect, the largest foreigners' colony in Moscow squatted like a dirty yellow ocean liner trapped in the mud. We made a U-turn, and drove in.

I knew I hadn't held out for enough money as Boris piloted the car through the single entrance into the block-long row of apartment buildings. Gray-jacketed policemen hovering around a square guardbox controlled access in and out. One of the officers recognized Boris and waved us by with a salute. As we drove off toward "Korpus D," I saw a guard check our license plate and scribble some notes in a book.

Boris escorted me to my entryway, unpacked the trunk, and bowed an awkward farewell. "We meet tomorrow," he said. It sounded like a threat.

Inside my stairwell, I met Ekaterina Sergeyevna, the regime's second line of defense. A fat, jowly pensioner, she cheerily explained that her job was to "monitor" the entryway.

"I sit downstairs, to make sure no one comes to steal your valuable possessions." She began tossing my suitcases into the elevator, eyeing them hungrily. Once she had wedged herself in among my luggage, there was barely enough room for me to squeeze in against the wall.

"I don't have any valuable possessions."

"Others do. So monitoring is necessary." She clucked like a genuine babushka, wrapped in a dirty shawl, wiggling her finger authoritatively.

"Are you married?"

"No."

"Aha! Maybe you will meet a nice Russian girl."

Not bloody likely, with you squatting like a toadstool in my stairwell.

"Here you are. Fifth floor." She held the elevator door while I wrestled with my luggage. "Your apartment—" she pointed to a door and handed me what looked like a set of duplicate keys, "—and your neighbors."

I saw an Arabic bumper sticker pasted above one door. "Fraternal radio correspondent from developing nation," Sergeyevna said, approvingly. Just as she spoke, the door opened an inch, and immediately closed, revealing only a yellow opal eye.

On the third door of the landing, I noticed a small British flag decal. "Who's over there?"

Sergeyevna waved her hand in disgust. "British spy,"

she grunted. "Enemy of the people." Worthy of extra "monitoring," I could tell.

Sergeyevna waddled back into the elevator, and descended. I unlocked my door, and entered my new home.

The apartment was huge, ravaged by children and the indifference of a hasty departure. Red and blue finger paints covered one bedroom, which stank of Play-Doh. In the parents' room, dresses and shirts were strewn around on the closet floor. Three empty bottles of vodka lay in the wastebasket, buried in a mound of cigarette butts.

I hiked across the oversized kitchen expanse to the refrigerator. Inside, I found a bottle of ketchup, four stinking eggs, and a note, drunkenly scrawled in magic marker. "To Whom It May Concern: Abandon Hope, All Ye Who Enter Here." Beneath an illegible signature the writer had added a final thought. "P.S. The eggs may be rotten. Welcome to Moscow."

I fell asleep in my clothes, exhausted from jet lag. In the middle of the night, shouts from the sidewalk woke me up. Two drunks in blotchy gray suits were careening along the river embankment, waving half-empty bottles at the night sky, screaming "God! God! Want a drink?" They paused for a moment, cocking their ears to the emptiness of the heavens, and the silence of the slow-moving city river.

The drunks staggered together and consulted. One rapped his finger excitedly against his chest and on his comrade's chest. Then he pointed straight up and shrugged. "*I'm* drunk, *you're* drunk, but *He's* still sober," I imagined him saying. In tandem, they bent backward to rocket their bottles straight up to the sky.

"Here you go, God," they yelled. "Drink up!"

Each ran off in a different direction. One tripped on

the curb and narrowly missed being run over by a solitary taxi speeding back to the garage. One bottle, pinwheeling, twisted a watery contrail of vodka across the dim sky, and shattered on the roadway. The other looped a long parabola, then banked away from God, dying in the river with a muffled splash.

Had I dreamed it? I couldn't remember by ten o'clock, when Boris phoned to say he was coming over. Five minutes later I found him slouched against my doorjamb, preening in his designer safari jacket from Bangladesh. He whispered conspiratorially that he had spent the early morning practicing his English with the help of the "Voice of America." "I haff come for office escort," he boomed proudly. Feeble from too much sleep, I dressed quickly and followed him out the door, on the condition that we speak only Russian for my first few weeks.

To reach the office, just a few hundred yards away in the same compound, we walked onto the street and re-entered foreigners' Korpus V through a second guarded checkpoint. According to a metal plaque outside the entryway, we shared the stairwell with the Bulgarian Telegraph Agency and the USSR-Burma Friendship Society. This must be the low-rent district.

Our two-room "suite" was laid out along caste lines. My room was large, bright, fully carpeted, and outfitted by the previous correspondent with stylish furniture imported from Austria. Boris inhabited an adjoining cubicle, ill-lit and darkened by colorless Soviet furnishings. His puce-colored walls were bare.

Boris steered me around my desk, showing me stationery, office supplies, and forms I would need to fill out. He flipped my desk calendar forward to my first appointments. "Tomorrow night there is a reception for the foreign community at the British Embassy. And an official of the foreign ministry press department invites you to lunch next Friday, at the Hotel Peking."

"Oh. Thank you."

He shuffled away, and left me sitting behind the desk.

I spent an hour and a half looking through a stack of Soviet magazines, and then perused a pile of English-language press reviews distributed to correspondents. It was dull stuff, the journalistic rendition of the agit-prop billboards we had seen on the airport road: "Foreign Potentates Praise Kremlin Peace Program"; "Maximal Leader Visits Textile Factory, Urges Un-flinching Efforts on the Garment Front." Boris's unenviable job was to read all this in the original, every day.

The phone rang several times, and Boris answered. A few of the calls were invitations extended to me as the new face on the block. From what I could overhear through the thin plasterboard wall, Boris used the office phone to arrange black-market deals for auto parts, frequently repeating certain ruble sums as "maximum" and "absolute maximum." Once, when I heard him complaining about the unavailability of an East European fan belt, I recognized a phrase from my army days: "Fucking Czechs!"

At noon, Boris dutifully invited me to lunch. I said I'd fend for myself. But where? Drifting past the guards—while one scrawled furiously in a notepad, his companion greeted me by name, showing he had done his homework—I wandered toward the river.

Ten yards after turning the corner onto the embankment, I wondered: Was I being followed? Stealthily, I pretended to read from a movie poster pasted outside a milk store while watching the street from the corner of my eye. For three long minutes, no one rounded the corner. Easily enough time for me to trade microdots with my agent, and whisper a few reassuring words of spy jargon in his—no, her—ear. Finally a middle-aged woman pushing a baby carriage turned onto my sidewalk. Her baby started to howl, and she buried her head in the carriage. I felt a glancing blow to my self-esteem. Maybe I wasn't worth following.

Further down the embankment, I stopped in at the Siberia, a cafeteria featuring *pyelmeny*, pudgy Russian ravioli. Waiting in line with the proletariat, I couldn't help but notice the stench from the bathrooms that permeated the serving area. From inside the kitchen, an obese woman in a soiled white uniform caught my attention by banging her ladle against a cast-iron *pyelmeny* pot that matched her ample dimensions. She was screaming: I had forgotten to pay.

I shared a table with a young man in a tweed cap who had been standing behind me in line. He was bent so low over his food that his bottom lip almost touched the edge of his plate. He appeared to have conducted a personal time and motion study to optimize his eating style. With conveyorlike efficiency, he flicked a fresh dumpling in his mouth every five seconds. I stared, wondering if he was trying to break some record.

"What are you staring at?"

"You're eating very fast."

He glowered and continued his speed eating. I swallowed a few *pyelmeny* and mumbled sounds of approval.

"Very good."

My table companion ignored me. About 100 seconds after sitting down, he had finished his meal.

I decided to extend the hand of friendship across the gulf of ideology and etiquette.

"I'm an American."

He wiped his mouth with his sleeve. "Figures." His trailing leg rattled the rickety plastic table as he bolted for the door.

I ate the rest of the meal alone.

Bottom-heavy with the dumplings and some watery fruit leftovers labeled "kompot," I spent the afternoon reviewing some of Boris's suggestions for stories. As might have been expected, they were suitable for publication in *Soviet Friendship* and boring to a fault. To document one idea, he had included some newspaper articles announcing the completion of the world's tallest dam, in Siberia. Checking in the almanac, I learned that the Brazilians had finished one even larger. Would my mother want to read about the planet's second largest dam?

Before leaving, I cabled the magazine not to expect much in the first weeks, vowing to "gather string on story possibles," which sounded professional. I walked back to the apartment lonely, in the big city kind of way, when you push down avenues jammed with men and women of all ages and wonder: "Isn't there anyone here for me?"

4 / *Rule, Britannia*

I think the British Embassy was the first palace I ever
entered as anything other than a tourist. The gleaming
yellow Empire facade, topped by the Union Jack, sang
out from a line of dingy Soviet ministries slouched
along the river bank opposite the Kremlin. According
to local legend, the foreign ministry had repeatedly offered the Brits more modern and spacious accom-
modations elsewhere in the city. The sight of the
British flag cracking snappily in the river breeze sup-
posedly offended Brezhnev and his cronies, whose
Kremlin suites looked out over the Moskva. Predicta-
bly, this was one outpost of empire John Bull refused
to abandon.

As I approached the embassy, black Mercedeses flying flags of all nations whooshed through the covered
portico at the main entrance, where fresh-faced young
diplomats escorted the ambassadorial flotsam into the
reception. I flashed my invitation and proceeded inside.

The building's interior was even more splendid than
the outside. The party, which seemed more like an
open house judging from the throng, spread through
a succession of elegant, mahogany-paneled libraries,
each one jammed with serious-looking men and women

locked in conversation, sipping drinks, and simultaneously scanning the crowd for someone more interesting to talk to. I felt right at home; we might have been in Manhattan.

A squadron of barrel-chested Colonel Blimps paraded through the reception rooms, jangling their chestfuls of medals, greeting guests, and shaking hands. Each successive greeter pumped my hand, mumbling, "Marvelous, simply marvelous, isn't it?" What was so marvelous, I inquired of the fourth Pneumatic Hand. Didn't I know? We were celebrating Great Britain's Armed Forces Day. So delighted I could come, along with England's 1500 closest friends in Moscow. I had no regrets: Trays of red and black caviar mounted on white-jacketed retainers (could the British still hire serfs, I wondered?) sailed past and docked in front of me almost every other minute. A diplomatic career seemed an alluring option.

In the room farthest from the entryway, I found the bar. There, hanging together like shipwreck victims clinging to a life raft, I found a half-dozen members of the Moscow press corps. I introduced myself, and they each nodded me welcome, gulping the names of their publications.

One of my newfound colleagues remumbled the name of my employer and jabbed his old-fashioned glass in my direction. "This superpower stuff doesn't seem like your side of the street, buddy." In his gravelly, wire-service patois, he was alluding to the magazine's reputation for cheap sensationalism, developed before our new owners decided to "raise the tone." Although we had sent twenty-three reporters and photographers to cover Elvis Presley's funeral—and fully intended to be first with the story of the King's second coming—we hadn't exactly won our spurs in overseas reporting.

"We're trying to spread our wings a little, go after some of the bigger international stories," I explained.

My questioner scoffed. "'UFOs over the Kremlin' is a bit more your line, isn't it?"

"Not at all." In fact, our main competitor had scooped us on that story and slapped it on their cover.

After a few pleasantries, and several invitations to stop by their respective bureaus for a drink, the assembled correspondents resumed the activity that I had interrupted: grumbling. The Soviet Union was no longer a front page story, and it pissed them off. Many had staked their careers on covering the long-awaited leadership "succession," but no one was succeeding. The Kremlin story read like a script from "General Hospital"—all the top leaders were ill, but no one ever died. The gerontocracy was clinging fast to its American-made life-support systems, and reporters who had uprooted their families to bag a Pulitzer covering the "post-Brezhnev" era found themselves mired in the senescent, liver-spotted politics of the do-nothing ancien régime. Brezhnev, or someone who looked remarkably like him, was still wheeled out to burble a few lines on state occasions, like Police Day, or the monthly pin-the-medal-on-the-cosmonaut ritual.

Along with the top leadership, Moscow's other "money" stories had also lapsed into a coma. The dissenters had been shipped to faraway penal zones, and, except for the occasional state visits by Third World eminentoes begging military hardware, foreign affairs were at a standstill. Under the circumstances, expulsion would be a good career move, but the Soviets wouldn't kick out just anyone. The previous occupant of my apartment, I learned, had beaten up a policeman who tried to confiscate his camera for photographing a line outside a meat store.

Disconsolate, the newspaper people complained their stories were appearing "next to the crossword."

"That's the section my mother turns to first," I chirped.

"Fuck your mother," the wire service man replied, rattling the ice in his empty glass.

Another scribe related the sad story of Roy, a recently departed colleague. Roy had devoted two years of evening courses to studying Russian, and hoped Moscow would be a stepping-stone to the foreign editor's job at a prestigious daily newspaper. He had just ended his three-year tour and departed for his next assignment: Africa.

"Black Africa," one of the mourners added sorrowfully.

"Poor bastard." Another colleague wearily tapped his glass on the bar for a refill. Just thinking of Roy, surrounded by balloon-bellied drought victims and U.N. do-gooders, he shuddered fiercely. "Arrrrgh."

Indeed, Roy's story had so shaken him that he teetered sideways, toward me. I hopped backward one full step, bumping an innocent bystander behind me. I turned to apologize, but the offended party, a young woman in a bright green cocktail dress, had turned around first.

"Watch yourself, Yank. You're not in the colonies any more." She was rubbing a cocktail napkin across the front of her dress, where her drink had spilled. Without looking up, she held out her glass. "Would you mind? Or are you too engrossed with the hacks?" She flashed a brief, condescending smile.

"I'm a hack. As you call them."

"Yes, I can tell."

"Is it so easy?"

"In this room, yes, luvvy, it is. Because you don't look like you've just had an enema, all right? Now run along and get me another beer, will you?"

40

Knowing as little as I did about the English, I wondered if she had complimented me. Do they like enemas? Back at the bar, I noticed that the clutch of correspondents had disbanded, fanning out to work the reception. My British friend seemed happy enough to see a full glass of beer, even though it reappeared attached to me. The couple she had been chatting with politely excused themselves.

"They don't like journalists," she stage-whispered behind her hand.

"Who does?"

"Their mothers, I suppose. Someone has to." She looked me up and down, from my splotchily polished loafers, along the rumpled lines of my only suit, to my unstyled hair, still waiting for its first encounter with Soviet barberdom. "You don't look so bad." She swallowed a mouthful of beer. "Who do you work for?"

Happily she hadn't heard of us. In elevated terms, I explained our editorial mission.

"Sounds a bit like a comic strip. But I'm sure it's just lovely." She peered around the room like a girl attending her first college dance, then frowned. "Same old lot."

"What do you do?"

"Can't really tell you. You being a Yank and all." She smiled quickly, showing me an active pair of dimples hiding in her fleshy, freckled cheeks. "I'm a sort of librarian."

"You don't dress like a librarian."

She spun around on her toes, showing off a neat pair of calves wrapped in green tights streaked with golden tinsel. "Do you like the outfit? My mum just sent them over."

"It's not very bookish." The skirt barely touched her knees.

"This is a party, silly. I can wear what I want."

Her name was Susan Islington, and she never did

41

tell me what her job was. She was no diplomat, nominally or otherwise. Discreetly pointing with her pinky finger, she offered me the Cook's tour of the Moscow luminaries at the party.

Just emerging from the men's room, a charcoal black diplomat in a tight-fitting cotton suit giddily surveyed the chatting crowd. "Sampson, of course, Jamaican cultural attaché. Imports ganja by the kilo in the diplomatic bag. The Russians turn a blind eye, lay it all off to Third World high jinks, I suppose.

"See that fellow with a drink in each hand, surrounded by ambassadors?" Indeed, an unctuous group of grayhairs was lionizing a woozy little man who was working hard to control his gesticulations, so as not to spill his pair of gin and tonics. "That's Ragulin. You'd think he was in the Politburo, but in fact he's the ticket man at the Bolshoi. His title is deputy-vice-under-squat-pot at the culture ministry, or something. But he's one of the most powerful men in Moscow, if your boss is in town, clamoring for front-row seats at Schwan Lake. . . ."

She pointed my shoulders toward the center of the room. "Oh, there's an important one for you. Dzherman Werth. He's half English, or has an English wife, I can't remember which. He's one of these Soviet 'journalists,' very plugged into the Kiev Gas Board—"

"You lost me there."

"The KGB. See all the hacks hovering around him? He's very good on deaths, seems to have some kind of line to the respiratory tent. You should probably cultivate him."

"How?"

"Bring him stuff from the West. His children like video games, and his wife enjoys fundamentalist literature. It's hard for them to buy here, poor dears. . . ."

Susan's face was locked in an ironical pout. Staring at

her in profile, I saw an attractive woman with a sense of humor. I resolved to watch my step.

"Ah, yes, here comes T. J. Jarvis, amorous young American diplomat." Cutting through the crowd like a football halfback came a moon-faced young man, elegantly dressed in a three-piece pin-striped suit. His dress code was Bureaucratic Elite, and he flashed a disapproving glance at my mottled brown loafers, which I had once tried to shine with black shoe polish. He spoke in a honeyed purr, rounding his vowels with a hint of the Old South.

"Why, Susan, how nice to see you! An' lookin' so *beautiful!*"

"Why, T. J., thank you." She pirouetted again, showing off her emerald-stockinged legs. Why did I feel jealous?

"I'm glad I ran into you. We're having a Las Vegas night over at the compound next Saturday night, you know, real gambling with roulette wheels, and blackjack. I thought you might like to come as my guest."

"Oh, T. J., how delightful! The problem is, I've drawn double duty next Saturday, and I'll have to work through the night. I'm *so* disappointed . . ."

"Oh, that's too bad."

"I'm sure you'll find someone else."

"No one as charming as you."

"Well, you *are* a dear."

Both Susan and T. J. acted as if they had had this conversation, or one like it, several times before.

Turning to me, Jarvis's charm iced up quickly. "Who's your friend?"

"He's one of yours, in fact, a Mr.—"

"Perkins. Nick Perkins." We shook hands warily. "I'm a new correspondent. Just arrived."

He asked me who I worked for, and I told him. He raised his eyebrows. T. J. didn't see the magazine much, but his mother read it at the hairdresser, naturally.

"Well, give me a call over at the embassy, and we'll watch some Redskin tapes. I've got all the games they've played so far. Theismann's red hot." Jarvis drifted back into the cocktail-consuming public.

"You certainly cold-cocked him." My vocabulary was still in the locker room with the 'Skins.

"Pardon me?"

"You were pretty blunt with that guy."

Susan wrinkled her lips impatiently. "He's sweet, I suppose, but he's a nuisance. The Americans are always inviting one to these strange expatriate events, like 'gumbo fest,' or 'yahoo night.' You'd think we were all living on ice floes in McMurdo Sound."

Here only two months, Susan was already itching to leave. She hoped to be "rotated" out of Moscow within a year, to a job in Western Europe. She didn't think much of the foreigners, and she was no friend of the locals, or the "Sovs," as she called them.

"If you want to know the truth, they're bloody awful."

"In what way?"

"This stupid system they have here, for instance. Starving the people half to death, making them line up for some frizzle-frazzle clothing from East Lahore you wouldn't wipe your bum with. It's shameful!"

I asked if she spoke Russian, or had any Russian friends.

"No, luv, it's a pity, but I'm not allowed to. Nature of the work and all that. Can't fraternize with the enemy. Hardly know why I'm talking to you."

"It must be my charm."

"You're right, luvvy. It must be that." She turned on her heel and disappeared into the reception. She hadn't even asked for my phone number.

44

By now my colleagues had begun to congregate around the door, debriefing each other on the "results" of the party. The consensus seemed to be that the British didn't have any better idea of what was happening in Russia than anyone else did.

Mike, the raspy-voiced wire service man, offered me a lift home, and I accepted. Since our arrival, night had fallen. Across the river, the Kremlin glowed under floodlights, which washed over the plaster walls of the imperial palaces and glinted off the gold-leaf domes of three majestic cathedrals. From the opposite bank, streams of headlights poured across the bridge, and parted at the near corner of the Kremlin's vast, red brick walls.

I was thunderstruck. "That's one of the most beautiful sights in the world."

Mike had already unlocked his car door, and dumped himself in the front seat. "I wouldn't mind dropping a nuclear bomb on it," he grunted, gunning the engine. "Let's get out of here."

In just one short week of "pours," "video parties," and "happy hours," the prospect of finding salvation—or even getting laid—inside the urine-colored walls of the foreigners' ghetto grew more and more remote. The diplomats I met often acted parochial, bridging or picnicking "within the European alliance" to limit contact to the Anglo-Saxon-romance gene pool. Friendships "with the nonaligned" opened doors of transracial fraternizing best left closed.

The masochist in me—or maybe just the red-blooded American boy in me—wanted to see Susan Islington again. But that didn't seem possible. At the British Embassy, she was an official nonperson. The switchboard denied she existed, and refused to put through calls or tell me her address. That was a very special library she worked in.

Colleagues told me governesses imported from Finland by diplomatic families were the prescribed sexual outlet for single men. Unfortunately, most of them had been corraled by the priapic platoon of U.S. Marines assigned to guard the American Embassy. My one approach to a sad-eyed Finnish blonde was cut short during an embassy "disco night" when her marine boyfriend joined us at the bar. This crewcut, peach-fuzzed killing machine laughingly recalled his combat training, when he learned how to interrupt an assailant's breathing by twisting the Adam's apple against the man's windpipe. "It's the dangedest thing—just like turning the water off in a faucet," he said. I couldn't remember any countermoves from my army days, and politely excused myself.

For sex, friendship, or anything on either side, locals were out of the question. "Stick w'yer own kind," a drunken Australian visa officer (a "nominal ally," my American escort explained) advised me during my only visit to the Dirty Diggers' Down Under Club. "Them Rooshns' a nasty piece of work."

Which came first, the ghetto, or the ghetto mentality? I couldn't tell. There were plenty of reasons to feel trapped. Foreigners weren't allowed to leave the city limits without applying for permission two days in advance. All our cars had specially-colored license plates, segregating us into various categories of undesirables: diplomats, businessmen, and journalists. The Russians had locked the foreigners away in their concrete cruise ship, and posted guards at the entrances and exits. For their part, the foreigners took pains to go ashore as little as possible. The ambience was pure Maugham: Russia was far upriver, and removed from civilization. Staples, like newspapers, appliances, and food, had to be imported from abroad. While we played the topee-hatted colonials, the Russians played the coffee-colored natives—spiritual, naive, inept, and of course, thieving. I heard one West German loudly complain that his Ukrainian maid had been stealing "carpet bits, to weave one of their quilts, or something."

So far, the only Russians I had met were Boris and Ekaterina Sergeyevna. Boris kept his distance, perhaps saving his energies for spare parts haggling, or for writing reports to the foreign ministry on my behavior. What was there to say? I ate, I slept, I read the press voraciously, looking for a needle of a story in the mountainous haystack of propagandistic silage. I had yet to transmit a word to New York.

Jonas's crew hadn't been very communicative themselves. The only message to come over the telex in the past seven days had been a memo from Boris's employers at the foreign ministry press department, reminding all Western journalists of the USSR's photography regulations, listed below. Summarized, the regulations prohibited all independent picture-taking by Western newsmen, who were encouraged to purchase their photos from "competent organs" like Tass and Sovfoto. If we had to take our own pictures, the message said, please obtain the permission of a policeman. He'll say no, but don't punch him out like the last fellow did, was the unspoken message.

While Boris kept his peace, Ekaterina Sergeyevna was a blabbermouth. She could prattle endlessly about the weather and the Second World War, two politically acceptable subjects that held deep spiritual meaning for her. Pinned to the huge bust of her cotton print dresses, she always wore a bulky medal, the Soviet equivalent of the Purple Heart. She claimed to have fought at Stalingrad, or perhaps her husband had fought there. She mumbled her war stories so deep in phlegm I never knew who was fighting where.

I quickly became her favorite audience, partly because I was the only foreigner in the entryway who spoke Russian, and also because my nationality afforded a handy foil for her exaggerated accounts of Soviet wartime hardships.

"We were eating grass cakes baked in mud while you Americans dined every night on stuffed pheasant and champagne," was a typical Sergeyevna jab.

"My father was sixteen years old when the war ended," was one of my typically lame replies. "He wouldn't have known a pheasant if it bit him in the nose."

"Plenty of sixteen-year-olds died at Stalingrad, while your father was watching Ronald Reagan movies and stuffing his face with popcorn." And so on.

Irascible with fellow Russians and "Germans," a category into which she bundled all white foreigners who couldn't speak Russian (nonwhites she called "monkeys"), she hadn't given up trying to charm me. Her patch of entryway smelled faintly, of an acrid animal odor.

About two weeks after my arrival, I worked up the gumption to inquire about the smell. By way of an answer, she opened the door of her broom closet and showed me foot-long slabs of salted pork fat hanging next to her change of clothes. She pulled a kitchen knife from her tent of a dress, and as a gesture of friendship, she cut off a slice of lard, which she offered me on black bread. I declined, holding my sinuses.

Shutting myself into the elevator, I realized I wasn't sinking any roots among the foreigners, and I wasn't making inroads into Russia either. My only speaking acquaintances were Boris and Ekaterina Sergeyevna, and they were paid to spy on me. I felt like the first twenty-nine-year-old exile, a million miles from home.

5 / *The House on Liebknecht Street*

We were halfway into October, and *Babiye Leto*—the "grandmothers' summer"—was in full bloom. We Americans call it Indian summer, but no one's sure why. Some say friendly Indians told New England's first settlers they could expect a "second summer" for last-minute field work before winter set in. Others say the Indians took advantage of the two smoky weeks of warm weather to launch the last, most furious burning raids before winter. With enemies, there are always two explanations.

Why grandmothers' summer? Ekaterina Sergeyevna, weather maven, gladly explained: "Because this weather is like . . . a mature woman." She tried to rub her hands along her hips, which had long since disappeared into the folds of her monstrous stomach. "A woman has her second blooming, Mr. Pairkins. Soon you will learn all about this."

I stepped out of the entryway into the unseasonably welcome sunshine and began navigating toward the Hotel Peking. Shouldering through the crowds on Kutuzov Prospect, I had a premonition I would be stood up. On the phone that morning, my foreign ministry host warned me he might have to cancel our lunch, if he were suddenly called away to the Presidium. When I asked what that might be, he insisted it wasn't important. But if it wasn't important—well, never mind.

As I took the measure of the teeming masses around me, the Russians looked as unappetizing as ever. Moscow worked the people like dough, squeezed into subways, buses, and sidewalks behind masks of pasty, resigned indifference. Collectively, the people looked vanquished; they had given up the fight, and abandoned all hope of moving their lives beyond the front door of the apartment, the assigned spot on the factory floor, the speck of allotted beach.

As an experiment, I had been smiling provocatively at store clerks, waitresses, and even passers-by. Without results: The orchestra of flat, angry faces harmonized on a single note—nyet. I could speak their language, but rarely communicate; Soviet power had effectively sealed the borders of its citizens' minds. In my brief exposure to the country, I felt foreign, unwanted, outside.

Ahead of me, I saw the Hotel Peking, just as Boris had described it. "You'll come to the planetarium—that's shaped like a box—and opposite there's Tchaikovsky Hall—it's shaped like a box, too—and then you'll see a fifteen-story red and yellow pagoda rising off the square. . . ."

There it was, the incongruous monument to Soviet-Chinese friendship, which had lapsed so badly since the hotel was built. Thirty years ago, Mao-suited economic "experts" jammed the lobby, assiduously parroting Soviet failures in industry, agriculture, and management. At the same time—I got this from a book, not from Boris—Lavrenti Beria, Stalin's most brutal police chief, directed the purges of the early

1950s from the Peking's twelfth floor, where the elevators still don't stop.

The Peking does boast the loveliest restaurant in the city. Immense red and blue columns shooting out dragons and gargoyles support warehouse-sized ceilings of shiny lacquer inlay. A colorful frieze of almond-eyed workers and peasants marches above the thirty-foot-high plate glass windows. Boris warned me—look, but don't eat. Expelled at the time of the Sino-Soviet rift, the Chinese chefs took their cooking secrets with them. The waiter will dutifully suggest the soy marinade, Boris predicted, and the bird's nest soup still appears on the menu, if not on the table. But the "chef's special entrée" is a sign of the times: *kotlety po-kievsky, po-kitaysky*. Kiev cutlets, à la chinoise.

Moving from the warmth of the second summer into the wide open chill of the cavernous restaurant, I found my premonition quickly fulfilled. I had been stood up. A cheerless, white-jacketed waiter led me to a table.

To kill time, I called for the menu and eyed the borschts, stroganoffs, and pilafs, born-again Chinese. I asked for tea. No tea, the waiter explained, only Baikal, a fetid Soviet cola drink. Between sips, I watched iridescent red and green peacocks flutter up the moulting blue wallpaper and wondered if Sharon would be happy here. The Peking wasn't her kind of restaurant, I decided. The service was slow, the portions filled the whole plate, and it didn't take credit cards. On the other hand, there weren't any Ecuadorian waiters pretending to be French. Maybe I should write her a letter.

Without enthusiasm, I thought of ordering. A few feet from my table, a commotion was brewing. A man and a woman were arguing with the waiter and pointing at my table, which had three free chairs. The man was carrying a huge briefcase, and swung it about, perilously, to show that the hall was full, and they must sit at my table. The waiter was actively discouraging them. I saw him shake his head gravely, muttering the words "foreigner . . . reserved . . . correspondent . . ." as if they were part of an ancient curse. This pair was ready to sit down with Attila the Hun—they wanted lunch. While I looked irresolute, the man shoved his briefcase past the waiter and planted himself and his wife at my table.

For Moscow, the woman was elegant, in a close-fitting nylon print dress worn underneath a lace shawl that highlighted smooth shoulders and perfect European curves. She had high, round cheekbones and a small, slanted nose. Like her husband, she had once had red hair. His, thick but receding, had darkened and flecked with gray. Hers was evolving toward an artificially induced gold.

The man was dressed in an open white shirt, unbuttoned over a strong, convex chest. His eyes were bright and smiling, and he exuded more energy than his age, which was probably close to fifty. His face was open, happy—should I say it?—un-Russian.

His first gesture was distinctively Russian. He reached into his bulging leather briefcase and pulled out a small bottle of vodka and a full liter of Arbatskoye, a fruity Byelorussian wine. He splashed two fingers of vodka into his wife's glass, served himself, and then lifted the bottle in my direction.

I pointed to my full glass of Baikal.

He motioned with his hand: Drink it up, and I'll pour you some vodka.

I scrunched my face, and wagged a finger at the vodka bottle: I don't like vodka.

He wagged his finger at the glass of Baikal, and grabbed his throat: Yecch!

I patted the cola glass with my palm: I'd better stick with this.

He shrugged his shoulders and turned back to his wife: Suit yourself.

I scanned the menu, then stared back at the couple, already filling their glasses with wine. Either I would try to talk with these people, or spend a stomach-churning ninety minutes watching the peacocks crawl up the wallpaper.

"What's good to eat?"

The man looked across the table, first at me, and then at his wife. "You speak Russian?"

"Yes."

"Then why the pantomime?"

"I thought you started it."

We both laughed. "Maybe I did. Only a foreigner would turn down vodka. Want some?" He brandished the bottle again.

"Sure." I drained my glass.

He poured. "What did you ask?"

"What's good to eat."

"Where?"

"Here, on this menu."

He smiled. "There's nothing good to eat, here, on this menu. There hasn't been anything good to eat here for twenty years." He spoke slowly, to help me understand.

"Then why are you here?"

"Well, of course, we should be at work." The man feigned gloominess.

"As should you!" The woman waved her finger.

"I am working, theoretically." I complained about being stood up.

"Ah, yes, the waiter warned us about you."

"You're one of *them*," the woman muttered darkly.

"One of what?"

"An American correspondent. A slanderer. The enemy."

"He warned us not to talk to you. That you'd be spreading lies."

"Or else you'd get us drunk, and pry information from us—"

"About our classified electric mixer blueprints—"

"Or the secrets of Soviet motherhood."

"Perhaps it's better not to talk at all."

"No!" My pent-up loneliness made it almost a shout. Since when had I been so emphatic? "No. I want to talk. I'm no—what's that word?"

"Forget it. My name is Andrei."

"I'm Lilya."

They repeated my name. I tried to steer them away from "Pairkins."

"Like a cat, Prrrrkins, Prrrrkins."

"Prrrrkins . . . Prrrrkins . . ."

"That's good! That's fine!"

The waiter approached, frowning at our good spirits. Andrei ordered for all of us, referring to me as "our guest."

He picked up the conversation after the waiter drifted out of earshot. "You're a journalist?"

I described my job at the magazine before the Moscow assignment, how I had divided my time among caption-writing, letters, obituaries . . .

That caught Lilya's attention. "Oh, you mean the articles with black borders, where you write what year the dead man joined the Party, and all that?"

"Ours are a little different."

She had one more question: Was it true that journalists had to pay for interviews in the West? A reporter friend of hers had sent a list of questions to Alfred Hitchcock, and never received a reply. She concluded that her interview subject was holding out for an honorarium. I answered that Mr. Hitchcock wasn't venal, just dead.

"Does your magazine have to pay to write obituaries?"

"Some things are still free."

What did they do? Lilya had worked "in television" as an actress, and seemed sensitive about not working now. "I know how it is in America, all your women work. . . ." She shrugged. "For now, he makes money, and I take care of the family." An un-Slavic touch of guilt? I was starting to feel at home.

Andrei worked as an engineer in an electric appliance design institute. His lab was thrashing through a "special assignment," which sounded suspiciously like the reverse engineering of a Cuisinart. He and Lilya were celebrating. He had just passed before a "scientific review board," which had renewed his five-year contract.

"It's supposed to be routine, but . . ." he lifted a finger.

"'Incorrect attitude toward socialist obligations,'" Lilya said. "He's not a model citizen."

I could relate to that.

"I missed both of 'Lenin's Little Saturdays' last year," Andrei explained. "I confused my obligation to load bricks at some hotel construction site with my obligation to stay in bed. And somehow I forgot to 'volunteer' to dig potatoes at the collective farm last September."

"And the vegetable depot—"

"Oh yes, I never could find time to load cabbage at the vegetable depot."

"Don't judge our great country on the model of this lazy man," Lilya insisted. "We will find you some Heroes of Socialist Labor to interview."

"I think I have the privilege of working with some of

your model citizens." I described Boris and Ekaterina Sergeyevna.

"They are . . . very special citizens," Andrei replied. "Unfortunately, we can't all aspire to their status."

"Some people can't be trusted. The kind of person who forgets about vegetable work, for instance." Lilya patted her husband's cheek affectionately. "Incorrect attitude . . ."

"But good attitude toward life?" Andrei raised his eyebrows hopefully.

"Not so bad. Not so bad." Lilya turned her feathery sense of irony on me. "Do you have attitude problems in America?"

I grinned. "I may be one of them."

"Oh, good. Perhaps we will be friends."

When our meals arrived, Andrei fished a second bottle of wine from his briefcase. He pointed to the label. "Arbatskoye. Do you know the Okudjhava song?" He hummed an unfamiliar melody. "'Arbat, Arbat, you're my religion, my happiness, my salvation . . .' Don't know it? Hmm. You've got a lot to learn."

Lilya began eating, then pointed her fork at me. "He looks like the man in the movie . . . Goffman . . ."

"Kaufman?"

"Hoffman." Andrei aspirated the H. The Russian language hardens H's to G's: Goward Gawks of Gollywood Gills. Gubert Gumphrey at the Gilton Gotel.

The movie *Kramer vs. Kramer* had just played in their district theater. "Lines around the block," Andrei moaned. "But it was worth it. Unfortunately, they cut the shower scene." Which shower scene? "The dirty one, of course." I made a mental note to see the film again.

"You do look a little like him."

Actually, I'm heavier and lighter-haired than Dustin Hoffman. If the light is right, I resemble George Segal.

If the light is precise, I'm the double of Richard Dreyfuss playing the tubby intellectual in *American Graffiti*. Maybe to Lilya all American men looked the same.

We ventured into politics and exited quickly. None of us was a tremendous booster for our native country's system, nor for the other fellow's. We shared antipathies toward all political parties, an attitude that probably had more consequences for them than for me. I told them I had registered to vote as an Independent in New York, an idea that intrigued Andrei.

"Maybe we can introduce that party here in Russia."

Lilya stroked his hand. "Not for a while, dear. Let's just leave things the way they are."

When I told them I had voted Democratic in the last election, Andrei grinned churlishly.

"Democracy . . . Let me tell you a story about democracy. . . ." With un-Soviet hoopla, a leading newspaper had recently challenged its readers to a chess match with Boris Spassky, the former world champion. Spassky's move was printed, then the readers voted on the response. "The majority always voted for the obvious play," Andrei laughed. "Spassky won in twenty moves. Of course, a few Jews sent in the right answers, but they were always in the minority. So much for your democracy."

Civics class ran deep. "The only thing worse than voting is not voting at all."

Andrei hunched his shoulders. "Maybe. We'll never know." I had an intuition that we didn't give a damn about the same things.

"So, how do you like it here?" Lilya was the blunt questioner.

"Do you mean here in this hotel?"

"No, here in this country."

"I'm enjoying this lunch."

"And the rest?"

I grimaced. "It's OK."

"Just OK?"

I summarized my experiences in and around the foreign community—the parties, the isolation, the idiocy.

"That doesn't sound much like Russia."

"It's not, unfortunately."

Andrei looked at Lilya. "We'll take you on an expedition to Soviet reality. You can be our guest."

Over lunch, we had confessed a shared weakness for not working on Friday afternoons. "Your bosses will never know, and mine will never care," Andrei said as we strode tipsily up Gorky Street to the subway. Andrei hadn't taken a Friday afternoon "on" in memory. My work habits were as yet unspoiled, or retrograde, in his eyes.

"A real man goes to work once a week, twice at the most," he grumbled ominously. Lilya patted him on the back and urged him to take some deep breaths of fresh air.

"Come on, Andrei, you don't want to give this nice American the wrong impression." She knitted her eyebrows. "We really are a very hard-working people."

"I can see." We clattered into the metro, and rode ten long stops to the Kolomenskoye station. The subway carriage, with yellow walls lit by oval amber lights, glowed like an incubator. The passengers sat frozen as if in suspended animation; still, irradiated, and calm.

The trip ended in the country. As we rose up the escalator, the cerulean blue of the Kolomenskoye cathedral tower filled our rising vision of the landscape. But beyond the monastery complex, the city erupted again in square gray rows of modern housing, lined like dominoes to the horizon. Walking the mile to Andrei's apartment, we took a shortcut through an unmowed field, Andrei lifting Lilya by the waist to keep her spiked heels clear of the cow patties.

"We used to buy milk over there." Andrei pointed to an abandoned brown hut. "Now they've chased the old woman away. They're building more apartment buildings, fewer cows."

"Well, we cleaned the cows out of New York quite a while ago."

"We don't mind being second," Andrei smiled, turning out of the field onto the first paved street of his "microregion".

On our left, Lilya pointed to two huge empty concrete basins, linked in a figure eight. Behind them rose a half completed skyscraper, gunmetal gray. "Post-Olympic objects." She frowned. "The hotel wasn't ready for the Olympics; I think we blamed the East Germans. So they never bothered to finish it at all, or even fill the pools." A shallow wash of rainwater and algae festered in the bottom of the basins, smelling as far as the sidewalk.

Walking through the gray symmetry of the postwar housing, I remembered the insipid street names of the factory-built American neighborhoods we had shuttled through during the 1950s and 1960s, where Maple, Pine, and Cedar Streets intersected Hawthorne, Camellia, and Rose. The Soviets, too, had succumbed to the neutering instinct. Here in the Kolomenskoye microregion, Rosa Luxemburg, Walter Ulbricht, and Klement Gottwald crossed Red Banner, Revolution, and Uprising streets. When capitalism and communism finally converge, real estate developers will strike the first blow for détente, erecting the Paris Commune Condominiums within easy walking distance of the Karl Marx Shopping Mall. We turned left on Karl Liebknecht, and entered the first courtyard.

Andrei lived in a *khrushchevka,* one of the thousands of five-story apartment buildings thrown up in a hurry by Nikita Khrushchev to house the homeless hordes pouring into postwar Moscow. German prisoners of war built many of them—"the ones with right angles," Andrei joked.

Unfortunately the POWs had returned home with their measuring tools before Andrei's apartment block was built. On the facade, you could see the jagged outline of uneven floors. The front door opened onto a three-foot dip. Someone had thoughtfully placed a plastic milk crate under the threshold as a makeshift step into the entryway. After descending, we walked up a dark flight of stairs, which heaved to the left. Happily, they lived on the second floor.

"This is home." Lilya shrugged off her shawl, and waved gaily at one of the smallest apartments I had ever seen—two tiny cubicles, each about ten feet square, joined by a corridor. Andrei and Lilya slept on the foldout couch in the living room, and the two daughters, Natalya and Anya, took the second room. "Eighteen square meters," Lilya noted. "Slightly under the norm." The floor felt spongy underfoot.

"I wish I could give you some of my meters, I have a lot more than I need."

"But you're an enemy of the people," Andrei said, ushering me down the corridor. "You deserve special treatment."

We jammed into their pocket of a kitchen for tea. The three of us couldn't fit. Andrei sat with his back to the window, huddling his head beneath a projecting wall cabinet. Across the folding formica table, I sat in the place of honor, next to the door. Lilya slouched on the waist high refrigerator, apart from the table, waiting for the water to boil.

"So where did you learn Russian?"

"In the army, many years ago."

"So you are a spy!" Lilya seemed excited.

"Used to be." I explained how we guys with college educations beat the draft by volunteering for Intelligence.

"Do you ever use your Russian in America?"

"Speaking to a cab driver now and then. Maybe on the phone to the delicatessen."

"Sounds like the emigrés have nailed down all the prestige jobs."

"It's tough to get started. Where's that from?"

Tacked above Andrei's head on the wall cabinet I saw a glossy Pan Am airline calendar, open to February of 1979. The photo was the stock panorama of Manhattan viewed from Brooklyn, backlit by the setting sun.

"We call that our window on America," Lilya joked.

The calendar was a present that had arrived exactly a year late. "I guess they liked it at the post office," she said. "We like it too, so we switch the pictures only every four or five months. We have a friend in New York. He—you know . . ." She fluttered her hand in the air.

"Defected?"

"No, no, the other thing—emigrated, legally. Here—" Lilya squeezed out of the kitchen, and returned cradling a shoebox crammed with onionskin letters. The side of the box was marked "America" in a charcoal scrawl. "Our newspapers." She giggled. "All we need to know."

That was my first meeting with Aron, strumming my finger along the row of red and blue airmail envelopes. Aron, Andrei's first cousin, had left the country with his wife and nine-year-old boy in 1978. Assistant director of a collective farm outside Moscow, he left via Rome for Israel, where he spent nine months waiting for a job in a Brooklyn accounting firm. Each month since his departure, he had written long, newsy letters to his mother, and after she died, to Andrei, who inherited the collection. The envelopes had often been opened, or arrived late. But they never lost their freshness for Lilya, who loved Aron's tales of life abroad, and made several copies of the letters, by hand with carbon paper, to distribute among friends.

"Sometimes in the afternoon I just curl up on the couch with one of his letters, and take a trip. I've arranged them by geography, see"—she pointed to hand-cut blue file tabs for Italy, Israel, and New York—"so I just grab a ticket"—she plucked a letter from the shoebox—"and go. I've toured the Vatican a dozen times, at Jerusalem we waited in line to see the Dome of the Rock, we even saw the Yankee football team play in Yankee Stadium. I know everything! Here, this jam—" she tapped the tiny saucer of black currant preserves next to my glass of tea. "You don't have this jam in America." She reached for one of the ruffled pages and quoted:

And as to berries, America is a backwards culture. In the stores, you have nothing, unless you make exception for their blueberries, which are bloated, dead, and tasteless, unlike anything you could imagine in Russia. Perhaps that was to be expected, but worse yet, there is no countryside around New York adequate for berry-picking. And mushrooms? Don't get me started. . . .

"Apparently New York isn't rustic enough for him," Andrei commented.

What else was in there? "Come back, and we'll read you more," Lilya said, shoving the shoebox under the kitchen table.

We drank tea and talked for several hours in the darkening kitchen. The conversation cycled with the level of liquid in our glasses. Details of my life in New York carried us through a service and a half, when Lilya took over with stories of her childhood in Georgia, the southern republic. I had suspected she was too pretty to be Russian, and I was right. Mooning over Tbilisi, her home town, she sounded positively Californian: "Sunshine all day long, fruit trees in the city, nuts and berries in all the stores—"

Andrei dropped a turd on the parade. "Stalin."

Lilya shrugged her shoulders. "No nation is perfect."

For the duration of half a glass of tea, Andrei remembered the frozen December of 1941, when as a small child he watched his mother and hundreds of other women hacking trenches into the icy earth to stop the rapidly advancing German tanks. The Russian lines backed up to the outskirts of the city, just a few hundred yards from where we were sitting.

"It was a thrilling time for a young boy," he said. "Each night, orange and yellow starburst flares lit up the horizon like fireworks. For three months during the siege, I would stand up in bed, hypnotized by the ballet of searchlights weaving around the columns of fire and smoke. We had an artillery battery down the block—they finally lulled me to sleep when the firing started just before midnight." Andrei pumped his fist against the table, slowly. "Thoomp . . . thoomp . . . thoomp . . . I thought we were seeing the end of the world." Instead, when Moscow was evacuated, his mother took him and his brother to Kuybyshev, in the Urals. None of them expected to return. When they did, their old neighborhood had been flattened by shelling, and they spent a year living in captured German mess tents. "For the first time since the Revolution, everyone was equal," he mused. "No one had anything at all."

During the last glass of tea, we indulged our complaints and worries. Lilya fretted that their eighteen-year-old, Natalya, had failed her entrance exams to library school, and would fail them again. Three-year-old Anya's eye had swelled up, and there would be trouble getting the medicine. Their grandmothers were complaining that foreigners were buying up all the subscriptions to performances at the Moscow Conservatory.

"Damned foreigners!" Andrei laughed.

What were my problems? My apartment was too big, though I could hardly pitch for sympathy here. Loneliness? Maybe if I didn't talk about it, it would go away. Besides, the Russians were the problem, not the solution.

Andrei seemed to have been reading my thoughts. "It sounds like you're a little lonely."

"Maybe I am. Home seems far away."

"To hear you talk, you were lonely in New York, too."

"That's possible." I placed my hand above my eyebrows, and felt my forehead heating up. "I'm not sure this tea is mixing well with the wine."

Andrei reached above his head into the cabinet, and set a slender bottle of white fluid and three thimble-size cups on the table.

"More vodka?"

He grimaced. "*Spirt.* Moonshine. Made it myself." Proud of his craft, he pointed out a jumble of *apparatura* thrown under the sink—pressure cooker, a beaker, condenser, and the distinctive, spiral "snake."

"Since vodka prices went up," Lilya explained, rolling her eyes. She was not a drinker. "The latest craze of the Moscow intelligentsia."

Andrei waved her off. "Nonsense—necessary economies. And in the given instance, for medical use. This will cure your sickness."

"But I'm not sick."

"No? Then it will make you feel better, generally."

I remember the faintest fruit taste—pear?—then a ravaging fire in my throat, and a rush of blood to my head. The headache was forgotten. Three shots later, everything was forgotten. When next I remembered, I was floating out of the apartment. In the entryway, Andrei lifted my right foot onto the milk crate, and eased me out into the street. Standing still, I had no sense of balance. Andrei's elbow was my anchor to real life.

"We'll make a Russian out of you yet," he said, gently releasing me into the street. Just before he let go, he clapped a five-kopeck piece into my hand.

"You have my phone number. Don't lose touch."

I arrived home just as Ekaterina Sergeyvna was packing her stool into the broom closet, blasting the entryway with the smell of pork lard. She had kicked off her slippers and was trying to wedge a pair of pumps onto her mammoth feet. While her back was turned, I began to slip up the stairs.

"Nikolai Pavlovich! You're drunk!" Why was she using my patronymic? How did she know my father's name? Maybe that's how one addresses drunks.

"You're drunk! I can smell it!" She spun out of the closet and stamped her feet down into the tight-fitting shoes. "When my husband comes home drunk, I bash him!" I meekly raised my foot onto the first step of the stairs. "Where've you been?" she demanded.

I stumbled over the words, and confessed.

"My God! That Chink place! Filled with little monkeys, I bet. Who were you with?"

Always on the job, I thought. But who was I with? I conjured up blurred images of Lilya and Andrei, and sheltered them in my memory.

"A girl, Ekaterina Sergeyevna. I met a nice Russian girl."

"Good boy! Good boy!" she shouted up the stairs. "You should see more of them!" She lifted her coat over her shoulders, and marched out the door.

Walking up five flights of stairs under the influence

of *spirt* felt like climbing Mount Everest on crutches. I paused for oxygen, and a brief nap, on each of the last three floors. I finally arrived at the fifth floor, but I couldn't find my keys—in fact, I couldn't find my pockets—before I fell asleep, crumpled in a heap just in front of the elevator.

I spent the night there, waking only once when one of my neighbors, arriving home late, repeatedly shoved the elevator door against my stomach. Was I dreaming? I thought I felt a light foot dancing across my rib cage, and heard a familiar, British voice.

"Well, well. If it isn't Mr. Charm. Gone native, I see."

At dawn, I located my keys, opened my door, and slept through to Saturday noon.

6 / *Deadline Now*

I had been in Moscow for almost a month. The time had come to file my first story.

Unfortunately, there was plenty of truth to my colleagues' complaints about the shortage of material. The town was a reportorial Lilly tank; I felt comfortably suspended in an environment devoid of journalistic sensation. Spurred by guilt—after all, my salary checks still arrived on time—I opted for the first refuge of a reporter with nothing to say: I set to work on a "situationer."

Boris fired up the telex and I transmitted my first message to New York: "Onworking 3000 wds Kremlin politicker. Delivery ASAP."

Just twenty minutes later, New York's reply crackled over the ancient East German teletype like machine-gun fire. "Tally ho. Holding inside spread. Need file soonest." The magazine was making space for me. Now all I needed was a story.

My first idea was to drop down two flights of stairs to visit my opposite numbers at the Bulgarian Telegraph Agency. Peeking in their open door, I realized I might have done better waiting for a second idea. Their news bureau looked like a zooful of Pet Rocks. Five pallid, immobile heads drooped over prewar typewriters, occasionally pecking letters onto dusty gray copy paper. A yellowing portrait of the Chief Rock (the Boulder?), probably the commissar for journalism back home, hung akimbo on the wall behind them.

I cleared my throat. Bulgaria didn't stir.

"What's new, fellas?"

Eyelids on the iguanalike head nearest the door rose slowly, then settled back into the half-closed position. A pudgy hand snaked out from under the typewriter and gestured toward a clipboard. There I found the bureau's latest dispatches. Just filed: "Bulgarian Engineers Exchange Fruit-canning Knowhow with Soviet Comrades." Beneath that one, I found "Holidaymakers in Dmitrovgrad—Summer of Fun." These weren't the stories Jonas was holding space for.

I replaced the clipboard, and backed slowly out of the room.

"Thanks, fellas. Have a nice day."

No one said a word. Halfway down the stairs, I heard the typing resume, tap—tap—tap, like a faucet with a very slow leak. So much for the "democratic" press.

Just three entryways away in Korpus D, the Amalgamated Press bureau was hopping. Typewriters clattered away, while Reuters, Tass and Agence France Presse news tickers gobbled up stories by the yard from around the world. You could feel the tension of deadlines, and smell the sweet aroma of cutthroat competition in the musty air. *Their* clipboard had plenty of action—sports scores, business deals, even some worthwhile disasters, including the recently transmitted "Siberian Tiger Rampages in Downtown Vladivostok; Dozens Feared Dead."

Mike, my gravel-voiced acquaintance from the British Embassy reception glanced up from his swivel chair. "Hey, bud. Great tiger story, huh? My maid told me about it. Her son-in-law's sister has a cousin out there." He introduced me around the bureau. Each reporter grunted in turn, then all resumed their furious hacking.

"Whaddya need?"

"I need a story."

Mike waved toward the clipboard. "Right there. Tigers. Go with it. Flesh it out. Call some zoos. Expert comment. Cover story for you guys." Wire service people talked like they wrote, as if some Universal Speech Authority was charging by the word.

I reminded him that our publication had changed its spots. "I need something serious. Politburo-level stuff. Real Kremlinology." That staccato delivery was infectious.

"Kremlinology, huh?" He scratched his head, then jotted down a name and phone number. "Jean-Luc. Couple of other names too. First secretary with the Frogs. Has the inside stuff." Mike slapped my fanny and pointed me toward an available phone. "Go get it."

Over the telephone, Jean-Luc d'Etienne de Montfort said he would be happy to share his insights with me, and invited me over to his office. I sped the famous Soviet Fairlane through noontime traffic up to October Square, where the elegantly architected French Embassy clashed with its surroundings—a molded concrete subway stop and an aging pile called the Warsaw Hotel—like a Dior gown parachuted onto the rack at Woolworth's. From the reception area, bristling with the latest fashions in electronic security devices, a dapper flic escorted me to Jean-Luc's office. Strolling through the embassy, we passed a capacious cinémathèque and a Montmartre-style cafe oozing authentic details, like red-checkered tablecloths and a high-tech espresso machine. I wondered if they imported rude waiters, or tapped the local supply.

We found Jean-Luc in his tiny cubicle, hard at work behind a slender desk, marooned among yellowing piles of unread regional newspapers. On each wall, he had tacked dozens of photographs of Kremlin ceremonies, with little numbers drawn above the head of each official, ranking the leadership by formal precedence. Stacks of fat reference books in French, English, and Russian jammed his desk.

Greeting me with a slight bow, Jean-Luc waved his hand over the debris, as if presenting his credentials. *"Je suis Kremlinologue,"* he announced proudly, lighting a foul-smelling French cigar. "How ken I help you?"

I explained my dilemma. I needed to write 3000 words about the state of play in the Kremlin, and I'd only seen the place twice—the first time, driving in from the airport, and the second, during a brisk walk-around organized by the state travel bureau, Intourist. That visit had featured a peek into Catherine the Great's cavernous clothes closet, and a memorable quote from our egalitarian-spirited guide: "When Catherine dies, ten thousand dresses in wardrobe, not one ruble in state bank."

My limited experience was no handicap in Jean-Luc's eyes. "Sree sousand words—eet is nahssing." He sucked on his cigar and gazed at the walls around him. "Zee current situation ees very complicated. I suggest you take notes."

I pulled out my spiral notebook, and off we went. Within moments, I switched to shorthand to keep pace with his animated docudrama: The Siberian technocrats had seized control of three key Central Committee departments. . . . Brezhnev's cronies were packing the Politburo staff, preparing for a showdown . . . the army was choosing sides. . . .

"Zare is Bonapartism in zee air," he commented, with no small hint of national pride. "If Brezhnev should fail to appear at the October Plenum, zat could be very significant."

I looked up from my notebook. "Suppose he does appear?"

Jean-Luc rubbed his cigar along his bottom lip, pensively. "Zat too would be extremely significant."

In between thoughts—paragraphs would be a better term, as he was dictating finished copy—he yanked down a photo of the leadership posing above Lenin's mausoleum, and proceeded to examine it under a magnifying glass. "Yes, Blatov's hat has zee brown ribbon—I should have noticed before!" Then he buried his nose in the coffee-stained pages of a Soviet reference book. "And born in zee Ukraine, just a few hundred miles from Brezhnev's home town. Of course zay are allies!"

When he finished, the Soviet state stood on shaky ground. Powerful factions were forming all over Moscow, anxious to seize power. *Après Brezhnev, le déluge.*

"Of course, all zis could be complete—what is your word?—puppycock?" Jean-Luc concluded. "I overheard it last night at zee Bolshoi, where I sat behind zee Bulgarian Telegraph people. Not zee most reliable fellows, really."

Perhaps they were intellectually active at night, I thought. I thanked him for his time, and sped back to the office to file the story, minus the French diplomat's disclaimer. Jean-Luc, who insisted on anonymity—"so as not to compromise my sources," he explained—was the "knowledgeable source" in paragraph three and the "experienced Soviet affairs analyst" of paragraph eight. In my conclusion, he became a "consensus of Western European diplomats," which would have pleased him no end.

While Boris typed the article into the telex, I think I

saw him smile. I went home, drank three beers, and collapsed on the sofa.

When I showed up at work the next day, a "herogram" from Jonas lay on my desk: "Worth the wait. Work those sources. Live stuff. Keep it up."

Now Boris really was smiling. And he smiled for the rest of the day.

Buoyed by my journalistic triumph, I decided to make some progress on the woman front. Susan Islington being an official nonperson at the British Embassy, I concluded that she worked in the registry, or code room, where the British keep their secret files—at least in spy novels. I also knew that I didn't need to find her, as my sleepover in front of the elevator door had indicated that she lived right across the hall. All I had to do was flush her out.

Proceeding on the assumption that it takes a spy to catch a spy, I approached Ekaterina Sergeyevna.

Just after lunch on Friday, she was rummaging inside her utility closet, packing shopping bags full of produce to take home. Apparently she too disapproved of working Friday afternoons.

"Going home already? Who's going to look out for my valuables?"

She continued bending over her parcels, presenting me with a panorama of fat brown stockings and billowy buttocks. "As I recall, you own nothing of value, Mr. Pairkins. Besides, I am not alone in concerning myself with the security of you and your home." She gestured toward the militia men guarding the compound. "And this isn't your New York, with tribes of monkeys roaming the streets."

"Thank heavens for that. But suppose that British spy tries to recruit me into crimes against the Motherland?"

Sergeyevna stood up slowly, and maneuvered out of the closet. This was not the kind of activity she condoned on her watch. "Has she tried to recruit you?"

"Not yet. I wish she would."

"You find her pretty?" The mental tape recorder was running.

"I wish I could find her at all. I've only seen her once."

"She works nights, so help me. It's a very unhealthy situation, Mr. Pairkins." Sergeyevna glanced furtively to both sides, then leaned closer to whisper in my ear. Her breath smelled like mustard gas.

"She receives air mail letters from London, and bursts into tears right in front of the mailbox. I think she has abandoned her husband and children to pursue a career in spying. She won't be interested in you, Mr. Pairkins. You would do better with a nice Russian girl." She hefted her shopping bags and waddled out the front door, wagging her finger. "Don't consort with the enemies of socialism, Mr. Pairkins."

I went back to the apartment, and scrawled out a brief message. "Susan: I know you're in there. How about a drink tomorrow evening? Your friend, the sobersided Nick Perkins." I tiptoed across the hallway and slid the note under her door.

7 / The Wolf of Capitalism

When I woke up on Saturday morning, I found a neatly typewritten note slipped underneath my door.

Dear Mr. Perkins,

Thank you for your kind offer. I am not free tomorrow—or today, when I suspect you will read this—but do not give up hope. Knowing how you enjoy yourself at English holidays, and most other days, if one is to judge from the temporary campsite where we last met, I hereby invite you to join me for a celebration of the queen's birthday, on Thursday of next week. The favour of a reply is requested. As liquor will be served, I am confident of your attendance.

S. Islington
Third Secretary of
Her Majesty's Embassy

Yes, little Susan. I would not miss your queen's birthday for anything. I snuck across the hallway and slid my acceptance under her door.

On the ground floor landing, I found a letter from Sharon protruding from my mailbox. I read through it slowly, while climbing the five flights of stairs.

Sharon was writing to close the door on the idea of a

visit to Moscow. "Period of personal transition . . .
loosening of the bonds . . . distance more than geographic . . ." were some of the phrases she used. I
looked beneath the signature for some kisses, a hug, or
a hastily scrawled "I miss you." Nothing. Well, I missed
her, but I didn't intend to say so either.

Saturday morning. I wondered what she was doing.
Sleeping late and screwing Jimmy, of course. Soon he'd
have no drawer space left for his monogrammed shirts
and pastel bikini underwear. Some people adore ice
cream. Envy is my vice.

Looking down at the lead-colored river inching between its concrete banks, I noticed the thermometer
mounted outside the living room window. Twenty degrees centigrade, in October, with fat white clouds flying fast and low in a deep sky. Good football weather.
Maybe I would buy a cat.

For a week, no one had come as close to being
friends as Andrei and Lilya, but they had disappeared.
I think his phone number wafted out of my pocket in
front of the subway entrance that Friday when I ran-
sacked my clothing for change. If his five kopeck piece
hadn't tinkled to the floor, I never would have arrived
home. Now I was facing the weekend with no one to
call.

Across the avenue, I saw that the Barricades Cinema
was offering a double feature: *Lenin in Paris,* and the
sequel, *Lenin in Geneva.* A colleague had invited me to
the American Embassy Film Club's Saturday Morning
Special, yet another movie with a geographic theme:
Debbie Does Dallas. Should I picnic with an ally? The
phone rang.

Andrei was upset. Despite his plea at the subway station, I had "lost touch." The word in Russian is *propal,*
literally "to drop through," or fall out. Russians live life
on thin ice; some people fall through.

"Why haven't you called?"

"I lost your number that day, in the subway station." A true and good excuse. Moscow has no phone books, so I couldn't have called. Not good enough, however.

"Well, why didn't you just come over? You know where we live." At the intersection of John Reed and Jennie Marx? I couldn't admit to forgetting the street name. That would be a sign of uncaring.

Andrei was quick to forgive. "Come to our family dinner. I'll pick you up at noon."

Behind the wheel of his bug-shaped Zaporozhets compact, Andrei described the ritual of the Saturday dinner, "with grandmothers." Lilya prepared the meal, and in return one of the grandmothers took three-year-old Anya home for two nights, freeing the weekend for the parents. I asked after the grandfathers. "They disappeared," he replied, waving his hand toward the street. "Out there somewhere. In the thirties. No one knows where." The stepfather who had raised Andrei died in the 1960s.

When we arrived in the apartment, the grandmothers were in high gear. Andrei's mother, Liza, hovered over a pot of soup, stirring it occasionally, yelling marital advice to her teenage granddaughter Natalya, who was setting a small table in the bedroom. Lilya's mother, Aya, huge, smiling, blind in one eye, was dandling little Anya on the sofa bed, simultaneously criticizing Natalya's silverware placement.

"Fork on the left, *dushechka*, knife blade facing in. Can't you remember from week to week?"

"I've got other things on my mind!" Natalya snapped, slapping the cutlery onto the tablecloth.

"She's thinking about marrying that clod boyfriend of hers," Liza shouted. "And throwing her life away."

Andrei introduced me. I was an unstartling addition.

Liza gestured toward me with her soup ladle, and Aya murmured a distracted hello.

Lilya pulled me onto a tiny kitchen stool, and pressed some onionskin papers into my hand. "I found some of Aron's letters that might interest you. Put them in your pocket, and read them when you get home."

Liza overheard her daughter-in-law's whispering. "That nephew! He'll find out what America's all about soon enough!"

Liza didn't like Americans. At table, she expanded on her feelings: "Americans are arrogant, self-satisfied, and think they know everything. I know Andrei likes Americans. He may even like you—" she jabbed in my direction with her spoon. "And now that idiot nephew thinks he's going to outsmart all the New York Jews! Ha! I never thought he was worth much anyway."

She punctuated her speech by grabbing the sides of her soup bowl and pouring cabbage broth into her open mouth, spilling gray rivulets through the troughs of her jowls. Andrei and Lilya hushed and tutted, although no one suggested she hadn't meant what she said.

Rallying charm, I asked if she might consider me a *good* American, at least until I disappointed her. She slammed her soup bowl down on the table. Nyet.

Grandmother Aya, on the other hand, *loved* Americans. "Tom Meeks! Merry Peekford! Dooglass Fairbanks! Djon Kennedy!" She gushed like an Iowa farm girl raised on *Tiger Beat*. "I'll show you, Lilya keeps my album."

Abandoning her soup, she trundled over to a large mahogany armoire and took out a tattered leather souvenir album bulging with mementos of her favorite silent stars. Her trembling fingers sifted through fifty-year-old newspaper cuttings, autograph cards with strange, florid postmarks, and grainy studio stills of long-forgotten movie legends. Aya's voice quavered, but she hadn't forgotten a face: Irina Voronina, the Russian Pickford; Heinrich von Fromann, the Weimar heartthrob; Theda Bara. "The Look! The Look! See how beautiful she is! Her hair curled like seashells!"

Lilya snuck up behind and wrapped both arms around her mother's waist, dragging her back to the table, tossing the album onto the sofa. The mountainous old woman took her seat, still bubbling.

"America! Djon Kennedy! How could you kill Kennedy? And Reagan, this awful man, this awful actor! He will make war on us! Why did you choose him?"

"The bosses chose him," Liza grunted. "Believe me, this one wasn't consulted."

I mumbled a few apologies, and Andrei jumped in to save me, praising the tasty Georgian delicacies: *lobyo*, a baked bean dish, and *hatchapouri*, a cheese pie. With unflagging enthusiasm, Aya launched on a discussion of her recipes, which she offered to the other women, not for the first time.

Eighteen-year-old Natalya was not the recipes type. An inflated version of her mother, she was *à point* for Russian men. This Saturday she had resurrected the idea of marrying her current boyfriend, Alyosha, an artist. The discussion had dragged on for several months. Where would they live? Alyosha's parents had three rooms, but his mother despised Natalya. Natalya's parents had no room. Ten thousand couples were waiting for apartments in the Kolomenskoye microregion. A clerk had told Natalya she could have a flat in five years, perhaps.

Aya found the housing talk dull, crassly un-Pickfordian. "In my day, we married for love, and then found a place to live." I noticed Liza raise a heavy eyebrow. Not everyone had the same experience. . . .

"In your day, there were places to live," Natalya shot back. This triggered the familiar lamentation of spoiled youth, and the eclipse of the Golden Age. While the debate raged, Andrei told me how his family had lived for seven years in one room of a communal apartment. "Four people in one room, with the kitchen in the hall, and the toilet outside. Our parents tacked a blanket to divide off their 'bedroom.' We had no running water. Before going to school each morning I drew ten buckets from the pump in the courtyard."

"Sounds gruesome."

"To me too, now. Then it was postwar Moscow. The building boom hadn't started yet. People were happy to have survived. We lived across the river from the Kremlin, in Zamoskvarechiye, where the thieves and lowlifes congregated in the last century. They put us in an old three-story house surrounded by four big elm trees, and of course with the pump in the courtyard. The thieves had gone, but it was still quite a bazaar. I think fifty people were living on top of each other, with rickety floors and cardboard walls. A big family of circumstance."

He watched the conversation for a moment, then turned back to me. "Chocolate! Imagine it! The whole place smelled of chocolate! What a memory for a boy! When the warm wind blew from the south, it picked up the fumes from the Red October candy factory just upriver, and smothered the stench from the boiling cabbage and the group toilets. Each night I went to sleep sailing on chocolate ships in a chocolate ocean. It was heaven.

"Next door to us there was a math professor just back from the camps who helped me prepare for exams, tutoring me in the kitchen at night, when no one was cooking, or doing laundry. Just a few yards away a fat gypsy woman evacuated from the Volga spent her evenings telling fortunes in the stairwell." He shook his head. "It was strange. We weren't unhappy."

The women were still "advising" Natalya. Andrei leaned back from the table again. "Where did you grow up?"

"Me?" He nodded.

Me? I could hardly remember, it seemed such a long time since anyone had asked. "All over, I guess. My father worked with the airlines, he changed companies several times, and they were always transferring him places. Let me think . . . Los Angeles, Chicago, Portland, New York . . ."

"That's a lot of shifting around."

"Is it?" Glancing through the window to the courtyard, I saw a band of little boys kicking a soccer ball. I remembered a basketball hoop in a driveway in Pittsburgh. We must have lived in Pittsburgh, too.

"The neighborhoods were quite similar—houses with little lawns, and a garage over here to the side. . . ." Digging my fork into the tablecloth, I etched the American Dream.

Andrei nodded recognition. "The famous 'private houses.'" The words have a pejorative ring in Russian, which frowns on the idea of keeping something exclusively for oneself.

"Yes. We call them homes. Mostly we lived in ranches"—I outlined the squat, box lines—"though sometimes we had two floors."

"Ranches, like in the Westerns?"

I laughed. "No, no. It's just a name for the style of building. They're almost the opposite of a real ranch. Out there, you have a house every ten miles or so. Where I lived—" I lined several little boxes alongside one another—"the houses all fit close together, sort of like dominoes."

"That way everyone can have a ranch."

"Yes, I think that's the point." I hadn't really thought of it that way before.

"Do you have brothers or sisters?"

"I have a younger brother. He's with the airlines, too. I can never keep track of his assignments. Do you?"

"Yes, a stepbrother. He's with the military somewhere. I can't keep up with him either."

"Why are you asking me these questions? Are you interested?"

We exchanged glances. "Yes."

The meal was dry, until Andrei pulled out his slender bottle of moonshine, and proposed a toast to me, their newest acquaintance.

Aya shook her head. "My son-in-law, with a university education, brewing spirits," she fretted. A far cry from Dooglass Fairbanks.

"He's done worse, I can assure you," Lilya ventured, stroking her mother's thick arm.

For most of the meal, three-year-old Anya had been on her best behavior, feeding her stuffed animals on the sofa bed, cuddling quietly with Liza between mouthfuls. The toast awoke her to my presence, and she interrogated her grandmother in loud whispers:

"Who is he?"

"Some friend of Andrei's."

"Why doesn't he speak Russian?" I *was* speaking Russian. Apparently she thought I didn't understand Russian either.

"Because he's an American."

"What's that?"

Liza glanced slyly in my direction. "He's a wolf of capitalism."

Anya's political consciousness was unformed, but a

wolf was bad all the same. She pouted. A year later, she still didn't understand why her father had befriended a wolf.

I left the meal after sunset, and my sixth glass of tea. Liza had removed Anya, and Andrei and Lilya were preparing for a "night on the town." As I left, Lilya tapped my breast pocket. "The letters," she reminded. "Don't forget to read the letters."

Alone in my cavernous apartment, dictionary at hand, I had their cousin Aron to myself. His script was clear and rock-steady, a throwback to a time when teachers squeezed their pupils' wrists, and pressed the pen nibs against the paper time and again until the cursive flowed right. I began reading his first letter, sent from a transit housing camp run by the Hebrew Immigration Aid Society outside Rome.

It's done, we're out. All the evil and good of one world exchanged for all the good and evil of the next. Samuel was the first to react: "We're in a *camp*!"

We are in a temporary settlement, surrounded by barbed wire, out here with dozens of other emigrés on the Ostia plain. What should I tell him? It's *their* barbed wire? Lena is sitting on the cot, sobbing half the morning and night, stopping only for Samuel to fall asleep. He and I are acting like men, though I doubt he's acting.

Thirty-six years of my life erased. I know we have some hope for the future—where did we pack it? There's no hope for the past; the farm administration called a meeting even before I left, expelling "the renegade Jew Klein" from the collective, confiscating my diploma, my work medals. Attendance was required. All my friends were there.

The last evening my secretary Rosa and three colleagues knocked timidly at our door, pressing fingers to their lips. No talking. They embraced us, and gave us presents for the road: a jar of honey from their hives, some bread and grapes, and a little aspirin bottle of that soil we used to blame all our troubles on. We bent over each other and wept. Finally, Lena and I recovered, and released them back into that last night, starless and dark as death.

Here in Italy we are prey for "case workers," pale-skinned American girls from New York who coach us on how to answer the questions of the United States visa officials. If we answer correctly, we can travel to America as "refugees from oppression." Say the wrong thing, and you end up in Israel. The girl handling my case suggests I talk about anti-Semitism on the farm: "You know, how the Jew-baiting peasants made life miserable for you." When I tell her I was the deputy director, she agrees to work out a different approach. . . .

The next letter launched a new ink, and even a letterhead, in Hebrew. I skipped over some personal messages.

Israel. Outside the cities, the country is flat and dry, the desert sky as open and blue as a dream. It is always summer. For winter they have a throw of rain. The nature is harsh, but not monotone. Washes of red stain the hills at sunset, and dawn flares yellow on the horizon long before the sun comes up.

After years of living inland, I've seen the ocean for the first time. From the beach at Jaffa, the water expands west like a broad gray road, traveled for centuries, leading to places I never knew existed. This afternoon, two dark old fishermen had pushed their boat on shore to untangle some lines. They spoke English, from Cyprus. Where is that? One of them points across the water. Yes, but America is across the water, too. At the sound of my voice, a dozen big fish start flapping impatiently on the deck, their silver scales glistening with blood: Let's get going! We're not dead yet.

There are other new sights, less pleasant. Soldiers are everywhere, carrying assault rifles. This evening I walked out beyond the university to watch dusk drop down on the plain, and two fighter bombers screeched a hundred meters above my head, tearing my mind off the sky. I had never seen a fighter plane before. I hadn't seen a gun since the army. A new collection of landscapes for me to learn, all at the same time.

And then, Aron's first description of America:

Perhaps there are no good first impressions. There are certainly no good first impressions of America. Stepping off the airplane in New York City, I thought I was the Pope, and the ground would rise to my lips. But the ground was macadam, the heavy August air was filthy, and the airport is as ugly as Tashkent.

There is no sign of that distinctive ridge of sky-scrapers you see in the airline posters. Following a short discussion with a Negro customs man concerning Cuban cigars—all Russians smuggle them, he insisted— Pasha picked me up in his car, and immediately drove me over to Manhattan so I could see the mythical city.

We drove for forty minutes, or rather crawled in an endless line of cars through a succession of depressing neighborhoods. After a rise in the road, a huge hillside full of graves loomed into view. It seemed that the life in the tiny houses of the landscape, with their cramped, affected individualness, was not accidentally juxtaposed with this exhaust-choked graveyard, buried here, in the heart of the middle class.

Manhattan is another world. Pasha parked the car near Wall Street, which had finished business by the time we arrived. The dusk was a gorgeous purple, sometimes bursting between the monstrously tall buildings, sometimes burning in the silver window glaze. We chose an avenue, and began walking.

Lower in the city, the streets were not crowded, so you could look more closely at each person. Everyone tries to look different, so that during the one evening I saw ten women dressed in leopardskin tights, many Negroes with beads fastened in their braided hair, and even six or seven people wearing T-shirts saying "Kiss Me, I'm Italian!" In front of a jewelry store on Sixth Avenue, we saw a group of Soviet diplomats, crowding together. I wished them good evening in a loud voice. By instinct, they huddled closer together, and shuffled past the windows, guiltily.

Fifth Avenue is the main shopping street, and still crowded at night, with people walking from cinemas and plays to restaurants, and back again. It's as packed as Gorky Street, without the lines in front of the Arctic Ice Cream Cafe, without the Armenians peddling jeans, without the glaring blonde Siberian girls walking arm in arm, unsure how much fun to budget for the night ahead.

First seen, the Americans are more purposeful; walkers are off somewhere, rather than just walking. When you know them better, you see that they are too much purpose, but for now the worst that can be said is there is no Ice Cream Cafe.

We spent the evening talking about you, wondering if you would ever join us. We decided you wouldn't, and blessed you the more for it. Geography has less to offer than people. Have you heard from Rosa? Is she using my guitar? Tell her I had my portrait painted by a computer—how about that?

Would he like us? How would it end? I let the letters slide to the floor, and pulled a beer from the refrigerator, finally purged of the rotten egg smell. I stretched out on the sofa and squeezed my eyelids shut, to stare back at America through Aron's eyes.

What did he mean, too much purpose? He should talk to my editors. . . .

Let him make his discoveries, and I would make mine. This evening, with Andrei and Lilya, I had felt the welcome encroachment of a friendship. I suspected I was going to be adopted, in a most pleasing way.

8 / God Save the Queen

The next story I transmitted was headlined "Waiting for Winter," properly illustrated with photos supplied by the "competent organs." I bought pictures of unsold sleds piling up at Children's World department store, of Moscow's famous fleet of snow-removal equipment idled in a suburban staging ground, and of babies pre-emptively swaddled in wool blankets, all waiting for the unseasonably shy winter that lingered at the city's door, yet refused to come on in. Here it was November, and Moscow hadn't seen a hint of its favorite white powder: snow.

"*Snega Nyet!*"—"No Snow!" the headlines moaned. The dogmatically atheist press seemed to be taking the news hardest of all, as they couldn't counsel their readers to take the only prudent course of action, and pray for snow. The state-controlled television contributed to the despair by broadcasting pictures of the southern republics, Armenia and Georgia, and even faraway Washington, D.C., immobilized in snowdrifts, while Moscow broiled in *plusovoy*—above zero—temperatures.

In the text, I tried to convey Moscow's ever-deepening pessimism. With the snowless, slate-colored clouds pressing down on the omnipresent gray concrete of Soviet architecture, the city felt like the inside of a submarine. The Russians, addicted to the suffering and bitter cold of "real," minus-fifty-degree winters, were morose, angrily blaming an epidemic of respiratory ailments on the warm weather. Worse yet, with the public transport system unencumbered by snow and ice, everyone had to show up at work.

Again Jonas cleared out a spread in the middle of the magazine, and cabled his delight: "Folksy stuff. Rockwell feel. Keep it up."

The following day—yet another sad, snowless morning—Ekaterina Sergeyevna clamped onto my elbow as I was leaving the entryway.

"What do you Americans want with our snow?" she demanded.

I jerked my arm free. "We're entitled to our own snow. Let me go!"

"My fur hat is in the closet, shedding. The moths are eating up my overcoat . . ."

"The television said there was plenty of snow north of Moscow, and in the Urals."

"The Urals! My family spent a hundred years trying to get out of the Urals! Who cares what kind of weather those fatheads have?" She escorted me out the door and stared up at the uncompromisingly unsnowy sky. "To hell with the Urals! We want snow!"

I headed off for my office, and noticed she was accompanying me.

"I'm just taking a little walk," she explained, cleaving to my side as we passed through the anxious shopping crowds on the avenue. Each face was glancing nervously at the sky, pining for snow. Just as I rounded the corner of the shoe store to enter my office, she pulled me next to her, against the display window.

"What do the Western papers say?" she whispered.

"About what?"

"About the weather, of course."

"They don't write about it. We have our own problems. You remember—mass poverty, racism and social disease."

She was unconvinced, staring first at me, then feigning interest in the store window. After a pause, I shifted my stance to walk away. She grabbed my arm again, and planted me in my tracks.

"It's the cosmonauts!"

I tried to move away, but she yanked my arm up against her huge chest. "Why don't you write the truth? And that space can of yours, whatever you call it. They're punching holes in the ionosphere, they haven't stopped since they crammed that poor little puppy Laika into one of those awful capsules. That's the shiny stuff that Gagarin saw outside his capsule—it was snow! But the papers censored it! The snow has been escaping into space for twenty years! The warm air is coming in—the sun's pure rays, without filtration. Write the truth for once!"

Somehow, across vast geographical and ideological distances, my mother and Ekaterina Sergeyevna had been reading the same magazines.

She slipped her hand inside her dress, just underneath the Stalingrad medal, and pulled out a tiny gold crucifix on a chain. "It's the Devil's work, this heat." She massaged the cross between her thumb and forefinger, then pressed her face up against mine. It occurred to me that her breath might be used to stun small laboratory animals. She whispered: "Are you a believer?"

I whispered back, "In what?"

"In God, you fool."

"No."

"Oh. Neither am I." She tucked the cross back in between her huge breasts. "We were better off in simpler times, God knows." She forged ahead of me into the crowd, acting as if we had never met.

Susan insisted she had spent the Queen's official Birthday at home, preparing for her party. Some of the time had been devoted to pouring herself into a strapless blue velvet evening dress, ceding at the knees to blue stockings, again flecked with gold tinsel. Pulling open the door, she executed her trademark pirouette.

"Silver slippers, too. You must have spent all day shopping at GUM."

She leaned forward to kiss me on the cheek. "More imports from the decadent West, I'm afraid."

"Happy birthday."

"Well, happy birthday to *her*." She pointed to a government issue portrait of Elizabeth II, hanging behind a large fern plant. The portrait, not the queen. The queen was hiding behind a bouquet of scarlet roses, probably a gift from hubby Philip.

"You're quite the civil servant."

"Hardly. It's not even her birthday, you know."

"I didn't know."

"I knew you wouldn't, so I let it go. It's actually Guy Fawkes Day, but I thought putting that on the invitation might confuse you. You might think he was a football player, or some cricketer."

"Who was he?"

"Revolutionary chap, at least when it was revolutionary to be a Catholic. Wanted to blow up the Houses of Parliament, but never quite brought the idea off. The students build big bonfires in his memory. I like to take the day off."

"Oh. Before I forget." I handed her a small box of White Nights chocolates, from the Red October candy factory.

"How sweet!" Susan kissed me on the cheek again. "You're so charming when you're sober."

I took in the apartment. Her quarters were cramped. On the space continuum she came in about halfway between Andrei and me. The living room set, a bland sofa with two plush chairs and a glass-topped coffee table, had a purchasing office look. To be fair, Susan had tried to brighten up the environment. She had covered her walls with splashy art exhibition posters, and huge blowups of rock and roll concerts, featuring U-2, Clash!, and of course Queen.

"Is that your kind of music?"

"I *abhor* it." She had an accent right off public television: I ab-haaaw it. "The music posters add a touch of spiritual decline to this otherwise monotone Socialist country. I've got Mozart on in the living room. Drink?"

I joined her next to the fold-down bar. While she pointed at bottles, I stared down her low-cut dress, ogling her full, lightly freckled breasts. God, it had been a long time.

For my trouble, Susan elbowed me gently in the solar plexus. "Mr. Perkins. If you would be kind enough to stop looking down my dress and choose a drink. Or are you addicted to sex, as you are to alcohol?"

"I'm suffering withdrawal symptoms. Sex doesn't come in bottles."

Susan's quick blush briefly extinguished the freckles on her face and neck. I silently prayed the other guests would arrive, to prevent me from pouncing on her.

She handed me a delightfully dark scotch and water, and plopped down on the sofa, dropping her slippers and folding her bare feet beneath her. I noticed she had poured herself a stiff vodka and tonic. At least she wasn't allergic to alcohol. We touched glasses. "Cheers."

"So. How are you settling in?"

"All right, I guess. Ten more months to go."

"Then what?"

"Western Europe. Maybe Paris."

"Yes, that was my agreement, too. A season in hell, a

lifetime in heaven. I often wonder how it will all work out."

"Maybe we'll meet again on the Champs-Elysées."

"Don't count your chickens. I'm as likely to end up in the Black Hole of Calcutta. How's the comic?"

I was vetting the apartment for boyfriend pictures, and saw none. A good sign. "What's the comic?"

"You know—your publication, your magazine."

"It's not really a comic. You've never read it, have you?"

"No, but I mentioned it in a letter to my mum, and she said it's rather an *extraordinary* production. Are you the ones that write about cows with three heads, and lobotomized baby stranglers?"

"Not any more. Now we write about stagflation and foreign policy."

"Oh dear. My mum will be disappointed. She says you cover 'Dallas' better than anyone."

"Well, thank her for the compliment. I don't think our pages will be completely purged of 'Dallas' material. And now she can read about Russia, too." I winked, to no response.

I was trying to sip my scotch, but the fluid level was rapidly lowering. "How did you get into this line of work?"

"The Foreign Office? I don't know. Early toilet training, carefully pressed uniforms, good grades in school. I couldn't escape the stigma of being well brought up. How about you—how did you become a . . . writer?"

"Same procedures, just in reverse. Frequently changing schools. Lots of demerits for poor conduct, sloppy dress habits. Lack of enthusiasm for a legitimate career."

"Mmmm."

"But, if you don't mind my asking . . . you're not exactly a diplomat, are you?"

Her eyes were laughing above the rim of her glass. "Whatever do you mean, Mr. Perkins?"

"Well, the embassy won't give out your phone number. And you're not supposed to fraternize with the enemy, which apparently even includes me."

"This is fraternization, isn't it?"

"Too fraternal for my tastes." She giggled, which I interpreted as another hopeful sign. "You must be a very important librarian."

"Oh, it's all just formalities." She leaned across the sofa and touched her lips to my ear. "It's really none of your bloody business, is it, what I do with my little friends in the dark basements of the embassy when everyone else is asleep? We still have an Official Secrets Act, luv, and *she*—" Susan gestured toward the portrait of the queen—"still pays my salary. And little Ivan has big ears. So let's change the subject, right?" She kissed my cheek, trailing a pleasant odor of perfume.

"Hole in your glass, luv?" Inexplicably, my portion of scotch had run out. "Let me fix you another."

While she mixed drinks, I checked out her bookcase. Before leaving England, she had stocked up on the great nineteenth century Russian novels, which sat on the top shelf of her cabinet, spines uncracked.

"Buy these by the yard? Or were you planning to visit Russia some day?"

"My, you are condescending. And whatever for?" She glided across the room and handed me my drink. Her velvet dress shimmered in the lamplight. "Yes, I thought I would read those, given that I wouldn't be meeting the citizenry." She led me back to the couch. "Do you know any Russians?"

"I met a nice couple recently. At least they seemed nice to me."

"How do you know they're not reporting on you? They all do, you know."

"Do they? I wouldn't know. They don't seem like the types."

"People don't always look the part." She giggled again. Clearly, the vodka was taking hold.

"What's to report, I wonder? That I eat peanut butter and mayonnaise sandwiches before I go to bed? That I wipe my fingers on my socks if there's no napkin around? What am I doing that's so secret? What's everyone afraid of?"

Susan assumed a preachy tone. "They hate foreigners, Nick. And worse than foreign spies they hate the foreign press. We're enemies, Nick, all of us. Read your Marx."

"I did, a long time ago. The sentences were too long."

"You're not ready for the ideological front. I'll have to warn my mum about you."

Happily the conversation took a less formal tack. I learned that Susan had grown up in Kent, the "garden of England," where her father, a Tory pharmacist, had laid the groundwork for her bedrock anti-Bolshevism. She seemed intrigued by my peripatetic childhood. How interesting, she thought, to have traveled so much as a family. Until she was accepted to university, she had hardly left the township of Dover. We agreed to exchange identities. The fantasy of a Trollope-y childhood in Kent appealed to me. Susan envied a lifetime spent within commuting distance of a major airport. She loved to fly.

As she said, she had embarked on her diplomatic career the way the English do these things—by excelling at competitive examinations from the age of seven on. She freely confessed the exams hadn't prepared her for the British Embassy in Moscow. Even from her vague description, I confirmed my suspicion that she worked as a super-secret registry clerk and was expected to provide a pattable fanny and even warm sheets for some of the senior spooks.

"It's really quite horrid, the things these married men try. And the area is rather enclosed—sound-proofed, actually—you can't make a fuss." She sighed, and rested her head on the sofa back. "I don't suppose your American women would put up with it, would they?"

"Who knows?" I decided to test the quality of Ekaterina Sergeyevna's intelligence. "What does your London boyfriend think?"

Susan didn't miss a beat. "My, we have been snooping, haven't we?" She closed her eyes for a moment, remembering her lover, half regretting and half relieved by his absence. "Sam? He's very proper now. A chartered accountant—a mother's dream. Bottom-pinching isn't quite his style."

Susan drew a deep breath, and curled sideways on the sofa, eyes closed, as if talking to herself. "He grew up in Kent—we went to school together, and fetched up in London after university. He never finished, of course, he was too busy being a Bolshie, mobilizing the masses, that sort of thing." She paused, and smiled at the memory. "You'd like him. He's very Left.

"We were together for quite a while. I sorted papers at a bank, while he lugged his megaphone around Battersea and the Isle of Dogs, drumming up rent strikes. He was a true believer." She opened her eyes to see if I was still listening. I was.

"Then I took the civil service exams, you see, and did very well, and the diplomats wanted me. Sam's reaction was just the opposite of what I had expected. Instead of turning against me, he turned with me, and rebelled against the Cause. He latched on to accountancy, of all things. I shamed him into going straight, and then flitted off to Moscow. Here I am, miserable in the workers' paradise, and there he is, tallying up the books for the lords of capital." She sighed. "It's terrifying to influence someone. Now he wants to marry me."

"By return post? Despite what you read in the comics, many married couples live together these days. It's the latest thing."

"You *are* difficult. What about you? You must have left a trail of broken hearts back in New York."

The scotch had plunged me into a vertiginous state of candor. "Not me. I don't really go for the heart."

Susan raised her eyebrows, and smirked. "Ooooh. Great script. Very American. Very frontier. Slam, bang, thank you ma'am. Does that approach work in New York? I thought the women shot back."

Potent with liquor, I laid my hand on her dark velvet thigh. "Susan, I can't hold out here much longer alone. You're too beautiful, and if your birthday people or fox people don't show up soon, I'm going to make a pass at you the likes of which your spy gang could never imagine."

Susan lowered her eyelashes demurely, and laid her hand on top of mine. "But Nick, this is the party. I wouldn't have wanted to share the holiday with anyone else but you."

I pounced.

Sleeping next to a woman must have triggered memories of Greenwich Village, when Sharon sometimes woke me three or four times a night to ask about a creak in the floorboards or the pinging of the radiators filling with water. Without waking Susan, I stood up next to the bed. On her bureau, I spotted a portrait of her parents, earnest and cheerful, arm in arm at a county fairground. And next to them, a picture of smiling, hapless Sam, posing with a briefcase and umbrella in a narrow alley of the City, London's Wall

Street. He looked awkward and out of costume. I lay him face down on the chest of drawers, where he wouldn't be disturbed.

From the center of the room, I walked over to the window facing the street, and gazed at Kutuzov Prospect below. I had traveled a long way from Greenwich Village. No sirens, no car alarms, no "jive people" screeched in the Moscow night. Every few minutes, one or two stray taxicabs wove slowly down the eight-lane avenue. Quiet and settled, all of Russia lay below, unknown to me. I resolved to see more of it.

Suddenly, I realized that I might still be asleep. Looking down on the boulevard, I dreamed I was an astronaut in a faraway space capsule, my window on Moscow sparkling with bright white dots. But I wasn't dreaming.

The bright white dots were snow.

9 / Martinou

By the time I tiptoed back to my apartment the next morning, the nighttime snowfall had vanished without a trace. There was no accumulation; the ground wasn't even wet. Maybe those really had been phosphor-whizbangs falling from the sky.

A cousin of mine from California had once tried to explain the differences between the East and West coasts in terms of the "mind-body mix." Sipping on a canned herbalist potion that was later taken off the shelves by the Food and Drug Administration, he told me how far out of balance we New Yorkers had fallen. But in Moscow, my cousin would have been pleased to know, the mix had been restored, and even enhanced. I spent my days shuttling among the lives of my mind, body, and soul.

The mind lived at the office, with Boris and the telex. As time passed, I was less anxious to spend six or seven hours planted at my desk reading translations of Soviet newspapers and eavesdropping on Boris' burgeoning auto parts business. His commercial activities, which now included furtive meetings in the stairwell with mechanics in grease-stained overalls, in addition to constant phoning, absorbed more of his time. I began to feel his nominal job of translator—my Russian had become almost fluent—might be keeping him from his true calling as manager of Moscow's first Midas Muffler concession.

In truth, he was expanding his avocation to fill the time. He wasn't exactly shirking his translation work, but I had little need of his assistance. I had long ago instituted "bankers' hours" for myself, arriving after ten and leaving before four. Soon even that commitment seemed excessive. As I pared my office hours to the bone, I realized I was merely resurrecting a preexisting category, "foreign correspondent's hours."

I did, however, devote most of the daylight hours to my job—at least for my first few months in Moscow. During October and November, I embarked on a campaign of "preemptive lunches," to corral sources for my stories. My task was not unlike filling the ark. I wanted at least one of each species—a Japanese businessman, an African journalist, an East Bloc provocateur—from the Moscow bestiary, whom I could train to return my phone calls promptly, listen to my questions, and speak their piece, no matter how bizarre.

The strategy paid handsome dividends. Soon, writing stories became a matter of pushing the right buttons. If I needed a speaker to blast "big power hegemonism," Mr. Chu at the Chinese Embassy, whom I had wooed with back issues of *Playboy,* was happy to oblige. If I needed a "curse on both imperialist houses" quote, I merely dialed up the Libyans, the Burmese, or for that matter, the French. The recipe for Moscow journalism became deceptively simple: Start with a bit of background reading, or maybe a Tass dispatch to add body, season with a few well-chosen quotes. Blend at the typewriter keyboard, shove the mix in the telex, and repeat, once each week.

So much for the life of the mind. To Susan I had

delegated control over my body. Because of her complicated schedule—much of her job was to manage the traffic of classified messages to and from London at night—we had swapped apartment keys, and merged our living spaces. We even played musical beds. Some nights I would fall asleep alone in my apartment, and wake up to find her snuggled next to me. Other nights I snuck into her bed and hid under the covers. Once I even slept under her bed as a prank. Coming home at five A.M., she spotted me, and woke me up by roaring the vacuum cleaner against my ear.

"Thought I smelled something under the bed, luv." I wrestled her out of her business suit, and we made love on a precious Dagestan carpet she had just purchased in a diplomatic store. We fell asleep on the floor, with the clean, woolly smell of the freshly woven carpet filling our senses. I woke up first, after ten, and put in an appearance at the office before lunch.

Susan was exactly Sharon's age, but not driven by Sharon's compulsions. Prefacing my comments with a half-hour-long disclaimer, I had once asked her whether she intended to marry. "That's sort of putting the cart before the horse, isn't it, Nick?" was her welcome reply. Perhaps my disclaimers should have been more forceful.

Susan found it difficult to explain her professionally executed Guy Fawkes Day seduction in a manner that didn't make her seem . . . promiscuous. "I'm not really like that," she would begin, and burst out giggling while I rolled my eyes. "It was something about your style. . . ." That statement, which she repeated often enough for me to believe, both gratified and perplexed me. I was happy to learn I had a style; no one had remarked on it before. Now I wondered what it was.

Our relationship was blessed by distance, from family, from friends, and from pressures to "define" our situation. We knew only that we enjoyed each other's company, and bodies, and that in less than a year we would be somewhere else, with someone else.

Meanwhile, Andrei and Lilya were laying claim to that most un-American piece of spiritual anatomy, my soul. At the end of the day, I enjoyed the relaxing drive to Kolomenskoye, watching the city dissolve into country, then reassert itself again. Now I was making the trip two or three times a week, happy not to spend the evening in my half-furnished apartment hoping against hope that for once Susan's masters in London and Moscow would fall silent, and send her home to me.

On my first few visits to Andrei's apartment, I brought small house presents, like a bottle of wine, or a Western fashion magazine, to ease my welcome. After a month, Lilya pressed my bottle back in its plastic bag. "Nick, don't be concerned. Just bring yourself."

Inside their home, the geometry was always different, but hospitable. Sometimes the girls' room was closed, if I arrived after Anya's bedtime or during a visit from Natalya's unpredictable boyfriend. Lilya could be alone in the kitchen reading a book, or boiling a five gallon vat of macaroni for a crowd of guests. Many evenings I found Andrei sitting alone at one end of the narrow corridor, legs crossed, gazing at the television resting on a bookshelf next to the door. At my arrival, he would raise his eyes, undisturbed. "Oh, I just switched on some figure skating. Our people are trouncing yours. Pull up a chair."

As we drank tea, or watched television, all of Russia seemed to parade through the tiny apartment. One evening a relative from Stavropol burst in to spend the night, and told the story of the skating bear that had charged off the rink during a circus performance, slashing spectators with the sharp blades strapped on its paws until the police gunned it down.

Another evening, a colleague who had resettled in Vladivostok appeared, unannounced, of course, with a gift of Ussuri Balsam "containing seventeen medicinal herbs, including the legendary ginseng," according to the label. What about the downtown tiger carnage, I asked? Had it really happened? He couldn't remember. Vladivostok tiger stories outnumbered Vladivostok tigers about ten to one, he warned, and suddenly the glasses were full again.

In New York, I had learned to distiguish between spontaneity and its opposite. For people like Sharon and me, spontaneity meant seeing the *Rocky Horror Picture Show* for the nth time, or ordering in Chinese instead of making dinner. The opposite might be planning for a summer rental in the Hamptons, in November of the preceding year. But here in Moscow, spontaneity remained untamed. Time was always *now.* No one knocked and offered to come back tomorrow. No one phoned to propose dinner next week, or even for the next evening. No desire could be suspended. Why not now?

Indeed, that was Andrei's attitude towards the trip he had been proposing for over two weeks, hammering away at my increasingly feeble objections. For one, it wasn't legal. I wasn't allowed to leave the city limits without informing the authorities. For two, for two . . . I suppose it was the fear of knowing any one person too well. Perhaps Russia was the place to overcome it.

We would take the train. Anyone can buy a ticket without producing the internal "passport." If we ran into the police, Andrei assured me I could "pass"— "certainly for a Latvian or Lithuanian"—the worst speakers of Russian in the country. The real seduction was the description of our host: Daniel Mitrofanovich Martinov, "active crusader against the Soviet state."

Andrei had befriended Martinov at the university, where he was one of the most notorious signers of the short-lived Petition Era, when Moscow University students, anxious to keep pace with Berkeley and the Sorbonne, railed against the injustices of the time. For a while, the regime ignored the signers, many of whom were children of the Party elite or of prominent intellectuals with academic appointments. But eventually the time came to set examples, and one of the first was the twenty-eight-year-old graduate student in mathematics, D.M. Martinov, sentenced to seven years of exile in the town of Z——, 400 kilometers north of Moscow.

"We took it as a colossal joke, you know," Andrei said. "The ultramodern youth of the sixties. I mean, yes, Herzen, Pushkin, the Decembrists were exiled . . . but a computer programmer working on integer theory? It was hard to believe.

"We could travel there, and we did, even though he lived about seven miles from the nearest train station. His girlfriend stayed up there a lot; they were talking about marriage. I visited once in the summer and had a splendid time. We cut the hay, we trapped leeches, we kicked goats up and down hillsides, playing the little Tolstoyans. In fact—"

From a drawer in the huge commode he found a sepia snapshot of a dozen young people bunched around a wooden trestle table in glaring sunshine, in front of a bleached white peasant *izba*, or hut. All had stripped to the waist, the women wearing the bulky 1960s style brassieres, laughing. Huge porcelain pitchers of dark kvass, thick beer fermented from black bread, crowded the table, alongside slender bottles of 150-proof village moonshine.

Fifteen years younger, Andrei looked magnificent, with a thick mane of russet hair, and the chest of a railwayman. He slid his index finger under a taller man, bearded, also strong, standing behind the table with his arm around a husky blond: Martinov.

"After university I was sent out to the Volga for three years," Andrei continued, "and when I returned everything had changed. The student crowd had married and melted away into the new housing projects. One night, by chance, I met Martinov's girl, and she told me it was all over. I asked after him, and she closed up, said she hadn't been keeping in touch. . . .

"For three or four years I met other friends and began to hear stories. Martinov is drinking, Martinov has gonorrhea, Martinov is keeping a peasant woman. In short, no one is visiting any more, no one knows anything. Then when a group of us gathered for dinner five years ago, someone counted on his fingers, and announced that Martinov's sentence had finished the previous spring. He never came back."

Propal. Martinov had fallen through the ice.

To make the trip, I had to cover my tracks at the office, and with Susan. I told her I was leaving town for a week to go skiing at a foreign ministry-owned dacha north of Moscow. She agreed to phone my office every few days and tell Boris I was sick, a ruse that would probably keep him off the scent until my return. Eventually the same listeners who shoehorned little microphones into my walls, and for whom both Boris and Ekaterina Sergeyevna had to fill our monthly reports, would realize that I had disappeared. But by then, knock on wood, I would already be back.

Standing next to Andrei on the platform of Moscow's Yaroslavl station, I was making a great effort to look Soviet. Andrei had loaned me wooden skis, a floppy old knapsack, and canvas overalls to help me blend in with the landscape. My one indulgence—as Dostoyevsky reminds us, all criminals want to be caught—was a red and white Harvard ski cap I had bought at the famous Coop during a weekend sexual encounter with an intellectual superior. But, Andrei told me, red and white were also the colors of Spartak, Moscow's favorite hockey team. I "passed" with flying colors, as just another little pea in the proletarian pod.

The train ride north was like a journey through time. After Yaroslavl, a despoiled industrial city that had long ago formed part of the Golden Ring of the twelfth century monastery-fortresses surrounding Moscow, the train plunged into the steppe. We never saw a power line, nor a road, nor even a car. This was where they were hiding the snow, endless fields of snow, occasionally dotted with clumps of trees or houses, stretching away from us forever. In the distance, I saw several horse-drawn carts, inching across the landscape like sad, cold grasshoppers.

Andrei had warned me that the train might not stop at our destination, so we had prepared. As the carriage slowed alongside a fifty-yard strip of concrete, he jumped out and jogged slowly next to the wagon. Out the door, I threw him our two knapsacks, which he dropped to the ground, and then our skis. Then I jumped out.

Three carriages behind us, an enormous peasant babushka swathed in black waddled next to the restaurant car, handing small bottles stoppered with cloth to a white-sleeved arm in the moving door, and grabbing fat sausages in return. The frantic transaction lasted the length of the platform. Three times she tripped against our gear on the concrete siding, shrieked a curse, and slogged forwards.

As the train clattered off into the distance, she

stopped short in front of us, gasping for breath where the concrete ended in snow. She held open her mesh bag, displaying four fat pink sausages, bursting their seams of crinkly skin. "For six bottles of alcohol. It's a fair trade, huh?" She looked up smiling proudly, showing only gums. I nodded. Snapping her bag shut, she wobbled off the platform into the forest, grumbling, "Why doesn't that son of a bitch ever stop?"

I stared at the landscape. Six hours in the train, and we were deep in the heart of the missing winter. Ahead and behind, there was nothing but the railway line, cut flat and straight through the snowy black forest, ceding five yards on each side. No roads, no paths, no signs. Where were we?

Andrei ran after the village woman. They talked for a minute, her free arm waving like a black flag. She spat, and stalked off into the woods.

"Over here." Andrei pointed with a ski pole to a narrow trail cutting through the opposite line of woods. "To the river, then follow the river right." We shouldered our packs, and began to ski.

After an hour, the river descended into a valley, and scattered the forest. The open space, flecked with low, dark huts, was Z——. In front of his same bleached hut, stamping out a path from his door to the village road, we found Martinov. In a country devoid of communications, these two people had been drawn together like magnets.

The three of us stood completely alone in the frozen roadway. Martinov and Andrei peered at each other across a ten-year span of time. Martinov spread his arms, opening the folds of his dirty sheepskin cloak to embrace Andrei.

"*Bratets*! My brother!"

Andrei squeezed Martinov, and snuggled his head into his friend's fleece collar. "*Sinochek,*" he whispered.

"My son." They embraced each other in silence for over a minute. Andrei disengaged and pulled me into Martinov's hug.

"My friend from America."

Martinov grinned through a ragged mouthful of broken teeth, and bussed me on the cheek. "Welcome."

Standing up to his calves in the snow, Martinov talked in the unflappable village style, as if guests from Moscow skied in often, and he had prepared a tour. He pointed to the "center" of the village, a group of ten collapsing homes, and rattled off the names of the owners, all women. To his left, he arched a long arm over the white hillside, showing us a small clump of bare tree trunks in a miniature valley about a half mile away. "My neighbor, Praskovya Fyodorovna."

Behind us—he threw a thumb over his shoulder without bothering to look—stood the old cement factory, abandoned several years ago. Most of the men, including Martinov's landlord, had vanished when the plant closed, leaving the village a dwindling population of about forty old women. "They spend the days talking to their icons, and their evenings making moonshine for the city clientele."

Our host looked every inch the muzhik. The long-haired sheepskin cloak, once white, doubled his volume and lifted his shoulders above his considerable height. Underneath, he wore only a peasant's cotton blouse and homespun trousers tied at the waist with a drawstring. For footwear, he had *bast,* peasant shoes of woven straw. Seeing me stare, he laughed. "It's just an affectation—don't think I've 'gone peasant,' for God's sake! My boots are drying next to the fire."

But he took the look beyond clothing, burying his face in a vast brown beard beneath waxy, unkempt hair. His eyes betrayed the disguise; they illuminated the soft, blue gaze of the Russian urban intellectual, who understands more than he needs to know.

We left our skis leaning against the outside door, and shed our boots in a tiny anteroom built to protect the front door of the hut. We entered one big, cold room, with a floor of dark packed earth, hard as concrete, seeping the light acid smell of clay pounded by two hundred years of feet and straw. In the far corner, a huge blue tiled stove rose like a shaft of open sky in the dark interior. Andrei picked his way between a broken sofa and a handmade table to press his palms against the tile. He frowned.

"We'll stoke it up after some shopping," Martinov yelled from the "kitchen area," where a gas range and waist-high shelves full of cans and preserves separated a second corner in the room. "Throw your stuff down next to the stove, and let's go."

Outside, in the town, there was no attention to time. The daylight was somber, a gray commingling of dawn and dusk. Passersby were few, and they didn't wear watches. The village's three stores were all closed, and had no hours posted on the doors. Martinov suggested we buy vinegar and mustard seed for pickling the cucumbers we had brought from Moscow. But instead of walking toward the road, we set off into the backyard of his hut, flush into three foot snowdrifts.

"I thought the store was in town," I grumbled, as my boots filled with snow.

"The store is in town," Martinov replied, kicking a path for us with his knees.

We carved a trough along the muted hillside, and trudged toward the neighboring hut he had pointed out earlier, sprawled beneath a stand of bare, frosted trees. The roof sagged under a heavy burden of snow. Some sections of the outside walls had settled much further into the ground than others, creating an uneven roof line, and the suggestion of collapse.

Approaching from the rear, we came upon a bloated sow shivering in a covered pen. A ragged clothesline dangling tiny icicles hung around her neck, tying her to the kitchen door. A narrow path strewn with corn feed led from the pen to the door.

Martinov pulled off a wool glove, and banged heavily against the door. After a few moments, he banged again. "Praskovya! Open up! It's me, Martinov!" Andrei and I began stamping circles in the snow, trying to keep warm.

From inside we heard a noise like shifting furniture, a jostling of pots and pans, then fumbling with the lock. Heavy cotton batting lined the door, taped along the edges. It opened with a sucking sound, like prying open a sealed jar. A round face, jellied with wrinkles, molded by a fading blue kerchief, appeared in the doorway.

"What's the lock for? Don't want us to catch you praying?" He extended his hand.

"Never shake over a threshold."

The woman ignored Martinov's question to gaze at us visitors, rubbing a huge mole that hung like a polyp from her upper lip. "Who're your friends? They're squeezing their knees like virgins."

"Maybe they are. Look, give us the keys to the store, will you? I've got to get some things."

The crone began to agitate. "You know the rules! Store's not open. What time is it anyway? My radio's busted."

Martinov glanced over his shoulder at the bulging, gray sun. "About eleven. Look, let's have the keys."

A touch of color flowed to Praskovya's cheeks. "Who knows where the keys are? Victor Semyonich was rooting around there for vodka, ask him where—" Martinov pressed a ruble note into her chalky palm.

"What's this? What our Muscovite friends call an incentive payment? What must they think of us backwards country folk!" She chuckled, and brought an arm out from under the dark blanket draped across her shoulders, tossing the keys against Martinov's chest. "Bring them back soon! Store closes at noon, ha, ha, ha!" We heard her high-pitched cackling laughter from far down the hill, as we retraced our steps toward the village.

"Tea?" An old enamel pot sat on the bottom grate of the ceiling-high oven. Martinov dipped his nose into the pot, frowned, and walked to the back door to toss the stale leaves into the snow. From a warren carved out behind the stove, he unfurled a rumpled packet of tea and dropped a few fingersful into the pot. "Ceylonese." He laughed. "They stand in line for it in Moscow. Here it's all we have."

From a huge bucket of water standing against the wall, he filled the teapot. Next, he pried open the oven's metal trap at knee level to look for signs of fire or coals. "Ash, damn it." In another corner of the hut we hacked a few logs small enough to fit into the grate. Before tossing them in, Martinov dipped the kindling in a wide-mouthed bottle of kerosene. At the touch of a match, the wood exploded inside the belly of the oven, and ten minutes later cups of hot tea were warming our hands.

"Technology," he muttered, sliding onto the dirty sofa, balancing his tea on a moth-eaten arm. "It reminds me of a moment just before the trial. Four prosecutors had been in my apartment cataloguing my books and papers to use as 'evidence' for their case.

"Afterward, we were standing around in the entryway, smoking, chatting, as if I had invited them to come fix the pipes. 'A fine library, Daniel Mitrofanovich,' one of them said. 'If you should be leaving town unexpectedly'—of course he knew I was getting seven years—'make careful provisions.' He was especially interested in the Dostoyevsky centenary edition, and even suggested a price.

"Then suddenly, without warning, a little guy in a work suit forced his way past these secret police types and barged into the apartment. Who's this? The detectives get the scent up, maybe thinking in terms of a second arrest. This tattered fellow heads for my kitchen, and pulls out a pen, a notebook, and some measuring tape. He's down on his knees, writing all sorts of numbers on his pad."

Living without television, Martinov acted out his own dramas in pantomime. He was crawling on the floor with the unknown visitor, watching him scrawl messages on his pad.

"Finally, he stands up, and tucks his notes away in his jacket. One of the prosecutors flashes his red badge, and asks what's going on. The little guy puffs himself up, and proudly declares: 'We're putting in electric stoves! Your neighborhood's joining the twentieth century!' And he shoulders his way out of the place, ignoring the security men."

Martinov straightened up. "Of course, I got Article Forty-three, and that ruled out the twentieth century for me. Now I'm four hundred kilometers outside Moscow and two hundred years back in time. I could go further. Civilization gives me a headache. I've never been happier."

Martinov knew Aron, whom he called "the other exile," from his days at the university. Aron had stayed with Martinov for two weeks while he was waiting for his exit visa, to see what it was like, being away.

"It was meaningless," Martinov said. "Being here had nothing to do with being away from Russia. We dug up the garden, planted the spring potatoes, guzzled moonshine at night. Hell, he was closer to Russia than ever before. There—" he shook his head, then remembered me, smiling apologetically. "Sorry, but America, really . . ." From another niche in the stove, he pulled out a folded sheaf of onionskin letters, like Lilya's.

"He writes maybe twice a year. I'm not so sure he's happy over there. . . ."

"I think he's doing all right," Andrei said.

"Maybe." Martinov lumbered over to the sofa and pulled an envelope out from under one of the cushions. I realized there was no bed. The sofa was all the comfort the room had. "I was rereading one of them last night. I guess it's almost exactly a year old."

Andrei and I lowered ourselves onto the floor, leaning our backs against the burning hot tiles of the oven, which warmed the earth as far away as our ankles.

Martinov cleared his throat, and shuffled the pages back and forth. "Yes, here's the good part."

Lena is the censor: Nostalgia is forbidden! But what happened to winter? In New York, it's hardly a season at all. Heating bills go up, maybe some snow falls. But nothing stops—It's depressing. Life just keeps on going.

Remember during the 1968 blizzards, when we couldn't even leave the apartment buildings, and they had to send the army kids to dig us out? Or the time all the subways froze to the tracks in one of the switch-yards? I didn't go to work for weeks! The schools were closed; Samuel and I learned ice fishing on the Yauza. Not in America! The subway may be dirty, but it still runs. It's December, and I haven't missed a day of work yet! It's awful!

I was going to write that in Russia, winter is a season when you can finally relax. But hell, you can relax any season there—the winter's too cold for working, the spring's too muddy, the summer's too hot. Fall? Remember gathering chestnuts on the boulevards? In the fall, it's too lovely to work. But here come the Nostalgia Police. I must stop.

The fall here was not so good, but I'll save that for another letter. I've been offered a higher paying job, so I must rent a more expensive apartment. See how ambitious we Americans are? But there's no time to reflect, because we are in the middle of a period of great "happiness"—the American Christmas.

It's all very Soviet. The superpatriots here would strike me down for saying that, but it's true. It hardly matters if you're Jewish, Arab, or Hindu. You don't have to participate, you just have to be happy. I buy hemorrhoid ointment at the pharmacy and the clerk wishes me a "happy holiday." On the front of my office building, they've hung a twenty-foot-tall, smiling head of St. Nicholas from the third floor, so that his beard cuts off the sunlight from my window. I mentioned this to one of the bosses . . . he wasn't happy.

Down the street, on the sidewalk, there is a Negro dressed in a red and white St. Nicholas costume, wearing a combed fiberglass beard. He reminds me of Lenin—the beard's not right, of course—this I don't tell my boss. But this jolly fellow always wants you to be cheery, to think of the underprivileged . . . why, who else could it be, but Vladimir Ilyich!

Martinov folded the page back with the other letters. "Our friend's sense of humor seems to be darkening a bit."

"America can do that to you, can't it?" Andrei asked me.

I suppose it can.

10 / Natasha

Our second morning in the hut, Martinov rolled off his sofa, groaning, "I've got to go to work."

Martinov stoked the boiler for the district school, which burned soft coal in a basement furnace for heating and for hot water in the locker room showers. School was out for New Year's, but Martinov had promised to fire the boilers once a week, to keep frost off the blackboards.

In the summer and fall, a school bus circled the neighboring villages to pick up pupils. But in other seasons the country roads were impassable, so teachers, students, and help slogged to school in the spring, and skied in the winter. For Martinov, the pay was negligible, but the school director allowed him free coal for his oven, and never probed too deeply about his defection to the countryside.

"And her husband brews moonshine," he said of the director. "A pillar of local society."

The skiing took us behind Praskovya's house, about two kilometers further along the base of the long, oval hill. The school, a two-story weathered brick building, huddled in the crook of the slope. A faded agitational placard hung by one corner on the side wall: "Schoolchildren! Implement the Leninist ideal in—" The bottom half lay buried in a snowdrift.

In front, like a huge staple on the landscape, stood a set of soccer goalposts, foreshortened by the heavy snow. On the opposite horizon, we saw a thin pair of ski tracks winding out of a forest toward the front door of the school.

Inside, we found the director's husband splashing in a puddle of melted snow, filling a knapsack with bags of sugar for his still. "We get forty kilos a month, whether the kids are here or not," he puffed, stacking the square bags inside his pack. "Shame to waste it." Martinov grunted an approval, of sorts, and led us to his basement holdings.

The lower floor had been hollowed out of the ground. The walls were earthen, damp, and black with coal dust. In a corner, next to the tarred boiler, Martinov had created his den: a reclaimed easy chair, also soot black, and a low slung cot next to a night table cobbled from kindling. From underneath the chair, Martinov extracted a bulky shortwave radio, wrapped in a plastic bag. "Perfect reception," he chuckled. "Voice of America, Radio Liberty, Deutsche Welle. I pervert youth."

Next to the chair stood a small food cupboard, sealed with cotton to keep rats out. One lightbulb plunged from a cord run along the ceiling. Switching it on, Martinov lit a double row of waist-high bookshelves behind the sofa, standing free of the moldy earthwall.

While Martinov shoveled coal into the furnace, Andrei inspected the bookshelves. "A lot of those are from the district library," Martinov explained above the jangling of the coal scuttle. "I had about a hundred volumes checked out when it burned down. No one ever came for them. Between those, and what I hauled from Moscow, I'm not missing much." He tossed some kindling into the boiler, along with a glassful of kerosene.

"The kids like it down here, when the dust isn't so

bad. They come and take whatever they want. They're very impressed that I have *Lolita,* by the emigré insect Nabokov. And it's only intolerable in the summer. The cellar, I mean." He coughed at the bottom of his throat, and threw a match into the furnace. "Pow-woff! Work's over for today."

Andrei was fingering a pre-Revolutionary volume of Dahl's encyclopedic dictionary, frowning at the dark border of coal dust that had formed along the gold-edged calfskin covers. "I read it, I use it," Martinov pleaded, on the defensive. "Andrei, this isn't a museum, this is where I live."

"I know what you're thinking," he said as we clattered back up the fragile wooden stairs to the main floor. "The dust, the blackness. How do I put up with it? For privacy, I suppose. . . ." He jostled some keys, and closed the cellar door behind us. "I don't know. I've had worse than coal dust."

Looking out a window as we walked along a corridor to the front door, I saw a second thread of ski trails emerging from the forest opposite the school. Just inside the double front doors, a young woman was batting caked snow off her sweatpants, her skis leaning against the entryway.

"Hello." Martinov laughed and coughed at the same time. "You look a bit old for school."

The woman stood up straight, and squared her shoulders; her stomach and her voice tensed like an athlete. "I'm old enough," she threatened, to no one in particular. Underneath her canvas construction jacket, she was shivering. Glancing at the wall, I noticed that one of her skis had broken about a foot in front of the binding. After a moment, she spoke again, with less vainglory. "I'm lost. I said I'd ski back to the train station, but I can't find it, and it's turning dark." She looked across each of our faces.

"Could you take me home?"

She was Natasha from Moscow, and during the remaining days of our stay we became friends. Martinov dutifully fixed her ski that evening, with strips of rag and a plaster splint. "We don't want to make you our prisoner," he said to the young woman, who was still far from sizing up this university-educated hermit. Each morning we expected to find she had fled to the station, but she stayed.

Our first evening with her, life in the hut changed. Our cursing evaporated, and we stopped warming ourselves naked in front of the stove. None of us was modest, but there was a question of age: Natasha, just out of college, was almost ten years younger than I, and twenty years younger than the others. She was a dark-haired, dark-eyed beauty who claimed a dash of Kirghiz admixed with her Russian-Jewish parentage. Her slight figure was strong and healthy, and we couldn't help noticing she was tanned to the waist in wintertime. When the four of us laid our wet ski wear at the very top of the stove, and crowded in our underwear next to the grate, we men felt . . . excited.

For as long as a day, Natasha was uneasy, walking with locked knees close to the walls of the hut, a type of house she had never stayed in before. Every few moments, she curled her toes, then bent down sideways, as if she were wearing a skirt, to press her fingers against the black, packed earth floor. She shook her head in disbelief. "This is the way people used to live."

"This is the way I live," Martinov answered, minding some other business.

Toward dinnertime, she took more interest in the huge tiled stove, which Martinov had just fired with foot-thick logs. "For cooking?" she asked, pointing to the iron grate that was large enough for a man to crawl through.

"For everything!" Martinov laughed. "But we have a gas range, too." The remark passed by Natasha, who continued her halting quarter ambits of the huge stove.

For the first dinner, she helped set the table, laughed at a few of Andrei's off-color jokes, and held a rabbit's feet splayed while Martinov opened its stomach with the point of his sickle. While the rabbit cooked, we swallowed small cupfuls of *spirt,* and soon Natasha's knees began to flex. In the middle of the dinner, lisping slightly with drink, she proposed a toast to broken trails and broken skis.

Martinov, effulgent, thanked her for "decorating the table" of three lonely men.

To preserve our friendship, we strained the bonds of chivalry, urging one another to "show Natasha the village" or "take Natasha to the store." During the days, we skied together, gliding along the hillsides, or following Martinov through the web of forest trails, rattling our wood skis across the stippled ice of frozen rivers, stripped to the waist when there was sun.

Skiing, I sometimes let the others run ahead, while I propped myself next to a tree, to listen to the forest. Nothing moved; maybe a rush of wind. No map could ever find me—where was I? I had no idea. "Somewhere north of Moscow"? Slouching over my ski poles, I had no coordinates, no job, no assigned place. I felt so free, I almost wept with joy. I had stripped off the skin of someone, to stand alone as me.

I yelled ahead for the others, and the cry came back, in a faraway squeak muffled by the snow. "N-ee-ee-eeck!" Andrei's voice cast across the landscape like a hook, reeling me back to the company. For the first time in memory, I was in love—with myself, with nature, with these people. In Russia. Things were not going according to plan.

The woods had their most powerful effect on Natasha and me. When had we been so free? We reacted like children, playing with our elders through entire days. I organized a baseball game with pine cones and ski poles. Natasha teetered on a tree stump and "pitched," while Martinov's giant shoulders dominated home plate—my Harvard ski cap—blasting cone after cone back into the treetops. When Andrei and I tired of shagging "fly cones," we munched the tasty pine nuts scattered around the batter's box.

"Cone ball" led to "downhill slaloming," pointing our slender touring skis down fifty-foot hills, and hoping for the best. I vaulted spread-eagled into snowbanks, like charging waves on the beach. On one hill, Andrei tried a somersault on skis, and failed. For the first time since childhood I took a snowball square in the face, and wanted to cry.

After skiing, we enjoyed "quiet time" in the hut with books "checked out" of Martinov's basement library. *Lolita* fascinated Natasha, who squirreled the banned classic away in her ski parka, and flipped it open to read at the least interval, even a stop to check a binding on the ski trail.

The motel scenes absorbed her. She asked if I had had "experiences" in motels.

"With little girls? Certainly not."

"Well then, with big girls?"

"Big girls have their own apartments. They don't go to motels."

"I have my own apartment."

"Then you know what I'm talking about."

"We don't have motels. We have phone booths." She giggled. "But you, Nick, where do you take your women, just for company? To the country, like this?"

From the top of a small hill overlooking the village, she waved her arm across the snowy valley.

This kind of country? Last winter, Sharon and I had visited friends living in a renovated farmhouse outside of Lenox, Massachusetts. The year before, Bob had left his midtown law firm, his wife Marcy had abandoned the Soho gallery scene, and they had moved to the country to raise their two children. We four adults spent an hour and a half of Saturday afternoon skiing, then Bob and I watched basketball on cable TV while Sharon and Marcy labored in the appliance-laden "country kitchen." After dinner, we drove across the valley to see Fellini's *Roma* at a community college auditorium.

Driving back from the movie, Sharon stopped the rental car on the side of the road, to stare at the velvet black country sky, pecked bright with stars.

"The sky always looks bigger in the country," she said, leaning back on the fender. She burst out laughing, at herself: "Jesus! How profound!"

I put my arm around her shoulder. "It's beautiful."

"I wonder what it's like, living out here?"

"Marcy and Bob seem to like it."

"Well, they're lucky. He can practice here, and she still has her gallery contacts in the city."

"They are lucky." I was saying so, but I wasn't sure. "What do you think they do at night, when they don't have guests?"

"Watch the kids. And they have each other."

After a minute, I dropped my arm and jackknifed forward from the hood of the car. "Yeah. We're probably better off in the city." Unstated, but understood, was the death of our imagination: We wouldn't have each other.

"Our country is different," I told Natasha. That allowed for any possibilities.

Quiet time happened in the hours before dinner, after sunset, when we sipped tea and picked at small saucers of jam to replenish ourselves after skiing. Natasha sat on the floor, propping her back against the stove, nose buried in Nabokov. She read intently, but every few minutes jerked her head up to see if anyone was watching her. Sitting wrapped in a blanket against the opposite wall, I was often staring at her, and was often "caught." She smiled. She liked being observed. I would smile, and go on pretending to write in my diary, or scrape down my skis.

Andrei and Martinov talked on the couch, lying at opposite ends and scissoring their legs. They spoke in low tones, mostly about their student days, chuckling to themselves. Andrei confided to me that he was trying to talk Martinov back to Moscow, and that he was having no luck.

We introduced Natasha to Aron. Martinov fumbled in his packet of letters, and chose a long excerpt to read at late afternoon tea. "This one is about making friends," he announced, settling his huge frame on the ramshackle sofa.

It was strange to me, this sort of gospel. I knew more about America than Aron ever would, but his pronouncements were received as holy writ. If I challenged his testimony, my comments were politely dismissed. What did I know? I only lived there. He could anger me. One evening back in the apartment, Lilya had read this passage to me:

In America, friendship is a handshake, a forced smile, your first name on the lips of someone you've never met. They have a myth, that friends stride cheerily across the lawn, borrowing cups of sugar. Go next door sometime—if you can get past the burglar alarm, and the chain pulled across the door, and if the cast-iron police lock isn't engaged, a cup of sugar is about all you'll come away with.

"What crap!" I hammered at Lilya's kitchen table.

Lilya was a professional soother. "Nick, maybe it's just something he's feeling."

"But you let him feel *for* you."

"Someone has to. We can't go there and feel for ourselves."

And here we were again in Martinov's hut, a million miles from nowhere, hanging on Aron's every word.

The Americans know a little something about us, and that is the first problem for a Russian here. Half the people I meet think I'm a Communist, which means a very bad person. They are fortunate to have no Communists, so they are at ease with their vision of Orwellian evil. What haven't the Communists done, one wonders? Poisoning the water with fluoride wasn't enough. . . .

If a conversation lasts long enough for me to explain that I left Russia disenchanted with the system, suddenly we've traveled to the Gulag. How many years was I in the camps? Did the guards loose the dogs on my wife before or after the gang rape? When I explain—at my peril—that I sat quietly on a suburban farm for fifteen years trying to fulfill my cabbage plan, drawing salary until one day my exit visa came in the mail, well! The eyebrows shoot up; I can hear the phones ringing at the FBI.

So the Americans can be a problem. For a time I mingled with other recent emigrés, to whom one doesn't have to explain oneself. But together we drown in our own pond, talking Russian when we should be studying English, reminiscing about the good life in Moscow (when the Nostalgia Police are asleep), cursing the Americans' piggish obsessions with money and sex.

You see how useful these sessions can be. So after several months Lena and I decided to seek out new friends.

The process began in earnest when we moved away from Brooklyn. Now we rent part of a house in the suburbs, with an extra room for Samuel, and some new treats like a hi-fi and television. Samuel learned baseball on TV. He was sure it was *lapta,* and he had the idea that by coming to America we had simply moved to some sixteenth republic they hadn't talked about in school, one where the big shots lived and spoke a different language, where the houses were spread from side to side instead of top to bottom, and where a more complicated version of *lapta* had become the national sport.

Knowledge of baseball rolled up to our steps one evening while Samuel was playing Chalk Man on the sidewalk. Samuel held the ball at arm's length, until an American boy appeared and asked for it back. Samuel handed the ball over, and practiced his English at the same time. "What is it?" "A game," the American replied. Samuel pointed at the chalk figures he had drawn on the pavement. "Also a game?"—but the boy had vanished back to the baseball field.

A few days later the boy returned and asked to play the chalk game. So Samuel was the first to make a real American friend. Stevie quickly won Samuel for capitalism, though it was no chore, given his "cosmopolite" background. In just a few days Samuel was chewing gum everywhere, wearing a baseball cap, and asking why we didn't own a home computer! He now insists on accompanying us to the supermarket, and pilots the cart down each aisle, piling it high with festively colored boxes of breakfast foods, snacks, and candies. This country was made for children.

Stevie's parents were the first Americans who invited us to dinner. They lived in a modest house, by New York standards, in a different town called La Rochelle. They were surprised to learn that we had no car, and as there is no public transportation, Mr. Stevie had to drive fifteen minutes to pick us up, and of course the fifteen minutes back.

This did not ease our relations, nor did our discovery, during the first car ride, that we had little in common. Mr. Stevie owned a small clothing factory in New Jersey. He was surprised to learn that both Lena and I had taken degrees in accounting. He had finished high school and taken over the plant from his father. Only in the car did he realize we were Jewish—I saw him frown at the mention of Israel—and I sensed that Russia cannot claim a monopoly on anti-Semites.

As you probably fear, many things here are artificial, but our first evening as guests showed us more than we expected. The interior walls of the house, which appeared to be mortared brick, were plastic. Inside the fireplace—also plastic—burned an artificial fire, the first of many I have seen since. A jet of gas shoots up between two cast-iron "logs." The worst moment came when Lena tried to pull a volume of Dickens off a living room shelf, and brought the whole shelf down with her! The "books" were a false front of spines, stenciled on a piece of tin, nailed to the cardboard shelf. . . .

It was a bad evening for détente. From their son's description, the Stevies (I really have forgotten their name) had the idea that we had escaped from Russia, guns blazing, along a remote frontier crossing. Mrs. Stevie's imagination had been stirred by a recent television movie about a young couple who tunneled under the Berlin Wall. In our wavering English, we described the reality: the application, the harassment, the wait.

But our story had little impact. After Lena finished talking about the last night, when just four of our friends dared to come to say goodbye, Mr. Stevie jumped in: "So you left Russia by filling out some *forms*?" We were not model Russians. Happily Stevie had spent all evening showing Samuel videotapes of old baseball games on his television, which Samuel vividly described during the ride home.

When the letter ended, Natasha sprang up off the floor and started to lay out her sleeping bag. "Fat targets, aren't they, with their phony book collections and their private cars? And all these dirty books they publish—" she waved her arm at the tattered *Lolita* on the handmade table. "Of course, it could be worse for him," she snapped, folding herself into her bedding. "He could have stayed here."

While she lay down, Martinov reassembled the letter, folded it back in with the others, and slid them into the chink in the huge stove. He patted his dark, wrought hand against the sky blue tile.

"In America, you'd be electric."

11 / The Schism

Sunday morning began just like the other mornings. The "Muscovites" dozed while Martinov crept about the hut, stoking the oven and dipping the previous night's dishes in a bucket of heated water. Andrei stirred next, bumping me as he wiggled into his clothes under his sleeping bag. Soon we were in gear, splashing water on our faces, chatting, sizzling eggs, mounting a gradual crescendo of noise until Natasha woke up.

The weather was static. The sun hadn't yet broken through the gray yolk of winter fog when the four of us finished our breakfast and asked Martinov where we might ski today. He suggested we leave the skis for a morning and walk to church.

"Church?" Andrei asked. "I didn't see any church around here?"

Natasha repeated an atheist nursery rhyme, comparing God to a pig. "That's how we're brought up, and you're trying to take us to church?"

Martinov muttered that "this is a different kind of church, hardly even a church at all . . . over behind the hill where the cement factory used to be." He offered me use of his *valenky,* pressed felt peasant snow boots, for the walk, converting me to the idea.

We dressed for the weather—deep snow with "warm" air, minus five degrees centigrade—not for church, though none of us had presentable clothes anyway. Natasha asked if she should bring a kerchief to wrap under her rabbit's-fur cap. Martinov grunted noncommittally, and she tucked the kerchief into a pocket.

There was a path to the church. Indeed, this late in the morning several paths, like strings hanging from a maypole, ran up to the crest of the round hill looming behind the hut. We plowed through the knee-high snow straight back from our kitchen door, half a mile to the summit, where the paths joined. From there the tracks dipped down several hundred feet into a flat wash, a meadow in summertime. Looking out from the hilltop, we saw thirty-odd figures milling about in the snow-filled basin below, clustered in two tight circles, black speckles on white. Martinov gestured with his hand, and we hiked down toward them.

This was church. When we joined the larger of the two groups, we saw three or four women doubled over in black shawls, cradling small icons against their chests. They mingled with about twenty other women, beating their boots in the snow, crossing themselves rhythmically, chanting and praying in muffled voices. Seeing strangers, several came up to us and made the sign of the cross on our foreheads. Each one stopped to greet Martinov, and reached out a thin arm to squeeze his elbow.

"Good day, Daniel Mitrofanovich."

"Happy holiday, Daniel Mitrofanovich."

"Christ be with you, Daniel Mitrofanovich."

At the edge of this circle we spotted Praskovya, and stamped over to her. "What's the holiday?" I asked, catching up to Martinov.

"Every day's a holiday for these old birds," he

mumbled, half smiling. "Look at the Orthodox calendar some time. You'll see why everyone was so religious—they never had to work. Happy holiday, Praskovya Fyodorovna."

She cackled quietly. "Is it a holiday? I'm sure it is." She stared at the three of us, most closely at Natasha. "New parishioners? One of them very pretty, I see. Nothing to confess, I hope?" She pulled a small icon from under her coat and offered it to Martinov to kiss.

He turned away and pointed to the smaller gathering just ten yards away. They were "worshiping" in the same manner as the group we stood with, fondling icons and rosaries, trudging about in the snow, praying in guttural monotones. "They seem fewer today."

Praskovya looked over her shoulder, turned back, and spat. "But it's been so long since you've visited, Daniel Mitrofanovich. Yes, a few of them have passed on, as it were, to warmer climes, ha ha!" She spat a second time. "Worse than Communists!"

I was about to walk over to the second group, when Martinov caught me by the shoulder. "Stay here. I'll explain later." He left me with Andrei and Natasha while he sought out some acquaintances to whisper business. I was searching the snowfield for some explanation of this "church" when one of the old women in black approached me, bobbing her head.

"You Orthodox?" she demanded. I told the truth. "Then get out of our church. Go join your friends—" she yanked her thumb over her shoulder and spat. Andrei intervened, explaining I was a visitor, interested in Orthodoxy, a friend of Daniel Mitrofanovich . . .

"He's not Jewish? He looks like a kike." I shook my head, and she drifted away.

"The One True Church." Andrei smiled wistfully.

Natasha wandered out among the old women, while Andrei and I stalked a large circle around the "worshipers." Soon Praskovya hobbled over to join us.

"Pretty silly sight for you city boys, isn't it?—these old women scratching around like frozen hens? Well—" she licked the huge mole hanging over her upper lip, anticipating a good story—"let me tell you . . ."

There had been a church where we were standing, until 1936, when Party zealots from a neighboring village looted its gold fixtures and icon screens, and burned it down. For a few years, priests conducted secret services in the back room of the grocery store, or in a believer's potato cellar. But soon the neighbors denounced them to the police—Praskovya crossed a grid of four fingers in front of her face, the sign for "jail."

Forbidden to worship, their priests shot or imprisoned, the few village believers created their own Sunday "service," walking the perimeter of the razed churchyard, furtively chanting prayers memorized from books that had survived countless house searches.

Praskovya rubbed the mole on her lip to invoke the genie of memory. "Then they tried to shut us down with the soccer idea—"

In the early 1960s, the directors of the cement plant built a modest soccer stadium on the meadow to displace the parishioners, now reduced to a band of old women. But each Sunday they gathered at ten, and stayed on until the hundred or so spectators, mostly drunk, assembled for the weekly soccer match.

For several weeks, drunk toughs accosted the women, insulted and ridiculed them, and snatched at their clothing. But the women reappeared each Sunday, and soon they earned tolerance, and finally respect from the factory workers. Eventually, the two sets of communicants became symbiotic. Around twelve-thirty, the drunks began to file into the bleachers, their voices hushed as if in church. And just before the one o'clock kickoff, the crones trooped off the field, and vanished over the top of the round hill.

The old woman covered a nostril, and emptied her

nose. "The fucking Communists. What haven't they tried? But come Judgment Day—" she waved her finger, thick as a pickle, in my face—"God'll fuck'em. Really fuck'em."

"And those people?" I pointed to the rival group just a few yards away.

"Ah! *Raskolniki!* God'll fuck them even worse!" Praskovya spat emphatically, hatefully. Schismatics!

Martinov showed up with Natasha in tow, eager to leave. He had rescued Natasha against her will, from a lecture on dogma. "It was so interesting," she protested as he led her up the hill by the arm. "They really believe much the same things . . ."

Natasha had been hearing about the Schism from one of the faithful. The famous controversy that had split Orthodoxy into Old and New Believers under Peter the Great spared the village of Z—— until 1963. Only in Russia: A white-bearded wanderer in a black sheepskin coat emerged from the forest one day, seeking work. He carried no identification, but as he had apparently committed no crimes within a five-mile radius, the cement factory hired him as a loader, throwing hundred-pound sacks into the back of a truck.

"No one asks too many questions around here," Martinov said, speaking from experience. "So they gave him a bed in the dormitory, and left him alone. I wasn't here, but they say he was a quiet sort, not a drinker, which is rare for these parts, and not around in the evenings much. That's all right, too, you don't need an excuse not to be around after work—people think you have a woman, or a still. But this guy was preaching gospel."

Real Gospel. The Old Gospel. The Byzantine Cross, no shaving, no fish, no fornication, no priests. "He was an Old Believer. He said he came from a big community in the north, which had chosen a dozen members as *poslantsy*, 'ambassadors,' to go out and spread the Word.

"Well, the fellow—his name was Ruslan—must have been convincing, because within just a few months of his arrival, he had this so-called congregation split down the middle. So out on the soccer field the women started lining up in two separate groups. The drunks thought their eyesight had finally given way, but no, week after week, a second small crowd formed down where the visiting goalposts used to be. Each week their number grew one or two persons larger, and the Orthodox group shrank correspondingly.

"Ruslan had the golden tongue. For a moment, it seemed the Old Believers would outnumber the original group, until—" Martinov paused at the top of the hill, panting vapor in the freezing air.

He licked his lips. "Until one night somebody laid open the charismatic Ruslan's throat from ear to ear. While he was sleeping. And left an Orthodox cross on his chest."

Natasha collapsed her shoulders. "How awful. . . ."

"No one asked who did it. A band of his women took the body off somewhere into the forest, and they made a little shrine, I think." He turned back to look down at the snowfield. "So there's our religion for you. Two flocks of feuding, toothless old sheep, cursing at each other, half blind in the snow."

We tired ourselves for night, perhaps deliberately. Hovering near the stove in our underwear, cooking dinner, we affected a lugubrious sexlessness. One evening, when Natasha leaned over a tub of heated water to rinse her raven hair, conversation stopped while we stared at the perfect curve of her back, and the finely formed hairpin of her legs tucked in at her side.

"So go on talking!" she yelled, wringing water from

her hair. Ill at ease, Martinov shifted his position on the sofa. Andrei got up off the floor and fumbled with kindling for the oven. I looked the other way.

Our friendship eroded the sharpness in Natasha. On successive evenings, tiny cupfuls of the village alcohol irrigated new blossoms of her personality. Chapter by chapter, she told us the story of her life.

Only twenty-one, she had been married and divorced, and had borne another man's child. She boasted of a brilliant university career in biology, and a promising future, married to the son of an eminent surgeon, a kingmaker in Soviet medicine.

While talking, she lowered her tongue delicately into the miniature shot glass, licking at the *spirt*, her eyes on the floor. "You know, everything was in place, like a story that was about to be written. His father had arranged an apartment, and even jobs for both of us at one of the big hospitals. My grades would fetch me a good salary, and I would study for the graduate degree at night . . ." she glanced involuntarily at the bottle, and Andrei filled her glass.

"It was perfect. We both loved to ski, we liked foreign movies, we made love, like everyone does." She raised her head, to check on our attention. "But we didn't *know* each other, do you understand? We were just ideas of people in each other's heads." I suppose we nodded some feeble understanding.

"So for some months we loved each other, worked hard, and nothing went wrong. Then, the summer before last, Volodya traveled to the Far East for three months, and when he came back, I was pregnant." She giggled.

"So suddenly all of Moscow was involved. His father examines me—can you believe it?—and concludes that I'm seven weeks pregnant, by someone else. Furor. I am quiet. I know whose child it is—" she giggled again, and tried to drink, splashing alcohol on her chest—"maybe. But maybe it's my husband's."

"Big deputation to my family. My father-in-law declares there must be an abortion, and offers to do it himself, with his West German equipment . . ." she dropped her face forward, and began to cry.

We were quiet for several minutes, lulled by the play of her dark hair in the ochre glow of the kerosene light. Once again I sensed the warm, yolky candescence of Russia, the same hospitable, incubating penumbra found in the subway, or in Andrei's tiny kitchen. Outside, we heard a rustling noise, like an animal breaking through the brush. When we looked back at Natasha, she had fallen asleep.

Andrei rose first, lifting her ankles from the floor onto his bended knee, where he pulled off her oven-warmed socks. I unrolled her sleeping bag, and Martinov found a blanket. She wore no other clothing we dared touch, so the three of us lifted her, breathing lightly, on top of her sleeping bag, while Martinov tucked the blanket under her feet and around her shoulders. Andrei pointed with his finger, and we slid her a foot or two closer to the stove. We handled Natasha like our most delicate possession. She belonged to us.

The next evening, she finished the story. "But I wanted the child, and now the world of sugar began to melt. My husband threw me out of the apartment—legally, because it was registered in his father's name. 'Complications' arose at the job, the laboratory was to be reorganized, someone had to be let go. . . . Next the graduate school says I can't carry the course load if I'm going to be a mother, there are so many other qualified applicants . . ." she swallowed a cupful of the home brew, and flung the last drops at the open grate, evok-

133

ing puffs of blue flame. "I said, fuck them. I had the child."

Her head tilted forward, then tears followed. Would she fall asleep again? After a few moments, she started, and looked around at each of us, smiling, embarrassed. "The baby is with its father now, its real father, a wonderful man. I have a job, though not exactly a dream job."

She smiled at a passing thought. "I couldn't be happier than to be sitting here with the three of you."

The dinnertime storytelling also returned Martinov to Moscow. He grinned lazily at the familiar place names, tales of apartments he had frequented, talk of new movies, vanished buildings. ("What do you mean the *new* Puppet Theater? What happened to the *old* Puppet Theater?") The pleasure of recognition clashed with the pain of renunciation. He was looking at Moscow through a window he had vowed never to open again. One evening, while Natasha was resting before dinner, he told us how a deputy prosecutor had traveled to Z——, to inform him that his sentence had been reduced, and he was free to go home.

"Of course, the court suspended the term in January, but this bird didn't feel like coming up here in the winter, so he waited for the roads to harden in May. He's arranged for a ministry car to drive him all the way from Yaroslavl, and he jumps out in front of this doorway, holding a briefcase. Those windows were just as dirty then as they are now, but I saw him coming, and let him beat on the door for a while, acting as though I'm not at home. Finally, I let out a little grunt, just what he might expect from the peasant type, and I ask who's there.

"'It's me, Soviet power.'" Martinov paused with his hand deep in his beard, questioning.

"'Who?'

"'It's me, the lawful representative of Soviet power.' I grunted some more, like a hog, to let the guy think I was drunk, then yanked the door open in his face. He's a small bird, dressed in one of those shiny blue Finnish suits the secret police people buy in the special coupon stores.

"'*This* is Soviet power?' I ask. He hops like a little rabbit over the threshold, mumbling his name and title, and starts unpacking his plastic briefcase, all in a great hurry, because the driver is already racing the motor in the car. He can't use the table, as I was gutting some fish that day, so he balances his case on one knee, and he shoves one of those documents that look like diplomas, you know, with the big red seal, right in my face. And he peeps:

"'You're free.'"

Martinov hesitated, reading a mimed document with his arms extended in front of his chest.

"The little one slithers out, and here in my hand—" he waves the imagined document for effect—"is a pardon, as it says, in connection with the sixtieth anniversary of the October Revolution, etcetera, etcetera. So I was free two years earlier than planned—but there wasn't anywhere I wanted to go.

"I put the thing away and went back to making the fish soup. There was a woman coming over for dinner, one of the teachers I was sleeping with. We ate, we talked, and I showed her the pardon after the meal. She almost fainted. 'I didn't know you were a criminal,' she said.

"'I'm not.'

"'Then why do you need a pardon?'

"It struck me: I had a different life. The people who knew I had been sentenced were either gone, or had forgotten about me. Even the tiny police station where they were supposed to keep tabs on me had disappeared years ago, along with the cement factory. I was an exile by choice, not by coercion.

"I hadn't thought much about it, but suddenly I liked my thick plaster walls, I liked my neighbors and their silly religious chicanery, I enjoyed the seasons happening outside my door. Everyone who came here from the city—please excuse me—seemed to be speaking of the same things with different names. This fellow was up, this fellow was down, such a movie could not be shown, such a play had pleased the bosses. Today red, tomorrow white." He was hurrying his sentences, feeling embarrassed to have exposed his articles of faith.

"If life is like a river, it moves more slowly here, but at least I am in it. Maybe as stupidly as dragging Praskovya's pig out of the spring muck, or shooting a horse for an old woman too in love to pull the trigger. We don't have *ideas* of people like she does—" he gestured at Natasha—"we have people. This isn't *like* life, this *is* life."

Martinov heard Natasha stirring, awakened by his voice. He fixed his gaze, first on Andrei, then on me, fearful that we hadn't understood. Grabbing Andrei's forearm, he jabbed his immense, muscled finger into his friend's chest, whispering through his beard.

"Here there *is* life, there *is* . . ."

Our parting felt like unraveling cords that had been knotted into rope. Andrei and Martinov did the packing and talking as we waited for dawn, and our trip to the station. Natasha, still in her pajamas, paced the hut in a daze, stamping her bare feet against the earth floor, pressing her palm against the oven tiles, which had chilled overnight. Every few minutes, of no one in particular, she asked: "Why is there no wood on the floor? Will Martinov be cold when we go away?"

Our host warmed little meat pies on the range for each of us, and handed around cups of heavily sugared tea, in silence. Only the blue flame of the gas under the teapot lit the hut, until the sky paled, and the landscape brightened. Andrei tiptoed among the packs, yanking at fasteners and straps.

Natasha had dressed, and was quiet. We planned to travel together as far as the Yaroslavl station, then part. The three men sat down for the traditional moment of silence before a journey. Natasha stayed standing, and walked over to Martinov, pulling his head against her thighs. Rising, he kissed her modestly on the cheek, then embraced Andrei and me.

"You're leaving Russia now," he warned.

"No, no." I buried my face in his beard. "I think I'm just arriving."

Looking back, I see that Martinov was the tinder who fired my imagination about Russia. He was a catalyst for me, like an exotic wildflower spotted among the ground cover that made me raise my head, and look at the forest. If *this* grows here, what other wonders will I find?

12 / *Pizza for Christmas*

By the time we returned, Moscow had been fed a spoonful of winter, and spat it out. A second flurry of snow had fallen and melted, then the temperature dropped through the floor. On the heels of the cold came the New Discipline.

For me, the timing was all wrong: I was just adjusting to the *Old* Discipline. Phones were busy, or never answered all day. The official I needed to speak with was sick, at his dacha, or "on academic leave," the excuse offered by the plumber who delayed six weeks before reconnecting the apartment's hot water line.

I collect hypocrisy, maybe for future use in a more straightforward world, one without our confusing mix of truth and falsehood. In New York, a secretary wards off calls by insisting her boss is "at a meeting," or "in conference," Sharon's euphemism for long-distance jawing with her mother. In Moscow, their Soviet counterparts would be "at the Secretariat" or the "Collegium," bodies as vaporous as the "Presidium" that swallowed my first lunch partner. While an American office worker might be "expected back after lunch," a Russian would hazard no such guess. Absence is no guarantee of return. Maybe the fellow had done the sensible thing and quit work for good.

Environment does affect behavior. I seemed to have grafted some of the village timelessness onto my rapidly shrinking work schedule. After a late breakfast with Susan, I phoned Boris for a digest of the overnight telex messages, if any had come. None required an answer—after all, it was past midnight in New York. I now devoted many mornings to my diary, letter writing, or catching up on twenty-nine years' worth of neglected reading. The Old Discipline confirmed one of the Russians' favorite folk proverbs: Work is like a bear; it won't run off into the woods.

Boris first alerted me to the New Discipline campaign when I found a heavily annotated copy of *Pravda* splayed across my desk one wet, gray snowless morning just before lunchtime. Major government decrees weren't just rough on the citizenry, they were hell on the eyes; I was staring at four tabloid pages of densely packed type. Boris—dull, underemployed Boris—had underlined each key provision using a ruler and a felt-tipped pen. He had read every word.

When he shuffled into my office half an hour later, I asked whom these decrees might apply to. He glanced out the window, hoisting his shoulders indifferently. "I don't know. The people, I suppose." That category excluded him. He *was* disciplined.

I was hoping for more information on the New Discipline when I encountered Ekaterina Sergeyevna in the stairwell before lunch. A lazy, shiftless chatterbox, she seemed the perfect target for the campaign. Yes, she confessed, she had been summoned to a meeting of the pensioners' *aktiv,* and there had been reprimands, even some threats. With what results? I hadn't noticed any change in her dress, her manners, nor her eagerness to abandon her post for a smoke, a chat, or a bit of shopping.

"Measures were taken . . ." she reported darkly. I

had noticed a fresher smell around the ground floor. As her "Socialist obligation" under the new decrees, she had pledged to stop hanging salted pig fat underneath the stairwell.

The holiday season, with its boundless potential for personal depression, was fast approaching. It looked as if I was going to be facing the festivities alone.

Susan was taking her yearly "out trip" to England, to spend three weeks with mum and dad in Canterbury, she said. She had invited me along, half-heartedly, and well after she made her plane reservations.

Slighted, I tried to slight back. "We wouldn't be popping into London now and again for sex bouts with old pal Sam, would we?"

A blush of guilt lit Susan's face. "I'm a big girl, Nick. And now you'll have more time to spend with your delightful Russkie friends."

Susan hadn't shed her embassy-induced Russophobia. Even though she often ridiculed the insularity of the diplomatic community, which huddled around their videocassette recorders and duty-free liquor cellars, she still disdained the "Sovs," her derisive catchphrase for all Russians. More than once, I had invited her to meet Andrei, and she always refused, citing the security regulations that forbade her from associating with "hostiles." (To her bosses, I must have been a "nominal ally.") Perhaps too generously, I suspected she wasn't really afraid of breaking the rules, but of sharing my enthusiasm for Andrei and his friends, and his way of life. Then the rules themselves would have to be called into question.

Shortly after I learned of Susan's plans, Andrei announced he too would be forced to leave town, because of the New Discipline. After years of evading undesirable *komandirovki*—business trips—Andrei was being packed off to Novosibirsk for six weeks starting in late December. "Some mixer breakthrough, I don't know," he complained over the phone. "No one else wanted to go."

With Andrei and Susan gone, I succumbed to the holiday "merrymaking" inside the foreign compound. Loneliness was the disease everyone seemed anxious to communicate; invitations from individuals, organizations, and even countries I had never heard of jammed my mailbox every day. I remember a blur of square-jawed Swedish secretaries, dozens of brainless conversations, and rivers of artillery punch. Plenty of parties, plenty of drinking, and plenty of distance between us and gray, subzero Russia hulking outside our double-paned windows. I was regressing.

To stanch the boredom, or allay it, I began attending national day receptions. I was never invited, but I did own a dark pin-striped suit, which satisfied most embassy doormen. My protocol directory wasn't up to date—once I showed up at the embassy of a country that had been partitioned since the last edition. One of the first sovereign acts of the Free State of Thingamabob had been to abolish all state holidays, according to a handsome young vice-consul who greeted me at the door in Nehru-collared egalitarian trim. But he assured me I could return to use the squash court any time.

Just a few nights later, at a reception in "Third World Alley," just off Embassy Row, I came across a sallow, pot-bellied man wearing a cummerbund, whom I asked to bring me a drink. When he identified himself as the North Yemeni ambassador, I inquired if he represented "our" Yemen or "their" Yemen. Sovereignty was not the stuff of diplomatic humor, I learned as I was gently escorted to the door.

Happily, all remained quiet on the work front. The

political story lay dormant in the Kremlin hospitals, allowing me to send back more of the anecdotal dispatches I enjoyed writing. The New Discipline, of course, proved to be a journalistic mother lode. Office workers showed up at their jobs for the first time in years, only to discover three desks for eighty employees. Policemen took up posts inside meat stores, monitoring the notorious "black exit," or delivery entrance, where the butchers sold their choice cuts at inflated prices to customers lingering in the alleyway. Beer parlors and Cognac bars opened their doors at 2:00 P.M., instead of eleven in the morning, giving rise to the joke that the state had extended the workday by three hours.

Jonas loved the tales of the New Disicpline, and never complained about missing political stories. Thank heavens for that. Superpower politics bored me. In disarmament talks, Russia and America were acting like two petulant children who refused to stop playing with firecrackers. When it came to propaganda, the emanations from the "free" world—the United States was romancing the "authoritarian" dictatorships—sounded just as absurd as Radio Moscow's dispatches from the Afghan front, where Soviet soldiers apparently spent long days helping old ladies cross the street, or passing out candy to children.

Clearly, I was losing the ideological edge. Aggression here, repression there; I cared less and less. The trip to the village had distanced me. Looking down an empty forest landscape, standing on a frail zipper of a train track nowhere at all, I had risen above the fray.

Christmas Day dawned, and I was alone. American Christmases had lost their power over me at the age when sweaters and underwear became acceptable gifts. A Fruit of the Loom 3-pack never stirred my imagination like a massive Nike-Hercules missile base, bristling with plastic, spring-loaded missiles targeted at you-know-where.

But the Soviets' complete nonobservance of Christmas tested my cynicism, and I was found wanting. I missed Phil Spector's Christmas album blasting out Crazy Eddie's double doors, and the West Indian Santa Clauses circling Union Square. ("Hey mon, it's Christmas. Need some smoke?") To lose Christmas entirely was like hearing that a tiresome cousin had finally died—you realized that he did have some good qualities, after all. Totally deprived of Christmas, I missed my parents and being a child.

My mother was present in spirit, represented by a large brown parcel that had fought its way to me through the international postal system, scarred by innumerable stampings, inspections, retapings and re-stringings. Inside the package, I found a yogurt maker, calfskin driving gloves, and some newspaper clippings about unusual phenomena witnessed by the Skylab astronauts. A Polaroid snapshot slipped into her Christmas card showed my mother and my brother eating Thanksgiving dinner at the Marriott Wagon Wheel, where Interstate 95 meets the George Washington Parkway. Why aren't they at home? Where is home, anyway? Shallow soil for putting down roots, I thought. No time to complain: Never, never cry.

I glanced quickly around my living room. The furnishings reminded me of Susan. She had sent away for some Finnish wall hangings, and hung a few phony icons purchased at the state-run "art" collective down on the embankment. Several glossy portfolios of pre-Revolutionary art lay on the coffee table, further evidence of her civilizing influence. I felt lonely, and jealous of Sam, who was probably trying to worm his way back into her heart. Merry Christmas. I decided to go out for pizza.

This winter, the "pizza cafes" were the talk of Moscow. Some ambitious foreign trade bureaucrat had bought thirteen fully-furnished pizzerias from a smooth-talking Italian restaurateur. With checkered tablecloths, and Chianti from Italy rather than Moldavia, the cafes were a galaxy apart from the brutal offerings of the Siberia *pyelmeny* bar, where I still occasionally ate during fits of masochistic indulgence. Just a few months old, however, the pizzerias were already taking the first steps down the assimilationist path blazed by the Hotel Peking. Long lines clogged the entrances, where barrel-bellied doormen demanded small bribes as entrance fees. Service had become surly and slow, and naturally there was only one kind of pizza available—"Moskovsky."

I started my pizza hunt on the Boulevard Ring, the circle of elegant pedestrian gardens that surrounds the center of the city. This was where the big shots in *War and Peace* lived. Their stately Empire mansions are still standing, still painted lemon yellow or lime green, reclaimed as clubs, ministries, or restaurants.

My favorite was the Gogol Boulevard, for its two Gogol statues: Andreyev's original, brooding writer, hunched in the courtyard of the former Trubetskoy estate, and the new, erect, post-Revolutionary Gogol 200 yards away in the middle of the boulevard garden. Of course, Andreyev's Gogol is the truer portrait of the narrow-shouldered religious fanatic who cadged money and story plots from more successful St. Petersburg writers. Some crooked lines can never be straightened. The New Soviet Gogol is a wish gone unfulfilled.

I was still scouting the horizon for pizza—a nice Gogol touch—when I saw Natasha trotting through the middle of the garden, swinging a kilo of oranges in a string bag. I hadn't seen her since we parted at the train station three weeks ago. I had spent the last thirty kilometers of the trip from Z—— badgering her for a phone number, or at least an address. She blushed and flirted: No, no. I gave her my number, and she promised to call.

When she first saw me, I thought she tried to back out of sight behind a group of brush-cut army recruits. Perhaps I imagined it—when she recognized me, she burst into laughter and kissed me on the cheek.

"Nick! How good to see you!"

I complimented her oranges, a conventional show of respect for canny shopping.

"Don't be silly! They're for sale just down the street. How have you been?"

"Hoping that you might call."

She blushed. "But Nick, in our country the women never call the men."

"But you wouldn't give me your number!"

"Ah!" She waved her hand. "It doesn't matter. We were fated to meet. How are you?"

"Fine," I lied. "Today is Christmas."

"I thought it was in January."

"That's the old calendar."

"No one cares about it anyway. Except you, Nick." She laughed and squeezed my arm. "Where are you going?"

"I wanted to see the pizzeria next to the Arbat."

"Why? Walk me to the subway instead."

I inquired about her job, and her home life. Was she visiting her child? I didn't know where she worked, or even what her child's name was. Each question went half-answered. She worked in an "institute." What did her child's name matter? Natasha wanted to be observed from a distance, not examined under a microscope.

"I miss Martinov," she confessed.

"So do I."

"That was an unusual time."

"It was." We were approaching the plaster colonnade of the Kropotkin metro station. I stopped her just in front of the steps. "I want to see you again."

Her eyes flared. "It could happen like this." She gestured toward the boulevard.

"No, I want to agree to meet, at a time and place. Say eleven o'clock next Saturday, at the entrance to the pet market."

"Oh, next Saturday is bad, I have an appointment . . ."

"Cancel it. I'll expect you there."

She shrugged her shoulders, neither accepting nor declining.

When I had first seen her, she was smiling. Now she walked into the subway frowning anxiously, as if I had spoiled her day.

Did I expect her to be waiting for me? My vanity said yes, and there she was, shivering in her tan construction jacket, pacing in front of the pet market gate. I smiled. "I'm cold," she said, taking my arm as we entered the market.

The pet market, like Moscow's stamp market and used car market, was an empty lot where buyers and sellers gathered to exchanged pets *sruk*—from hand to hand. Schoolchildren sell off litters of gerbils for five kopecks, alongside professional breeders offering Great Dane puppies for one hundred rubles each. In the "fish department," pensioners boil water on portable stoves to keep their aquariums from freezing. A few feet away, gypsies from the Kuban sell "parrots" and "papagaus"—pigeons and mourning doves streaked with housepaints.

"Whew!" Natasha held her nose. "What are we here for?"

"I want to buy a cat."

"Let's go, then."

We found the "cat department," a cluster of Young Pioneers cradling kittens inside their parkas. Natasha selected a dappled black and white sourpuss, which the seller, a young boy wearing a Baby Lenin pin, insisted was Siamese.

"Three rubles, for the pedigree."

"Ten kopecks and no more, you little swindler!"

"It's a Siamese . . ." the little boy whined.

"You grabbed it out of a garbage can, you liar. Twenty kopecks is my last price!"

Natasha settled at fifty kopecks, and gently lowered the kitten into the side pocket of her bulky jacket. "Not a bad deal," she chuckled. "Maybe it is a Siamese." She stroked its head, peeping over the edge of the pocket.

From the market, Natasha suggested we walk through the Bauman district park, just a few blocks away. I asked about her work week, and whether she planned to visit her child this weekend.

"Oh yes. Don't let me forget. Today at three o'clock. I'll need something to bring." She stopped into a store to buy baby food. The cashier scolded her for feeding processed food to a cat. "No, no! It's for my child!" The saleswoman shook her head in disbelief.

Once we reached the park, Natasha lowered the kitten to the ground, and watched it nose its way over small rock piles and inch-high tufts of dead grass.

"What shall we call it?"

"In America, all cats are Felix."

"After Dzerzhinsky?" The first chief of the Soviet secret police.

"No, after Felix, the cat."

"Is this a he?"

"How would I know?"

Natasha scooped up the kitten and parted its rear legs. "It's a she."

"I'll think of a name later."

We watched a small boy shaped like a beach ball bump against the low wooden wall of a sandbox until finally he somersaulted head first into the sand. Inside the box, the child stumbled to his feet, grinning proudly.

"You really didn't want to come today, did you?"

Natasha huddled tighter in her parka. "No, I didn't."

"Is it because I'm an American?"

"No, no." She touched my shoulder. "That makes you better."

"Why?"

"Oh, you might understand."

"Can you be more vague?"

"Yes, if you like." She laughed. "It's just . . . it's so hard to tell the truth." She sprang up off the bench, pocketed the kitten and set us off walking again.

I tried to think of a new approach, but I didn't know what I was approaching, or why. Natasha was one of the most attractive women I had ever met, but she was forbiddingly beautiful, wearing her beauty more like a shield than an adornment. Only a bold man, or a very naive one, would have married her.

Inside the park, Natasha spotted a movie theater.

"Oh, please, let's see a movie? I haven't been to one in years!" She was pulling at my sleeve like a child.

"What about it? I mean her?" I pointed to the kitten.

"Oh, she'll just go right to sleep, won't you kitty? Yes . . . let's go!"

"But what's playing?"

"What's the difference? It'll be fun!" I could accompany her, but I couldn't guide her. Natasha would not be redirected. She dragged me into the theater, and paid for our tickets.

We sat through forty minutes of East German cartoons starring a robotic porcupine that used its quills for intergalactic warfare. Then came the main feature—double length and thirty kopecks more expensive—a detective thriller from Uzbekfilm, the Hollywood of Central Asia. I latched on to the beginning and the end of the film: Counterrevolutionaries were plotting to steal gold from the fledgling Soviet republic. A confusing sequence of events set the Extraordinary Committee, precursor to the KGB, on the case, which ended with the "highest measures" of punishment meted out to the "enemies of the people."

Natasha's eyes never left the screen. During the sixty-second intermission, she stroked my knee excitedly. "I wonder how it's going to end." I glanced at her pocket, and I envied the sleeping kitten.

After the firing squad crumpled the last of the bandits, Natasha reluctantly lifted herself out of her seat. "Great! Let's have something to eat."

The theater housed a small cafe in the basement, where we filled a tray with "napoleons," the vengeful Russians' name for a languid heap of curdled sweet cream that is a far cry from the Parisian original. As at the Siberia, bathroom odors wafted into the dining area.

"Yecch." I wiped my filthy spoon with a napkin.

Natasha laughed at my delicacy. "I've had worse than this."

"At the university?"

She rolled her eyes. "Oh, the university."

"Bad memories?"

"No, it wasn't bad." She laughed. "Nick, do I look like a graduate student?"

"Sure, yes."

"Oh." She poked at her pastry with a spoon.

"Do I look like a journalist?"

"Not really. You look like that actor, what's his name—Kaufman?"

"I know which one you mean. But you are a graduate student, aren't you? That's what you told us."

"Is it? Then I guess I am." She slumped over the table and cradled her forehead in her palms. "I don't know." The kitten was trying to wriggle out of her pocket. Natasha set it on the table and let it lap at her dessert. "I never went to university."

"But I thought—"

"Yes, I remember. Biology, graduate work. The sad story of a brilliant career sacrificed to privilege and class in the classless society. I could even see tears welling up in Martinov's eyes." She rocked her head in her hands. "No, it never happened. I made it up for the three of you. It seemed appropriate."

"And your child?"

"The child?"

"The illegitimate child. The cause of your divorce."

"Oh, that. I got that all from some movie. I didn't think you would recognize it." She giggled. "No, no bastard child. No brilliant career. And no apartment like your free and easy American girls, my friend."

"Where do you go at night?"

"To a dormitory for postal workers. Where the cutlery is much dirtier than here."

"You deliver mail?"

"Right in this district, in fact." She stroked the cat along its back. "I deliver mail."

"But why—" A fat serving woman interrupted me, brandishing a grease-splotched soup ladle.

"Young woman! This is a workers' restaurant, not a zoo! Filthy animals walking on our clean tables! Disgusting! Get out!"

At the sound of the commotion, three more white-aproned battle cruisers sailed out of the kitchen, firing salvos of abuse at Natasha and me. Natasha held her own, but when one of the cooks drew a knife, I pulled her away, still screaming.

"You fat bitches! I'll come back and cut your tits off with a switchblade! I'll cut your fat fucking throats from ear to fucking ear!"

On the street she calmed down, nestling the kitten inside her jacket. I put my hands on her shoulders. She pushed the kitten inside my parka, the first warm feeling I had had all day.

Natasha grinned. "See? I can talk like a mailman." She handed me the bag of baby food. "Feed this stuff to the cat for the first few weeks. It's in all the stores."

"Taking food from babies' mouths?"

"To hell with the babies. There aren't any babies."

"Where are you going?"

"Home. To the dorm."

Suddenly, she rekindled the same protective urges that had nurtured our life inside Martinov's hut. I wanted to take care of her. "Let me come with you."

"No men allowed. It's time I got back."

"I'll take you to the subway."

We walked in silence. She took my arm, more as a formality than a sign of intimacy. Each time I reached across to hold her hand, she recoiled. A hundred yards from the subway, the kitten began to squeal inside my jacket.

I took it out, and Natasha ran her finger along the back of its head. I noticed for the first time a crescent slope in Natasha's eyelids, a shadow of the Orient.

"So how did you find the school that day? Why were you skiing alone?"

"If I tell you, will you believe me?"

"If you tell the truth."

"You believed me before." She smiled faintly. "The

truth is I had been skiing without a map for a day and a half. I was trying to lose myself."

"But we found you."

"For a while, yes. It was one of the loveliest moments of my life." She planted a quick kiss on the kitten, and darted off toward the subway.

I stopped back at the same grocery store where we had purchased the baby food to buy milk for my yogurt maker. I went home to play with my Christmas toys, and puzzle out Natasha's story.

13 / Testing the Limits

Natasha was a *limitchik*, a worker from the provinces who accepts a menial job for three years in return for a coveted Moscow living permit. The capital is officially closed to outsiders seeking employment; only those who agree to work as ditchdiggers, trash collectors—or postmen—can eventually look for jobs in the city.

"They're our Negroes," Andrei explained as "Zazie," his tiny Zaporozhets, bounced along a potholed suburban highway. "Second-class citizens. Is that the right analogy?" I didn't object.

Not officially Muscovites, *limitchiki* have no right to housing in the capital. Most live in dingy, overcrowded workers' dormitories an hour beyond the reach of the furthest subway lines—beyond the city limits. "They're legendary," Andrei said as we approached a set of apartment blocks aligned like tombstones in a vast, garbage-strewn empty lot. "Rape, burglary, murder—everything goes on there. They're the worst we have."

When he returned from Novosibirsk, Andrei phoned the Bauman district post office to find out Natasha's address. They gave him a room number in Korpus Three, the women's building. Outside, Andrei did something I had never seen him do before—he locked his car doors. I was surprised, both that he had never locked them before, and that he was locking them now. He caught my stare, and shrugged his shoulders. "Really, it's that kind of place."

Climbing to the third floor, I glanced into the communal rooms, some filled with ten triple bunk beds occupied by women sleeping through the Saturday morning. The rooms had no doors. A half-dressed man with a splotchy purple portrait of Stalin tattooed on his chest wandered the corridors aimlessly, hungover from the night before. A burned mattress lay heaped on a pile of broken furniture at the third floor landing. Someone had tacked a sign to the mattress: Trash. In a different handwriting, an obscenity was scrawled underneath.

I sniffed at the unpleasant smell from the kitchens. "Boiled cabbage," Andrei said. "It's all they can afford."

Most of the women in Natasha's room were still sprawled across their beds, snoring loudly. Natasha had stretched out on her top bunk with her feet on the pillow, staring through the window at the empty lot. She was wearing her construction jacket over a cheap flannel nightgown. Andrei snuck up on her from behind, and tickled her feet.

"Oh!" She spun around.

"Get your things," he said. "We're taking you home."

It's no accident, as the Marxists say, that I'm wearing a pair of Andrei's socks, and have three of his shirts hanging in my closet. Even though his standard of living was just a fraction of mine, he was oblivious to possessions. After tennis, or a swim, he often forced fresh clothes on me, some of which I forgot to return. I eventually left the country owing him money, which he wouldn't let me repay. And he was generous with his time. He would drive his precious Zazie halfway across town to help a friend move, or make deliveries. But he couldn't afford to be generous with living space. He simply didn't have enough.

Lilya's eyes widened when Natasha, Andrei, and I appeared on the threshold, carrying three suitcases. Andrei made the introductions as he brushed past his wife to stow the luggage in the girls' room. "Lilya—Natasha, our new guest."

Natasha shook hands sheepishly, and fled into the bathroom. Lilya confronted Andrei in the hallway. "She's *staying*?"

He nodded his head. "She can sleep on a cot in the corridor."

"What about the girls?"

"They'll get used to her."

"Andrei!"

"Lilya, she needs help."

"Let someone else help her! There's no room here!"

"It's not a question of room. She won't be with us long."

The bathroom door opened just as Lilya was about to explode. Natasha must have overheard the argument.

"Of course I'll pay for my room and board."

Lilya looked over to Andrei, who waved his hand dismissively. "Don't be ridiculous."

Natasha settled in quickly, helping Lilya prepare the lunch, eagerly setting the table in the bedroom. She seemed ready to wait on us, until Lilya scolded her into her chair. Halfway through the meal, Lilya's questioning brought Natasha out, slowly.

Warily, she provided some details of her background, knowing that Andrei and I had already heard a different version. She was born in Kazan, the capital of the Tatar Republic, of mixed parents. Her Tatar mother died when Natasha was four. Her father, a

Russian Army colonel, sent Natasha and her older brother to an orphanage when they were in their early teens.

"Where's your brother?" Andrei asked.

"They killed him."

"Who?"

"In the orphanage." All of us raised our eyebrows. "Natasha . . ."

"No, really, because he was this—" She pushed up at the edge of her eyelids—"slant-eyed. The boys called him 'Chink.' They were beating him up all the time, and one day his head struck a concrete pillar."

"But Kazan is full of Asians."

"No Tatar would give her child up to the orphanage. My mother never would have."

Only her eyes hinted at Asianness, although she obviously didn't think of herself as Russian. In the orphanage, she hid the bloodline that had caused her brother's death.

"They thought I was Russian. Russian enough to marry."

"You did marry?" Maybe I asked a bit too quickly.

"I had to get out of the orphanage. I married a construction worker. A Tatar."

"He thought he was marrying a Russian?" Lilya asked.

"He was. It says Russian in my passport."

"But—"

"That's right. The baby was Tatar, light brown and almond-eyed. My husband beat me for two weeks in a row. One night he tried to kill the baby with a hammer—"

"Natasha!"

"Andrei, I swear it!"

"Leave her alone," Lilya said. "She's telling the truth."

Was she? Wasn't this just the same horror story all over again, with different characters? Andrei couldn't believe that she sold her baby to the Kazan gypsies before she left for Moscow.

"You just said a Tatar mother . . ."

"The gypsies are Tatars. They understand."

Lilya filled her guest's plate with potato and vegetable casserole. "How did you come to Moscow?"

"With a man. I met him in a restaurant one night. He said he had an apartment, he'd take care of me. . . ."

"Like Andrei?" Lilya laughed.

"Not exactly . . . he kept several women in this apartment, as a . . . business."

Lilya and Andrei nodded knowingly.

"What kind of business?" I asked.

Natasha blushed and played with her food. "Nick, it's the . . . woman business. . . ." I sucked in my breath. "Yes, my friend. You think only America has these things—women for sale, narcotics, crime? Your country has much to be proud of in these areas, indeed, you are truly a world leader, but give us some credit! Even our New Society has its own achievements . . ."

Andrei slammed his hand on the table. "Natasha! Shut up!"

She bowed her head. Lilya stood up to clear the dishes.

Natasha looked up at us, her eyes welling with tears. "I just didn't want Nick to think that America had a monopoly on unhappy people."

Just a few days later, on a gray February afternoon, Ekaterina Sergeyevna ambushed me in front of the elevator. "Your girlfriend's back," she announced triumphantly. "And she's wearing a ring."

Without betraying any reaction, or even interest, I rode the elevator up five flights and knocked on Susan's door. There was no answer—she must have left for work. No chipper note of greeting, no funky postcard of Buckingham Palace guards in beaver hats awaited me on my doorstep. The scenario was clear: Susan had been unfaithful. She was engaged to marry Sam. Her mother was already sending out the wedding invitations. Susan was ashamed. She was avoiding me.

I had ten hours to kill until she came back from work. Some of the time could be consumed by sleep. But it was only five o'clock in the afternoon. I phoned Andrei.

"My woman's left me."

"Mine too."

"But you've got four of them."

In Russian, Andrei was "sitting in the strawberry patch," a folkism that described a man surrounded by women. Into his tiny apartment, he was cramming a wife, two daughters, and Natasha.

"They've all gone with the grandmothers to the Conservatory."

"I thought the foreigners had scooped up all the tickets."

Andrei laughed. "Turns out there were one or two left. Come on over. They're spending the night at Aya's. Valya's coming by to watch the soccer match."

During the drive to Kolomenskoye, I plotted revenge on Susan. Perhaps I could compromise her with M16—or was it M15?—by arranging a security breach with the dreaded "hostiles." I could ask Andrei to phone her apartment, posing as an indignant trick demanding his fifty rubles back. Surely the suggestion that she had been augmenting her civil servant's salary by hooking in the pizza cafes would tantalize the listeners, British or Russian. That would be my revenge:

expulsion, a delaration of persona non grata, maybe even an exposé in one of the Moscow papers, a propaganda coup for the "Sovs." Red faces and foot-shuffling on the Brit side. Bad bit of business, wouldn't have expected it of one of *our* girls . . . that would shut her career down mighty fast.

Just beyond the last row of housing projects, the peace of the emerging countryside, and the vision of the blue-domed Kolomenskoye monastery rising over the hill soothed my fevered brain. Why would I want to sabotage Susan's career? I liked Susan. I practically loved Susan. Why should Andrei be her enemy, when, living through me, they should be friends?

Andrei and I had already begun to deplete his case of Arbatskoye, Byelorussia's watery knockoff of a Beaujolais nouveau, when his university roommate Valya strode through the front door and joined us in front of the television set. Andrei and I had bet on the match, agreeing to finish a full glass of wine each time our team was scored upon. After the third goal against my team—I was backing the Armenians against the Georgians, and already regretting it—our guest shook his head disapprovingly. Valya, I learned, was a self-proclaimed contradiction in terms: a Russian who didn't like to drink.

Valya sat down at my right, rolling his fingers across his knuckles, staring nervously at our half-empty wine glasses. Andrei took a third tumbler down from the cupboard and began to pour.

Valya's hand shot out. "Oh no! Thank you, not now." He smiled apologetically. "I can't stay long, and . . . well, you know, I'm really not a drinker."

The conversation ambled on, with Valya fidgeting nervously while Andrei and I drank down the first bottle of wine. Leaning back in his chair, Valya reached for a dry breadcrust on the sideboard and gnawed it, noisily. "Maybe you'd like to wash that down?" Andrei tilted the bottle toward his guest.

"No, thank you." His gaze rested longingly on the slender, blue green bottle. "I somehow never developed the taste."

Just as I was about to launch into a discourse on the transient nature of human relations, embellishing my commentary with examples from my recent sexual past, the telephone rang. An acquaintance was calling from Kuybyshev to tell Andrei, who never checked the television listings, that his favorite pop singer, Alla Pugachova, was crooning on the other channel.

Pugachova was an overweight, bag-eyed "star" who had recently recorded several songs from Shakespeare plays, translated by Boris Pasternak, disco style. Her detractors accused her of pandering to intellectuals. If Andrei was any guide, they enjoyed the pandering. He lunged for the television, and flipped the dial.

While Alla trundled around the stage in a diaphanous cream-colored evening gown, Andrei leaned closer to the screen, tapping his foot to her latest hit, "Leningrad."

Valya continued to fidget. "Is this Pugachova? She doesn't look half as bad as they say. . . ." During a long pause, Alla thanked the band, her fans, and the cultural department of the Central Committee of the Communist Party for making this lovely event possible, before the electric guitars ripped into another Pasternak hit.

Stirred by the appeal to Party values, Valya piped up. "Andrushechka, you know, I've never seen Pugachova before. I think this calls for a bit of a celebration . . . give me a touch of your wine, would you?"

Tentatively, humbly, Valya edged his glass across the kitchen table. As Andrei sloshed out the final drops of the first bottle, Valya quickly shielded his glass with the back of his hand. "Oh no! Not so much, please." He licked a few spilled drops off his wrist.

A second bottle emerged, and evaporated quietly as the Pugachova special drew to a close. Valya was becoming garrulous, loudly savoring his personal discovery of the country's best known singer. "Really something, our girl, huh? Now I see why she filled the Olympia in Paris."

Just as I was reaching out to pour a final round from the second bottle, Valya helped himself to the last glassful. "May I? This Arbatskoye is impossible to find in the stores."

After the music show came the news, which soured Valya's mood. The Americans were threatening nuclear war, the Israelis were massacring Arabs, and even worse, the Central Asian republics, which just a few months before had been suffering unseasonable snowstorms, were basking in undeserved sunshine.

Shaken, Valya inquired just how many bottles remained in Andrei's case.

A third bottle materialized. Andrei began to yawn. I pulled a few buds of pickled garlic out of the refrigerator, in case a traffic policeman should ask me to breathe in his face on the road home. Valya was fumbling with the television dial.

"Hockey!" Valya pointed at the television screen. "I haven't seen a hockey game since we were in school!" He cooled his enthusiasm with frequent gulps of wine. "My God! The Canadians, what luck!"

Indeed, the hockey was excellent. The Canadians brutalized the Russians, who retaliated by scoring goals. Just watching those stubbly-bearded Quebecois provoking our boys was enough to dry up anyone's throat.

At the end of the first hockey period, Andrei padded

off to bed. He raised an arm in comradely farewell. "Good luck with your woman problem."

Thanks to the Arbatskoye, I had nearly forgotten my woman problem. If I were to move my body, I wasn't certain that my head would follow. That left Valya alone to search for more alcohol. Wine was out of the question. Rummaging behind crates of tinned food, burrowing beneath sections of Andrei's frame tent, which was stored on top of the refrigerator, Valya wanted vodka. Disturbed, a jar of preserves teetered on the edge of the cupboard, and smashed on the floor.

"Oh, Jesus . . ." Two pans spilled out of the oven, which Valya was examining on his hands and knees. Finally, from behind a barricade of hot-water bottles and cookie molds, he unearthed a small flask of clear liquid to which Andrei had attached a hand-written label with a rubber band.

"Aha!" Valya crowed. *"Spirt!"*

I ground the tips of my fingers into my temples, anticipating a headache. Whatever happened, it would be Susan's fault. She shouldn't have left town. She shouldn't have accepted a ring from that scrivener boyfriend of hers. I was the injured party, and I was damned well entitled to a last drink. Or two.

More breakage produced three lacquered shot glasses. After filling all three, Valya remembered that Andrei had left the party, and drank off his friend's portion. The hockey game had ended, and state television was displaying its nighttime holding pattern, a picture of the Lenin mausoleum, and emitting a slow beep. As always, the *spirt* tasted hideous, like a rotten blend of brandy and ammonia.

"Not bad, huh?" Valya poured out three more rounds. I didn't have the strength to reach out my hand over my glass. Valya drained the three cups, and then poured another round, all for himself.

His brow was beaded with sweat. He ran his palm back over his forehead, plastering his hair down against his scalp. "Andrei says you have woman problems."

Admittedly, I couldn't hear him very well. My hearing was deteriorating just as quickly as his speech. I think the dialogue unfolded like this:

"Well, I have a woman."

"You have a problem."

"She may have left me."

"Either way you have a problem." He paused for effect, allowing a few drops of sweat to trickle down his cheek. "I think I can help you."

"Uh?"

I distinctly remember his bunching a hairy, knotted fist just a few inches in front of my nose. For a moment I thought I was a meteorite, about to collide with an onrushing planet. Then I thought perhaps he was threatening me. Had I insulted him? Wasn't I drinking enough?

"Beat her."

"Uh."

He rocked his fist slowly in front of my eyes. "Beat her."

Yes, I had heard him right. Beat her. What a grand idea. With what, I wondered? I had left my riding crop back in the States.

He had read my mind. "With *this*." Valya brandished the fist again.

"Uh." To my credit, I never took his suggestion seriously. God knows what they had taught Susan at those sedate country manors where the James Bonds of the world learn to garrote sentries with their American Express cards. She'd probably tear my Adam's apple out. I tried to say goodbye.

"Uh."

Blind drunk, I found my car keys, then the door.

Just where I had left it, thank God, I discovered my car, then the ignition, and finally Leningrad Avenue that led back to the center of Moscow. The night traffic was a blur of yellow headlights and the gray brown road. I'm getting better at being drunk, it occurred to me. Just a few months ago I would have passed out by now. Driving in this condition is quite a challenge—maybe I'll get a medal. If I didn't slow down and stop bumping the grassy divider that ran between the lanes of the boulevard, I'd probably get a month in the pen. Still, there would a good first-personer in it for Jonas: "From Traffic Court to the Gulag." Not too catchy, really. And the "organs" probably wouldn't supply any pictures. I slowed down.

Back in the compound, wrestling with the elevator door, I collapsed in a heap on the fifth floor landing, and began to cry. I blubbered even louder when I banged against Susan's door and there was no answer. I wanted Susan. I needed Susan. For five full minutes, I squatted on my knees, my head pitched forward on her doormat, and sobbed. God, I thought, I'm really becoming one of *them*.

Summoning my forces, I sorted through the keys again, threw my weight against my own open door, and careened into my apartment. Half asleep, dead drunk, and still crying, I dropped my body on the double bed. My body hit something hard, like a briefcase. I tried to throw it off the bed, but it was too heavy. Then it moved. It was Susan.

"Crikey, are you bloody drunk again? You're turning into a blooming *lush*, Nick." She fled to the far side of the bed before I could search her fingers for rings.

14 / International Women's Day

Happily, there was no ring. What they had neglected to tell Ekaterina Sergeyevna at the Informers Academy was that British and American women wore engagement rings on their left, not their right, hands. Susan's mother had bought her a thin gold filigree ring at Harrod's, for Christmas. I saw no reason to protest.

But even with that misunderstanding accounted for, Susan and I weren't close enough not to be awkward at our first breakfast together in four weeks. Using words, we groped across the table like blind people, seeking for signs of the person we had parted with. My tentativeness wasn't all metaphorical: A crushing hangover was banging hot angry fists against the insides of my eyeballs.

Assuming I had less to hide, I began telling Susan about Natasha, while I toasted a plateful of her London-baked English muffins, which Susan insisted on calling crumpets.

After hearing Natasha's story, Susan tightened her lips. "It all sounds very romantic."

"It was, in a way." Wrong, wrong, wrong. I would pay for that.

"Did you sleep with her?" Susan smiled sweetly, like a landlord raising the rent.

"No."

"Did you try?"

"No."

"Did you think about it?"

I burned my fingers trying to wedge a muffin out of the toaster. "Shit! Who are you, anyway, the Thought Police? Back off, Susan! It's hard to imagine you with your knees soldered together for four weeks in London."

"Oh, they weren't."

In the silence that followed, you could hear the butter running down the crispy muffin craters.

"Oh." I thought those throbbing little brain fists were going to punch my eyeballs out the front of my head.

"In fact, Sam and I broke up."

"Oh. Am I sorry?"

"I don't know. I am."

"Then I am, too. What happened?"

"Oh, you know. Everything and nothing." Susan's diplomatic poise was showing. They had trained her for situations like this. "I told him about us. He didn't take it very well."

"Did you expect him to?"

"No, of course not." She was twirling her new ring around her finger. "He and I would have been apart for another year, you see. I received my forward assignment. To Paris."

"Incredible! They kept their word! Will you be . . ." I rolled my fingers into play binoculars, to mime the idea of spying.

"No, thank God. Consular section. Processing visas for Charles Aznavour and Marcel Marceau."

"And for Mireille Mathieu?" The French songbird was a fixture on Soviet television, where she always preceded her ditties with a resolute *"non"* to U.S. imperialism.

Susan turned her thumbs down. "Denied."

"Well. Congratulations." I didn't sound as if I meant it.

"Congratulations to you, too."

"What for?"

"To hear you talk, it sounds like you've fallen in love."

"Come on, Susan."

"Or that you'd like to."

"We'd all like to, wouldn't we?"

"Touché."

"So remain seated while I circle behind your chair, caress the back of your neck, and gently unbutton the front of your blouse."

Susan leaned back in her chair, and laughed.

I massaged the crests of her shoulders and her neck, and pulled her hair up from under her collar to hang free over the back of the chair. I ran my fingers along her neck, just below the tufty hairline, and drew them through her thick brown tresses like a comb. Susan closed her eyes, and sighed contentedly.

Then I pounced.

For the few weeks that Natasha remained in Moscow, her shadow fell across my affair with Susan. Natasha intrigued Susan, at one remove. Susan was intelligent enough to understand my fascination, and human enough to be jealous. For the first time, Susan seemed genuinely interested in one of my friends, and even suggested that she might defy her security regulations, and meet with us for dinner.

The suggestion came too late, however. One night, as I sat on little Anya's cot watching Natasha pack, I saw the shadow of the Other Woman passing on. Natasha was leaving Moscow.

During our five weeks together, over evening tea, or

chatting during movies, Natasha had explained herself to Andrei's and my satisfaction. I had trouble reconciling her sordid story with her pure, refined beauty. Perhaps I was still judging life on its surfaces. How petty of me, to let her exotic features blind me to her sadness, but I did. For me, she was too beautiful to bear a fissure, or a slight crack. But in fact, she had broken completely in two.

Recounting her past, she told us she had left the "woman business" quickly, and found her way to the post office dormitory. There, too, a clique of men had established a "business," demanding sexual favors in return for protection.

"With one woman, they threatened to cut her breast off. Another time, they kicked a friend of mine down the stairs."

"Were you protected?"

"I paid." She shrugged her shoulders. "We all paid."

"When did you decide to go skiing?"

"To commit suicide, you mean?" She was folding her clothes into the suitcase with the meticulous care of a seasoned traveler. To travel, she had put on a serious brown wool shift pulled tightly at the waist, and set her hair back in a bun. Her angular loveliness had turned severe. She spoke of herself distantly, as if of a former friend.

"After about five months. One of the other girls had just done it. But it was so awful—she broke a windowpane and cut her throat in the middle of the night, then screamed for all of us to save her. But with the dormitory lights out, no one could bandage her, because she was thrashing around her bed, slippery with blood.

"We lit torches of rolled newspaper, and saw her, grasping at her neck, trying to stop the blood from flowing through her fingers. From the next room one of the male 'bosses' told us to hold the noise down, or he would come in and beat us. Finally she lost strength, and lay down on the floor, to die. Someone called an ambulance, but they don't like to drive that far at night. When they arrived to clean up in the morning, it was just another horror—the black stains, the caked blood, the mess. I had to leave differently."

In the distance we heard a pop, and saw a roseate glow spread over the courtyard. Natasha looked up from her packing. "Oh, the fireworks. It's International Women's Day."

"I'm sad you're leaving." I was sitting slouched against the wall. Lilya and the children were out of town. Andrei hadn't returned from work.

Natasha reached back from the suitcase and stroked my hair. "I know you are. But I'm not the vision of purity you thought I was."

"That's not important."

"You'll go back to your motels filled with millionairesses courting you in their Cadillacs. You'll forget about us—"

"I don't think so."

"No, you probably won't. Anyway, so I decided to borrow some skis. I asked three of my friends, and they all refused. They were worried that I'd never come back."

"Why did you come in to the schoolhouse?"

"Dying wasn't for me." She snapped the last suitcase shut. "I changed my mind."

Andrei returned home, and the three of us sat down at the tiny kitchen table. From behind the refrigerator, he took out his last thin bottle of *spirt* to "celebrate" Natasha's departure. None of us felt like celebrating, however, and the first glass only deepened our despondency. Unwrapping a piece of newspaper, Andrei offered us each a dried *voblya,* the obligatory salted fish snack of the professional alcoholic.

"Special for Women's Day," he said, banging the fish carcass against the side of the table to loosen the meat from the bones. Natasha and I followed suit, chewing the tiny slivers of fish between our front teeth.

"God-awful," Natasha said. She swallowed her second shot of alcohol quickly. "Hundred grams are better than a hundred friends," she murmured, her voice already furry with drink. She poured herself a third glass. We sat in silence for a moment, listening to the fireworks pop against the night sky.

Natasha lifted her arm in an unsteady toast, her head already drooping below her shoulders. "To the Solovetsky Islands. No more Soviet power, just Solovetsky power!"

A huge starburst exploded lower on the horizon outside the window, like an artillery shell narrowing our range.

Andrei had shown Natasha a newspaper ad inviting young people to travel to the "Solovki"—twenty degrees north of the Arctic Circle—to restore the famous sixteenth century monastery, which had achieved a second fame in the 1930s as the first hard regime labor camp of the fledgling Soviet republic. For a lark, Natasha followed the ad to an obscure office in the Arbat, Moscow's sinuous old shopping district, and waited in an anteroom with a dozen other young people until she was called to meet Igor Vassilich.

A handsome young man with darkening red hair, wearing a frayed leather jacket, sat behind a badly scratched writing table. On the wall of the small office hung a portrait of Lenin and a framed quotation attributed to Leonid Brezhnev: "Restorers! Work with Pride to Reawaken the Beauties of the Motherland!"

Igor Vassilich smiled, and held out his hand. "Passport, please." He glanced over the document and entered Natasha's name on a list. Snapping the passport shut, he slid it back across the table. "The pay is a hundred and thirty rubles, with hardship raises after six months. We're all living in a dormitory, no rent. Mail twice a week if the plane can take off from Archangel. And visitors with permission only—there's a missile base next door." Natasha gave a start, and he grinned. "Ah, yes . . . first line of defense against imperialism, and all that. We won't be the last generation of restorers."

Natasha fumbled with her foulard, and turned her passport over in her palm. "But, this is happening much too quickly. What do I know of your work . . . and my friends . . . my things . . . my husband . . ."

"But your passport says you are divorced."

She winced, and looked at the floor. Igor Vassilich had been raised on the same movies as Natasha—Soviet *detectivy*—where leather-jacketed security agents hurry through interrogations in clipped tones, exposing the enemies of the people. "You came to us, we presume you are ready." Less brusquely, he added, "And we need people. You will enjoy the group, mostly young men and women."

"Perhaps I am unfit. Psychologically. Perhaps I am . . . suicidal!"

Igor Vassilich slapped his hand on the desk and burst out laughing. "All the more reason! No time for suicide in the north! Too damned cold! Too much work! Too damned beautiful! Have you been there? No? You won't believe it—wild horses, plenty of game, berries as fat as your fist. The air's so pure it chokes your lungs. You'll be coughing for weeks! Real winters—none of this city slush! Suicide! Ha! What a luxury . . . not at all—we're putting you to work!"

He thrust out his hand, stained tough as hide, and

greeted her warmly. "Igor Vassilich. Pleased to meet you. We're assembling at the Leningrad station tomorrow at ten, platform seven."

"And that was it," Natasha said. "It's always nice to meet an enthusiast. He was quite taken with the romance of it all. And I was glad to be wanted for something other than . . . the business."

Andrei had hiked in the north, and told us about tenting under the aurora, and the white nights. "It's like heaven. A very cold heaven."

"It'll be wonderful," Natasha said. Two long tears pulled pale lines down her cheeks. She slouched over the table until the center of her forehead rested on her tiny shot glass. Her body was jerking with sobs. "I'm going to miss you."

Andrei laid his hand on her shoulder. "If it doesn't work out, we'll always be here."

He lifted her head off the glass. "Just last night, Valya came over to watch the hockey, and it turns out his father spent fifteen years at the monastery, in a nonreligious capacity, so to speak. 'The main thing,' Valya says, 'my father always repeated is that there's no bullshit from the mainland.' The minute the prisoners arrived, they lined them up and told them to forget about Russia. That's where she got this slogan. 'Forget about Soviet power,' the guards said. 'Here we have Solovetsky power.'"

Natasha sat up, and squared her shoulders back against the kitchen cabinet. "No more Soviet power," she droned. "And better yet, no more goddam men!"

Suddenly, a cluster firework with a damaged fuse exploded in the middle of the courtyard behind us. Pink and violet sparks showered against the window glass, tinkling like sand. Pinwheeling fireballs streaked along the sidewalks. A cat screamed, a woman threw her body across her baby carriage. In the distance, a voice warned of fire. "They've found the range," Andrei said. "After the next round, we all disappear."

What did Natasha prove? That one could be unhappy under socialism? I hadn't doubted it for a second. Nothing had seemed to work for her, she was faced with permanent transiency. "No one can stay in the center," she wrote in her letter. I agreed; I felt far from my center, and better for it.

After Natasha left, the geometry of Andrei's apartment returned to normal. Her suitcases no longer blocked the narrow entrance to the kitchen, and Natasha's cot was removed from the corridor and folded under Anya's bed. Lilya was relieved. Andrei and I had mixed emotions. I regretted never coming closer to her. But I had never seen so many sad events embodied in one person.

We received our only letter from her two months later, neatly handwritten on six sheets of rustling onionskin. True to form, Natasha had a fantastic story to tell.

Dear Andrei,

I miss you all. Please thank Lilya for her hospitality, so much! I'll be happy to reciprocate—you've probably never lived in a monastery before.

We're all away now, aren't we? First Martinov, then your friend Aron, who fancies himself too good for America, and now me. Will Nick defect too? Perhaps we will collect a reward, for winning an enemy of the people over to socialism. No one can take it, no one can stay near the center. "When you chop wood, the chips fly." Did Lenin say that? Maybe we are experiencing the second revolution, and we are the little chips flying off the woodpile. Martinov was the pioneer, but I always knew he was better than all of us . . .

I've been here almost eight weeks, as you can count.

What to say, or what to say first? Start from the center and work outwards? Each of us lives in a cell in the monastery. I have become very monklike, with a low steel frame bed, a horsehair mattress, and the wooden table where I am writing this letter. Those are my furnishings, with a square window on the courtyard. Can you feel the table shake? Perhaps you can feel it in the handwriting.

Today is Sunday, our day off. This morning I walked to the dairy farm and helped with the milking. Also we collect the farmers' laundry, and wash it during the week. In exchange, we receive milk products. Explain this concept to Nick: socialism.

This room is white, as milk, as this paper. Who was here before, I wonder? Twenty generations of smelly monks, displaced by the pitiful detritus of Bolshevism, I guess. The courtyard is also white, peppered with hundreds of square black holes, the windows. There are still bars on them left over from you-know-when. Removing them is part of the "restoration."

There is a routine here. I suppose us poor old Russians (even us half-Russians) can't work without a timetable, or a plan. Calisthenics before breakfast—picture forty-three restorers in their underwear, shivering because the high walls keep out the sun, flogging off the cold. A solid breakfast, and to work!

I have a title: "painter-restorer, third class." So far, I've been mixing lacquers for one of the brigades touching up the iconostasis in the main cathedral. So I stare all day at the olive-eyed icons, waiting for my miracle. To me, they look dark and sad. I know that's not the "correct" response. . . .

We are a community here. Most everyone is quite young and friendly. Moscow types—you can explain to Nick what that means. Artists, even a writer or two. It is almost summer, and we are all happy. There are plenty of men and women to go around, with new pairs forming every day. Work for the midwife, but not from me; I'm the Virgin Natasha.

174

We are not the only community here. We have a brigade, a platoon—maybe I should say just a bunch of
about a hundred soldiers, conscripts from all parts of
the country. They have something to do with the base.
They run out of the courtyard in formation each morning, bouncing like a pack of rabbits, and they bounce
back in at nightfall.

We never see what they do, but two or three of them
are sweet on me, and hope that if they tell me military
secrets, I will go to bed with them. They are building a
submarine base. America, beware!

What a picture of harmony, the young soldiers de-
fending the Motherland, while the restorers serve on
the "cultural front." Would it were so. The locals are
great "brewers," and the moonshine flows freely. For a
time, it amused the soldiers to beat up our men, and
threaten to rape us women. One of our girls sank a
kitchen knife between the ribs of an amorous national
minority, and these incidents have stopped for a moment.

There is a third group in the monastery, a large
colony of paraplegic "samovars," who migrated here
after the war. They too are about a hundred, and re-
gard the rest of us as interlopers. They took the place
over when it was just a rotting prison and converted it
to their needs. They have wooden ramps for the little
trolleys they push themselves around on, and they oc-
cupy all the ground floors. They have their own vegetable garden, crosshatched with wooden planking for
their carts, cows, and of course their stills.

Who's so nice to the handicapped—is it the Swedes
or the Americans? They should meet this group: filthy,
evil people, most of whom melted down church relics
before the Ministry of Culture put the valuables under
lock and key. They are all men—don't any women lose
their legs?

The samovars tolerate us, but hate the soldiers. On
Lenin's birthday, the soldiers got drunk, and organized
a "gladiator match" between two of the invalids. Right

in the center of the courtyard, they trampled down a circle of earth, gave these fellows knives, and forced them to fight.

Many of the invalids hate each other, and the soldiers had picked two sworn enemies, and filled them with liquor. One of the men was larger and stronger—but remember, these are just torsos on wheels! The betting heavily favored the larger cripple, whose head wouldn't have reached my waist.

One hand was their "glove" hand, the fist wrapped in electric tape, which they pushed on the ground for moving and maneuvering. In the other hand they held the knife. To even up the betting, the soldiers gave the larger fellow a five-inch army dagger. The small one got a foot-long bread knife.

But they were still no match. The big man had the longer reach, and lurched forward, gashing his opponent on the arm and chest, even across the face. Each cut drew blood; after a few minutes the little fellow was trying to escape to the edge of the ring, where the soldiers spun his cart around and rolled him forward, into the knife of the big man. He seemed doomed.

Then suddenly, from the circle of soldiers, someone slid a broom handle along the ground to the smaller man. All in one second, he backed off, grabbed the stick, and jammed it under his opponent's wheeled trestle. He yanked the stick upward, spilling the big man on his back, wriggling like a tortoise. And in the same second, before he could climb back on his wheels, he was dead. The little fellow zipped over and slashed his throat.

I was watching from my window. You don't have such holidays in Moscow! I saw the rush of blood pour onto the invalid's fetid clothes, his gasp, his death. A great row broke out among the soldiers, because the broom handle had turned the tide, and men who had given odds against the smaller fighter had lost months of pay. Drunk, enraged, they disarmed the winner, dragged him down to the water, and threw him off the pier, along with the corpse of his victim. Even without legs, this man could stay afloat. So they heaved big stones at him from the shore, bashing his head until he drowned.

Now the samovars have threatened to kill the soldiers in their sleep. There was a fire in the soldiers' cells last week, but no one knows how it started. Meanwhile, we carry brushes and tins of solvents between the warring factions, restoring.

But the killing is just a sideshow, to my happiness. They could all die and I wouldn't mind. We have long blocks of time when we are untouchable. I've stopped drinking, and spend my free hours roaming the fields, or down by the ocean, playing hide and seek with the wild geese in the cattails. I don't think there's room for fantasizing here, about children or about a husband; it wouldn't occur to me to want them. Igor Vassilich was right—this land is too beautiful for suicide.

It's not even summer yet, and all the talk is of preparing for the winter. Are we ready? I don't know. The samovars have spent every day this spring rolling around the countryside, cutting down small trees for firewood. They have the warmest quarters, and now the largest supply of fuel. I suspect the soldiers will seize the invalids' wood when the weather turns cold, unless the base sends them some. We've begun some preparations, mostly writing to relatives in Moscow to send warm clothing!

Whose idea was it that I come here? Was it yours? Thank you. You knew it: I was monk material all along.

I'll send more reports on life under Solovetsky power. Best to you all, and of course Martinov.

N.

After receiving the letter, Andrei tried to put through a call to the monastery, but the operator refused to connect him, explaining that the one trunk line to Solovetsky was reserved for the Ministry of Defense. We never heard from Natasha again.

15 / *Pukh*

April surprised us all. I looked out my window, where a long alley of bare poplar trees ran between the buildings of the Kutuzovsky foreigners' compound. Just one day after the freezing rain stopped, thick clusters of leaves burst out on the gray branches, and white, fluffy poplar spores floated skyward. Spring in a day! I couldn't see the street any more—the bursting treetops hovered below me like a layer of green clouds.

At first, the kitten—I was still hesitating to call her Natasha—staged boxing matches with the billowy *pukh* seeds floating in my large casement window. Perched on the sill, she flailed madly at the airborne flotilla of fluff. After a day, she had exhausted herself, wagging her head helplessly as successive layers of *pukh* covered the apartment.

Walking on the street, I saw a young boy wearing a "University of America" T-shirt bending backward like a limbo dancer, trying to land one of the fluffy spores in his mouth. I lunged at the largest puffs, but just when I grabbed the seed, it would squirt off on an unexpected breeze. Passers by stared at me, hands waving, conducting my invisible symphony.

Ekaterina Sergeyevna accused the Americans of starting the *pukh* problem. According to her, Roosevelt sent Stalin a planeload of poplar seedlings to beautify wartorn Moscow. "Just the kind of present we've come to expect from you people," she said. "I've got Colorado beetles all over my vegetable garden."

But at the Saturday dinner, grandmother Aya firmly squelched this tale. "Heavens, no! I remember *pukh* from the 1920s, and even my poor mother used to complain how the stuff almost suffocated *her,* when she was a child. My grace! We can't blame the Americans for everything!"

The *pukh* sent us to the baths. Gossamer Ping-Pong balls clogged the air; the lint caught in one's throat, gathered in the sinuses, and brought on violent attacks of sneezing. I was certain I had contracted hay fever, or the local equivalent.

One morning, Andrei announced he had solved our respiratory problems. "I've bought us a month at the bathhouse," he informed me, pressing a fourteen-ruble subscription into my hand. On the back of the printed form, I read: "Use of ointments, branches, and alcoholic beverages forbidden." Our appointed time was scrawled across the print: Thursday, 8:00 A.M.

"Yowch!"

"It's all I could get," Andrei said apologetically. "It'll do you good to wake up early."

We owed our subscriptions to the New Discipline, which had just crested and crashed over Moscow's bathhouses. Police raids, newspaper exposés, even fevered citizens' groups scourged the baths, suddenly equated with brothels and foreigners' hotels as nests of vice. In one swoop, many of the houses' best patrons, the "men who know how to enjoy life," were turned out, and the administrators along with them.

When Andrei applied to the Kadashevsky Baths for a private sauna, he met the newly appointed director, a man who just three weeks before had been teaching

Marxism-Leninism to tenth and eleventh graders. "He needed clients to fulfill his plan—most of their regular customers were in jail," Andrei explained. "He treated me courteously, and filled out the forms on the spot. A most un-Soviet performance."

I felt like a scab, stealing bath time from men who had devoted their professional lives to the sauna. "If we're taking the place of the people in jail, does that mean we don't know how to enjoy life?"

"Not at all," Andrei assured me. "We're launching a new era of enjoyment."

The baths were tucked away in a side street across the river from the Kremlin, in the Zamoskvarechiye district, where Andrei grew up. To seal the circle of coincidence and personal history, Susan's cubicle in the British Embassy was less than 200 yards away, facing toward the river.

This was where the bad guys used to live, the absinthe drinkers, child prostitutes, and escaped convicts who swilled vodka at dead-end taverns named Wolf's Gulch and Lost Siberia. The industrial bourgeoisie cleared them out to make room for factories like the Red October confectionery just up the river. I sniffed the air, full of the freshness of sunlight, and the smell of leaves hanging over the sidewalk—but not a whiff of the chocolate oceans of Andrei's childhood dreams.

The serendipity of Russian planning, of Russian life itself, is ideal for searching, but not for finding. Walking down Kadashevsky alley, I had been told to look for the low-slung pink building behind iron fences. The first such building, gathered behind a small forest of flowering chestnuts, and sagging at the roofline, turned out to be a school. Further along, across a shoulder-high iron fence, stood an ancient church, one of hundreds left to collapse in this neighborhood, onion domes long since stripped of gold, silver crosses snapped off the gables by friends or enemies.

Perhaps this elegant wreck? But a small sign identified it as a vegetable and potato cellar for a nearby store. More walking, and I found three identical buildings facing into a fenced courtyard. One was the computer center for a city ministry, the second a police station, and the third—same broken staircases, buckling foundations and shedding paint—was the bathhouse.

At five of eight, the six founding members, as we fancied ourselves, had assembled in the courtyard. In addition to myself and Andrei, we had his old friend Lyonya, who had bought in to relax himself before a cataract operation later in the month, and his cousin Valera, a sports psychologist. Also a linguist and a physicist: hard core *intelligyents*. But don't let the briefcases fool you—bath men one and all.

"Where's your gear?" The physicist pointed to the bath towel draped across my arm.

"What gear?"

I noticed each of them was carrying a plastic shopping bag. Andrei opened his to show me the contents: vinyl flip-flops, soap, a shower cap, massage glove, and a gray felt hat for the sauna.

"I brought a towel."

"There are plenty of towels inside."

Would they cut me from the team?

"Forget it, you'll be fine," Andrei said. "Bring your stuff next time."

Lyonya brushed a cloud of poplar spores away from his eyes. "Goddam *pukh!*" United, we grumbled support, and forayed into the baths to save our lungs.

The interior was modest enough, for the pleasure it promised. Walking through a small changing area, we reached the sitting room, filled by a low, thickly lacquered pine table surrounded by benches. Pushing through a connecting door, we found a kitchen belonging to a squat, white-bonneted attendant named Natalya Andreyevna, who quickly shooed us away. From her side of the threshold, which she never again allowed us to cross, came many rattling noises, occasional squabbles among unseen voices, and the fat kettle of mint tea that appeared just after our first session in the sauna.

Above the door to the dressing room hung a giant electric sign, the kind that flashes in Soviet movie theaters, accompanied by a screaming alarm bell, to warn drunks and laggards to clear the hall for the next show: THE SÉANCE IS OVER.

Through another door, we found the shower, and a five-foot-deep, ice cold plunge. Outside the sauna, a caricaturist had painted a massive, benevolent bath god hovering over the padded door, welcoming visitors to the realm of the bath.

"An empire," Andrei crowed, as we completed our first walk around the premises.

"A country, a planet, for fourteen rubles a month," Lyonya sighed, heading for the dressing room, unbuttoning his shirt. "Let's get to work!"

Before becoming acquainted with each other's professions, marital problems, or political views, we met each other's bodies. Older by ten to forty years, these men were built tougher than I. Yes, they were carrying some white-collar fat, packed into round bulges underneath waistlines tightened by high, thin belts. But it wasn't flab—this was tense, Russian fat, like saddlebags, storage for an uncertain tomorrow.

Naked, I still showed traces of my childhood nickname, the Pear, and my ankles—well, my usually uncritical mother once compared them to tree trunks.

But the bath men, even the sixty-nine-year-old Valera, stood on muscled, wiry legs, fit from shoving through bus and subway crowds, or forcing themselves forward in early morning lines for cheese.

Valera was the most imposing, and one of the more mysterious. Six feet four inches tall, he was still slender in his late sixties, but badly stooped, almost broken at the collar bone. Two long surgical scars tracked blue railway lines along his left side, one on the rib cage, and one just below.

He spoke haltingly, his throat filling with liquid near the end of each sentence. His face was handsome beneath curling silver hair, but age had contorted his eyes, cheeks, and lips downward. Friendly and soft-spoken, he wore a tragic mask.

During our second Thursday visit, he told me he had been an athlete before attending medical school and embarking on a career as one of the country's first sports psychologists. I love sports, but with my equipment in full view, I wasn't sure he would believe me. I mentioned only that I played tennis and soccer "for fun."

Valera leaned back on the pine bench of the sauna, reaching his head toward the burning heat of "heaven," just under the ceiling. He took a breath, and blinked his eyes clear of perspiration. "Sports used to be fun," he began, dipping his head toward me, sitting one bench below. "I played in a different era."

He coughed to clear his throat. "What's happening in America? People play only for money now?"

"What's happening here?" I asked. "Athletes play just for the free car, or the exit visa and a handful of hard currency. The stakes are lower, but the principle's the same."

"Yes, you're probably right," he admitted, stepping

over the three tiers of benches to the exit. "It looks like we've finally caught up."

In the sitting room, we found Natalya Andreyevna's special mint tea set out for us, next to a neatly arranged plate of shortbread cookies. The rotund, bustling attendant had adopted us as her favorite charges, thanks to Lyonya's timely suggestion that we leave a tip the week before.

"Hardly anyone tips any more," she groused, studiously ignoring Andrei's Tai Chi exercise routine, which he claimed to have learned off Radio Hanoi.

Her complaint sparked my interest in the other "subscribers." Who, for instance, took over our quarters after us, for the ten to twelve shift, possibly a risky time to be caught in the baths under the New Discipline? Last week at ten on the button, I had seen a stocky young man charge into our dressing room, his shoulders stooped under the weight of two bulging briefcases.

"Oh, Misha! Yes, he always arrives first with the beers to cool them off in the plunge," Andreyevna said. "They still know how to live, that crew! Their biggest worry—" she lowered her voice to a whisper "—their biggest worry was that you'd run hot water in the plunge, the way some of the girls do. They need it icy cold, you see, to have the beers ready when they first come out of the sauna."

"Beer's not so interesting, without something on the side," Andrei remarked from his position spread-eagled on the floor, where he was "equalizing" his circulation.

"Oh, they do all right, don't you worry!" She was standing on the threshold of her kitchen, to keep an eye on the teapot. "I make them omelets, they bring their own dried fish. Sometimes even"— sotto voce— "caviar. They once gave me a tin. You know, I think

they work"—she pointed at the walls—"at the 'office.'"
In Soviet street code, there is only one office: the KGB.

"They must, to live so well during working hours."

"Well, you know, they work on a flexible schedule . . ." she pursed her lips, sealing the obvious lie.
"They seem quite, well, relaxed, especially when Victor
Sergeyich is around. They've become . . . friends." She
rubbed her thumb against her forefinger to help us
understand the nature of their friendship with the director.

She was itching to pass on one more little secret, but
ducked out to check on the tea. Within seconds, her
gray head popped back over the threshold. "One time,
they even had with them . . . a . . ." she broke into fits
of giggling, and pressed her head against the doorjamb, blushing.

"A woman!" Lyonya feigned shock.

Andrei sat up sharply. "A woman . . ."

Andreyevna had rushed back to her kitchen, rattling
cups, preparing the tea. When she brought in the tea
service, she was still giggling. "You must never tell Victor Sergeyich you heard this from me. The consequences—" She rolled her eyeballs. "They're nice
boys, really. You know, it's just hell where they work,
with all the pressures they face . . . they need to relax
and have a little fun."

Over the second round of tea, we asked Natalya how
we should approach the director to renew our subscription for the following month. She promised that
there would be no trouble, Sergeyich was a very decent
man, a former schoolteacher, and very modest, unlike
the previous boss. She crossed herself, as if we should
fear for the soul of the former director, whom we
knew to have found another comfortable sinecure.

"Victor Sergeyich wants people to respect him, of
course—" Another message in code: Even though Ser-

geyich had begun work only recently, he was already taking bribes. "And make sure you catch him early in the day. Also, you know, don't cause any trouble around here, with the situation . . ." She glanced around the table at our uncomprehending faces. "You know, keep the water cold for the beer. And keep your mouths shut."

Just that day, we overlapped with Misha for a moment, as he set his two briefcases down on the locker room bench, clanking glass.

"Empties," he explained brusquely, peeling off his shirt and undershirt. "The kids drink all night, and leave it to papa to return the bottles. Hey—" he kept his back to us, springing out of his pants and shorts, jogging in place, to have a running start at the sauna. "My friends and I really like the way you fellows keep the plunge ice cold. We're tough guys—we like to boil our balls in the sauna, and freeze them into little ice cubes in the plunge. Let's keep it that way, huh?"

He snatched up the briefcases with new vigor, and jogged into the shower room.

16 / Taking Care of Business

What can't you get in America, with money? Admittedly, some people can't get money; but the others, what can't they have? I remember how my New York crowd used to grumble. If the rent was right, the job was bad. If the job was good, the romance wasn't working. The horizon of happiness was always receding. But what a luxury, to be missing just one or two things! In Russia, Andrei couldn't get *anything*. This season, he needed some spare parts.

"It's the political economy," he explained, nosing Zazie through traffic toward the South Port car market. "You should read Marx."

"That's what Susan says. He's too complicated for me."

"Well, it's too late now. You're better off having me explain it anyway. . . . You see, if we spend all our time looking for spare parts we can't make revolution. If Lenin and Trotsky had owned cars, there wouldn't have been any 1917. They never would have left their garages."

Andrei was hoping that his six-week-long quest for front and rear brake shoes would end today. He claimed to have combed every classified ad, suborned every mechanic in Moscow, called in every favor owed him by his many friends. In vain: There were no parts.

"You know, in America, we'd go to the store."

"A store!" He slapped his hands on the steering wheel. "There's the New World for you! A store."

"Did you look in a store?"

He grinned slyly. "Only because I knew you would ask."

"And?"

He brandished his fist, with the thumb tucked between the second and third fingers. Soviet street semaphore: No more. They're out of it. It's gone. Nothing. Screw you.

He had scored a near miss. Traveling south in his spanking new Soviet Fiat, an engineer acquaintance had been run off the Kiev highway by a bus convoy of Young Pioneers, and was lying in traction at a local hospital, brazenly cursing every child in the ward. To make conversation, one of the male nurses joked that "It's too bad you didn't crack up a Zaporozhets, because I could get you all the parts I need from my brother at the factory"—which was just thirteen kilometers down the road.

The victim mentioned in a letter to his wife that "It will be a miracle if I ever get out of here alive, as the hospital has been turned into a spare parts dealership." The wife worked as a programmer at Andrei's institute, where the brake shoe search had replaced first quarter plan fulfillment as the top priority. Andrei dialed through to the hospital, and read the parts' serial numbers to a dulled floor matron, carefully noting that he would pay double the fifty ruble list price.

Two days later—the phone call had interrupted her crossword—the matron shuffled between the rows of cots and relayed the information to the patient. That evening, the nurse contacted his brother, who demanded triple payment, one hundred and fifty rubles, for the parts.

Of course, the patient still couldn't move. So the male nurse called the engineer's wife in Moscow, who relayed the latest demand to Andrei. Who again reached for his phone. "One hundred!" he screamed through the deafening static. "It's half a month's salary for me! I have a wife and children to feed!"

He winked telling the story. "Well, maybe a third of my salary . . ."

A day later, the brother sent word that the price was acceptable but called for half the money up front, for the risk. While Andrei was wondering whether to trust fifty rubles to the mails, the programmer delivered the latest message from the south: Security guards had arrested the brother trying to smuggle the brake shoes through the factory gate, and he was facing a three-year jail sentence for theft of state property. "The New Discipline claims another victim," Andrei chuckled. "I guess this brother didn't read the papers. So now we're thrown back on the invalids."

"Who are they?"

Bumping along the Varshavskoye Shosse, Andrei recited a bit of history. After World War II, the Soviet government decreed that wounded veterans would be first in line to buy the new automobiles rolling off the country's reconstructed assembly lines. But Russia's wounded were arguably the most disfigured soldiers in history; Red Army medics hacked off limbs indiscriminately, to dissuade soldiers with minor wounds from hanging around the overcrowded surgeries.

So in addition to twenty million war dead, the country lost ten million limbs. After a few weeks of lifting the legless "samovars," their thigh stubs swathed in stinking rags, onto the front seats of "Victory" roadsters, the authorities saw their good intentions perverted into a gruesome carnival.

From Moscow came a second decree: Half the output of the Zaporozhets bug-shaped compact would be specially modified for invalids, substituting manual levers for pedals where necessary. The veterans bought their cars in special stores, well stocked with spare parts. Within a few years, the invalids controlled the thriving black market in spare parts, charging up to ten times official prices.

"These are the paraplegics Natasha's living with?"

"Same ones. Honored veterans loved by the Soviet people, returning the love in kind."

To reach the invalids, one had to contact their agents, walking disabled who frequented the South Port car market. Andrei knew where to find them. This Saturday, a group of about twenty middlemen had gathered in front of a bread store, blocking the entrance.

Andrei thought he had once bought piston rings from the "Wolf," a towering monster dressed in tattered army fatigues, who had stuck a hooked piece of reinforcing rod into his wooden arm to use as a hand when he leaned on a wall, or a customer. The Wolf's gray eyelids hung like dirty curtains on his creped face. "You'll be my first business today," he grumbled. "What's the state out of now?"

"Brake shoes."

"Aha. . . ." Calculating the cost, and his cut, the old soldier ran a finger along the inside of his tobacco-stained gums, decorated with a half-dozen glittering steel teeth. "Big problem. Big money."

Wolf had the solution, but we had to drive with him to the "warehouse." As he hobbled toward the car, he faced down a brush-haired young policeman sent to shoo the malingerers away from the bread store. "Only an asshole works for a salary," he growled, loud enough for the policeman to hear, clawing at the car door with his twisted metal "hand."

The warehouse turned out to be a ground floor apartment in a shabby tenement overlooking the river. The entryway felt moist, and reeked of urine. Three boards formed a ramp over a short flight of stairs leading inside, and someone had ripped the rows of mailboxes from their braces, pulling them down to ground level. The world had been recast for the people on wheels; samovars live here.

Tacked above the black rectangle where the mailboxes had once hung, I noticed a typewritten letter from the District Soviet informing the tenants of the building's upcoming demolition, "in connection with the modernization of the South Port." Wolf jabbed his finger at the date: 1969.

"Can you believe it?" He barged into an apartment on the left corridor. "Fucking Soviet power."

We walked into a square, one-room flat, filthy, and empty except for a threadbare sofa collapsed onto the floor against the opposite wall. Yellow snakes of rolled newspaper crawled up the cracking plaster, to stopper drafts in winter. The soles of my shoes sucked grimy ooze on the wooden floorboards. I thought we were alone until what looked like a barrel-shaped pillow at one end of the sofa stirred, then rolled over to face us.

Like a nurse bored with the ritual of caring, the Wolf walked quickly to the divan, and lifted the legless torso by the shoulders onto a square wooden trestle with metal wheels, set next to the sofa. Planted on the cart, the samovar pulled a baggy sailor's jersey down his chest to hide his stubs, and looked us over. The three of us took up places around our midget-sized host, as if waiting on an unpredictable child.

The Wolf was spearing inside his nose with the steel hook. "Pavlovich, why don't you get somebody to clean this place up?"

"Take that construction material out of your nose and tell me what these people want."

"Brake shoes . . . '66 Zaporozhets."

Pavlovich stroked his sandy stubble. In contrast to his apartment, and his awful factotum, his face was open and handsome, with the clean Russian cast of the heroes of World War II movies. His voice was deep and strong, with an authority his body might once have conveyed. "Those parts could be a big problem." The Wolf growled his assent. "Not everyone can come up with the money. We tell them to write a letter to the factory with their complaints. See how far that gets them. Ha! I'll check the stock . . ."

Pavlovich planted his gnarled fists on the floor and propelled himself over to a closet, where he rattled his hands through piles of greasy scrap.

I looked around the room. A color portrait of Stalin in his white marshal's tunic, torn from a picture magazine, hung next to a dozen pornographic playing cards tacked—waist high—around a 1973 Aeroflot calendar. Just above the grimy sofa I saw a door-sized poster of a rowing squad, advertising the 1936 Berlin Olympics. From inside the closet, Pavlovich called for the Wolf, who brought four loops of grease-crusted metal out to the middle of the room. Andrei lifted them with the ends of his fingers, checking the serial numbers.

"Where'd you get the poster?" I asked. Pavlovich stared at me closely, suspicious of distraction.

"My brother was supposed to go, rowing. They trained for four years. They even went to Britain and beat the goddam English. At the last minute, he"—Pavlovich nodded toward the smiling portrait of Stalin—"called the whole thing off, said they couldn't go. Gave them all gold medals anyway, told them they would have won." He looked up at me proudly, beaming like a brother thirty years younger, before degradation. "They would have, too. They would have beat the fucking Americans." I mumbled some congratulations.

"They made him a big hero, sent him out with some agitational brigade during the war. The soldiers were so simple, they didn't know where he'd won the medal—they loved him. He even came to my regiment, and suddenly I was a hero, too, the brother of a gold medalist." Pavlovich pressed one nostril closed, and emptied his nose on the floor. "He always carried the thing around in his front pocket, ready to show to everyone. It was his life's treasure. Papa and mama were starving, but he'd never part with his medal."

Pavlovich pointed at the poster. "He's the third one from the right, the short one." I had my finger on the chest of his gray jersey. "See how handsome he was? Handsome but stupid. Someone knifed him for that medal during the siege of Leningrad."

Pavlovich's voice broke. He saved his pity for the tragedy of his brother, not for himself. His face was a rock, drained of tears, but his throat was trembling.

"After that, I ceased to care. Suddenly the war became attractive, as a way out of the horror. I turned into one of those fools you see in the films—the guy who's always leading the troops heroically into enemy fire, bellowing Stalin's name, throwing his life away for the Motherland. I even won some medals"—he gestured towards the closet—"they're in there with the scrap."

Pavlovich rubbed his thighs. Halfway down his legs, his wandering hands recoiled at the edge of the wooden trestle, the limit of his existence. He had been daydreaming about his body. "Then I stepped on a land mine . . ."

The Wolf coughed loudly, fearful of sacrificing his percentage to sentiment. Pavlovich ignored him, staring straight ahead at the yellowing poster, searching for the memory of his brother, lost in time. The Wolf coughed again.

"I don't know . . ." Pavlovich mumbled, fixing his eyes on his private dream. "Legs I don't need. But the rest . . ."

Andrei placed two fifty-ruble notes on the floor in front of the trestle. The Wolf cleared his throat disappointedly. Pavlovich glanced downward and nodded his head. Stooping, the Wolf plucked up one of the notes. Again a silent nod, and we filed out of the flat.

As we emerged from the dank corridor into the sunlight, the murky smell of the river supplanted the stench of the entryway. "You're lucky," the Wolf grunted, rolling the fifty-ruble bill in the palm of his good hand. "He could have asked for more. But he's nuts when anyone talks about the Olympics. I brought some big Jew in there a few years ago, who said he actually rowed with the brother. Pavlovich broke down, he fell off the cart—" the Wolf laughed. "We lifted him back on, and he sent me out for vodka. He and this guy went through three bottles, talking about rowing, and afterward Pavlovich gave him everything he needed for free!"

He tucked the bill into a crevice where his arm stump met the wooden limb.

"He's a good fellow, Pavlovich. But he's no businessman."

17 / The New Jerusalem

Three twenty-minute shifts in the sauna, followed by the paralyzing cold water plunge and soothing tea, sent me flying. Each Thursday around eleven I sailed back into my foreigners' ghetto, floated past the hostile stares of the militiamen, and ascended magically to my office.

Boris always laid out the overnight telexes on my desk, along with highlighted clippings from the six or seven daily papers he scanned each morning. Today, I noticed that the Supreme Soviet had sentenced three deputy ministers to death for illegal currency operations, and the chairman of the People's Revolutionary Council of Mozambique had arrived for his annual dip into the munitions cookie jar.

Maybe my neighbor would cover the visit. I had finally met the "fraternal radio correspondent from developing nation" ten days before, when I knocked at his apartment one evening to borrow matches for my stove. Warily, he cracked the door an inch, exposing only his Opal Eye.

"Unnnh?"

"A light for my stove."

He didn't understand.

I struck a pretend match.

"Unnnh." The Eye vanished. The door closed.

Moments later, the door opened, and scissored fingertips dangled a book of matches labeled Embassy of North Yemen through the narrow crack. The Eye reappeared.

"Who are you?"

"Perkins. An American journalist."

"Unnnh. Not the one who insulted our ambassador?"

I suddenly remembered my "Our Yemen or their Yemen?" gaffe. "No, no. We sent him home. Nasty piece of work. I've always supported brotherly relations with"—I glanced at the matchbook—"North Yemen."

"Unnnh. Tell your colleague he will be most unwelcome in our country. We have given his name to the visa authorities." He tossed the matches out the door, and slammed the conversation to a halt.

Back on my desk, I noticed an official news agency report that "sky pirates" had tried to hijack a mail plane to Turkey, but "vigilant security organs" foiled their plans. So Misha and his friends weren't spending all their time at the baths. Overwhelmed by ten minutes of work, I was sprawled back in my reclining desk chair when Boris lumbered in.

"You look relaxed," he said accusingly.

"I am relaxed." I straightened in my chair, summoning up my managerial affectations. "Anything in the papers?"

Boris nodded toward the pile of clips. "Not much. Your friends call. They never leave their names." He glared down at me disapprovingly.

"OK. Anything else?"

"I'll have to leave early next Tuesday. Political exercises."

"Getting out of shape?" He didn't crack a smile. Because he worked with a foreigner, he was required to attend a two-hour indoctrination class each month. His square-shaped head could accommodate any diagonals; after a full day of typing my dispatches (recently branded "slanderous" by the mayor of a provincial city I had labeled "New Jersey, USSR") and listening to the Voice of America, he could sit attentively in an unheated basement room in the foreign ministry while a pickle-nosed *politinformator* lambasted imperialistic intrigues around the globe.

Once, with the previous night's exercise fresh in his mind, he explained to me how CIA weather satellites were zapping the Ukrainian wheat fields with "ultrasonic rays," ruining the harvest. Naively, I brandished a news magazine report of a harsh drought in the American Midwest, flush with dramatic pictures of withered corn stalks and cracked, parched soil.

"See, we have crop failures in America, too. Without the CIA."

Boris smiled knowingly. "No one says we can't do the same to you."

Today, he reminded me of a press conference later in the week: Sixty Years of Soviet Railways. Boris was still angry that I had passed up the press bash for Sixty Years of Aeroflot and its trove of giveaways—glossy calendars, supersonic lapel pins, and the official Aeroflot record album, *Men of High Flight.* Surely the publicity-hungry railwaymen would one-up their flyboy rivals in the freebie department; maybe they would hand out sausages from the restaurant car.

"OK, let's plan on going."

Boris grunted acknowledgment, and loitered back to his cubicle. He was worrying that I would never attend the press conference, just as I had never found time to repair the office car, or once, for eight days, to pay his salary. He rarely complained, but at times I knew I had

let him down. Where was the legendary American efficiency, go get'em, chop-chop? Lying flat on a pine
bench next to a pot full of fragrant mint tea, cooling
off with a thin cotton sheet thrown over my waist . . .

I riffled through the telexes: "Need full details hi-
jacking soonest." That went straight to the wastebasket.
Additional details were not on the Soviet menu. Next:
"Unable to reach you three days fonely. Need promised contribution ASAP." Signed by some poor devil
who had been begging the overseas operators to put
through a call to Moscow.

Phone links to the United States had ceased to function about three months previously, "in connection
with improvement of the service," according to our Soviet hosts. Foreigners went apoplectic, quoting con-
ventions and charters to the indifferent Soviets until
blue in the face. I felt fine. Our literal-minded copy
editors had recently discovered the joys of transconti-
nental fact-niggling, harassing me with phone queries
in the middle of the night. ("Uh, Mr. Perkins, our
maps don't *show* a 'New Jersey, USSR.'") The phone
cutoff deepened my sense of being away. I liked being
away.

One last cable.

"Nick, onworking your forward assignment. Western
Europe possible as discussed. Please schedule July
leave for consultations. You're doing great. Hold on
for just three months—freedom beckons. Jonas."

Susan had been acting strangely. Ever since she had
learned of her Paris assignment, scheduled to begin in
July, she plunged herself into things Russian. Our
after-lunch constitutionals were no longer limited to
brief strolls around the compound. At Susan's insis-
tence, our walks became scouting patrols, infiltration
missions into the surrounding neighborhood. Who

would have thought it? We lived in an interesting part of town.

Hidden behind the hulking granite mass of the Ukraine Hotel, for instance, we found Beer Factory Number Four, one of the city's oldest breweries. Their flagship product was a delicious, malty beer called Golden Hops, which Susan and I began drinking during lunchtime, by way of supporting our local merchants.

Within walking distance, we discovered other marvels. Just behind the Siberia *pyelmeny* bar, we stumbled upon a farmers' market, where Susan learned to negotiate 300 percent price reductions from the peasant flower sellers. On another outing, we slipped into a tenants' meeting inside the *agitpunkt,* or "agitational point," of a neighboring apartment building. Like banners in a medieval banquet hall, ten-foot-high portraits of Lenin hung from the rafters. Lined up along the gray green walls were civil defense exhibits, illustrated with artists' drawings that showed the citizenry how to form a line in front of the subway entrance, in case of a nuclear attack.

Tenants must be the same everywhere. Here on Kutuzov Prospect, a restless band of about 100 renters, mostly women, was firing a barrage of complaints at a trio of dumpy housing bureaucrats cowering behind a card table set up at the front of the room. Naturally, much of the griping concerned the heating, the garbage collection, the plumbing, and the spasmodic elevator service. After each charge of malfeasance, an official nodded his head vigorously, scribbled down some notes, and solemnly promised that "appropriate measures will be taken."

After a quarter of an hour, I realized that the bureaucrats, who jiggled their knees nervously under the card table, and pulled at their sweat-stained collars, were far from inept. Quite the opposite, this was their job—to sit before a gathering of irate tenants, act contrite, promise help, and then disappear. These were the Soviet flak-catchers. They probably performed every day, to appreciative audiences around the city.

During that meeting we learned that the local women viewed the brewery—which employed most of their husbands—as a mixed blessing, at best. Many of the laborers brought their work home with them, and binged through the night. The brewery also spawned "hooliganism," a clunky circumlocution for street crime, in the surrounding courtyards. Young men were said to scale the barbed wire on the brewery walls, raid the plant's warehouses, and then practice "antisocial behavior" on passers by in the neighborhood. Hunkering down in the back of the room, we heard lurid tales of purse-snatchings, muggings, and even gang wars with stabbing deaths.

As I translated, Susan huddled closer to me, hugging my arm. "Cor! You'd think we were in New York." I noticed a pair of elderly matrons staring at our foreign clothes, paying special attention to Susan's spangled stockings. Lest we be denounced as imperialist spies on the trail of Soviet housing secrets, I ushered us out the door.

Just a few days later, Susan proposed our most ambitious outing to date: She wanted to visit New Jerusalem.

"What the hell is that?"

"Oh, Nick, it's marvelous! I've been reading all about it. . . ."

Susan had been burrowing deeply into the library of Russian novels and history books that she had brought from England, to experience as a surrogate for Russia itself. New Jerusalem, she explained, was a grandiose monastery complex erected by the patriarch Nikon, who really believed that his nondescript estate on the banks of the Istra River, northwest of Moscow, would one day be recognized as the "new" Jerusalem. To load the dice, he built a Church of the Holy Sepulchre—just like in Jerusalem—and changed the name of the hill overlooking the river to Golgotha. For good measure, he renamed the river, too. The section of the Istra flowing underneath the monastery walls was to be called the Jordan. Just like in Jerusalem.

"Susan, since when are you such a Russian buff? A month ago you wouldn't walk across the street, now we're off on the Cook's tour of religious quackery!"

Susan pouted. "Some things become more attractive when you know you can't have them again." She gave me a big stage wink, to help me understand: Yes, that remark was directed at you.

As we climbed into my car on Saturday morning, Susan casually mentioned that the monastery lay at the very edge of the forty-kilometer radius open to foreigners. "It's rather near a closed area, so do stick to the road, will you?"

"Not mixing business with pleasure, I hope?"

"We don't farm out business to amateurs," was her prim reply.

Her warning about the travel limit was reinforced by a gray-suited policeman who flagged us down at the traffic control point located next to the forty-kilometer marker. When we explained the purpose of our trip as "educational tourism," he grinned faintly, and repeated the directions to the monastery three times. He urged us not to deviate from his instructions, and, as surety, he dispatched a yellow and blue patrol car to follow us to the monastery gates.

Once inside, we fell prey to the clucking, brown-suited *ekskursavody*, or tour guides, who herded small troops of visitors briskly through the grounds. We were attached to a clump of swarthy Georgian tourists, visibly dulled by the lengthy speechifying on the part of our bull-dykeish, know-it-all tour guide. For twenty full minutes, she stood us in a patch of mud facing the main cathedral, while she recited every known fact in the 450-year history of the site. Several of the Georgians tried to slip away to their bus, in vain. Like a schoolmistress with eyes in the back of her head, our leader inevitably spotted them sneaking off, and tried to shame them in front of their indifferent comrades.

While the Georgians pecked at newspaper cones filled with sunflower seeds and grumbled incomprehensibly among themselves, Susan stood enraptured through the entire lecture, hanging on every word of my increasingly schematic translation. At each new factoid, she nodded her head vigorously, murmuring, "Da, da. . . ." The tour guide quickly found Susan on her radar, and smiled reassuringly at her prize pupil. I understood how Susan must have succeeded in school.

The outdoor lecture was followed by a forced march around the monastery grounds, with a minimum of time allotted for appreciation, wandering, or daydreaming. As might have been expected, Soviet power had drastically altered Nikon's grandiose vision. The monks' cemetery had long since been plowed under, to make room for an experimental potato field belonging to a nearby agricultural college. The dormitory and refectory had also been given over to the school's boarding students. The main cathedral had been converted into an "architectural museum" of questionable purpose. The remodelers had slung a false ceiling under the church's most astounding structural feature, its huge vaulted dome, which was now hidden from view. The museum—which was little more than a gallery of photographs of the cathedral's original interior—had been stripped of its altars and icons, crucifixes and prayer rails.

The gelding of the cathedral distrubed Susan. "It's not at all like in the book," she whispered, squeezing my hand. "It's incredible what they've done." Soviet Russia had eviscerated her imagination of this wondrous place, and she felt personally slighted.

"What's that?"

Back outside, Susan pointed behind the church, to a narrow tarpaper shed. Every minute or two, a woman pushed aside the smoky piece of canvas hanging across the doorway, and emerged into the daylight, clutching a small object to her breast. Occasionally, women scurried into the shed, furtively pulling scarves in front of their faces.

"It must be some kind of store."

Susan drifted over to the ramshackle shed just as the stiff-faced tour guide shooed us into a small chapel that now housed an exhibition called "New Jerusalem and the Great Patriotic War." She saw Susan walk off, and frowned harshly.

After ten minutes of wartime horror stories, none of which had any relevance to the monastery, the guide thanked us for our attention and hurried away to her next assignment. Free at last, the Georgians broke into smiles, and stampeded towards their tour bus. A few moments later, Susan came walking across the courtyard, with her head bowed, and her shoulders trembling.

Like everyone who emerged from the shed, she too was cradling something against her chest. We walked in step toward the car, where she unfurled her fingers, one at a time, to reveal a tiny gold crucifix.

She stared at the cross, and wept softly.

"There's a little altar in there, with a priest. He's

blessing bottles of holy water. That's what the women are carrying."

I laid a finger on the crucifix. It appeared to be solid gold, with a tiny inscription etched in Cyrillic on the back. The engraving said the cross had been presented at a baptism, in the nineteenth century. "Where'd you get this?"

Susan touched the edges of the cross delicately, as if it might break. "A woman came up to me, made the sign of the cross over my forehead, and asked me—in English—if I was a believer. I said yes, and she took this off her neck and—" Susan burst out crying.

She wiped her face with a handkerchief. "The woman said I should take this as a present from the Russian believers, and then she disappeared. I tried to find her, to give it back, but the little crowd had swallowed her up, and wouldn't let me move. When I looked around, it seemed that everyone was half smiling, out of the corners of their mouths . . . it was most extraordinary."

I squeezed Susan's shoulder, and escorted her to the car.

During the ride back to Moscow, she fell asleep, with her head resting against my shoulder. Halfway into town, a sudden twist in the road jerked her into wakefulness. Her eyes flicked open, then closed again. "Most extraordinary . . ."

Susan touched her lips on my neck, and fell back to sleep.

Our third Thursday at the baths was a slow time of the month for everyone. Payday was still ten days away, the monthly plan was still two weeks off, and I was four days away from deadline. Lyonya had been chasing all over Moscow gathering medical certificates for his cataract operation. Now the doctor had fled on a month's vacation, without telling his patients, and the forms would have to be filled out all over again. Borya, our physicist, had been luckier. He had finally found the three-person Czech kayak he had been searching for, in a hardware store.

"It was folded up and labled 'lawn chair,' so no one in the store knew what it was," he explained, dripping sweat onto the sauna floorboards. "They were a bit surprised no one had bought the thing, and they were more surprised when I took it off their hands."

The *pukh* was disappearing; that was news. To make conversation during the first sauna shift, Valera mentioned he had read in *Pravda* that 94 percent of Americans pay their income tax voluntarily.

"Yeah, that sounds about right."

Borya sputtered through thick trails of perspiration coursing down his lips. "*Voluntarily?* Whatever for?"

"Well, there's a government agency that enforces the tax laws . . ."

"Ahhh!" Something they could understand: the organs.

"But they only chase after two or three percent of the taxpayers."

"Oohhh." Valera spoke for the majority. "What an exotic country!"

Natalya Andreyevna brought in a second kettle of hot water, and reminded us to seek out Victor Sergeyich next Thursday at the latest if we wanted to renew our subscriptions. "He's a nice man, very modest," she said. "But be sure he understands that you respect him."

18 / Wings of the Soviets

Everyone has a way he wants to be seen, even countries. From my childhood, I remember the display America: boxy Colonial homes rising from green veloured lawns where the Beaver and his friends scrimmaged and scrummed. Ample space for all, and continuity. Donna Reed's voice playing across the one-acre zoning, clear and constant to her family, her way. For themselves, the Russians call it Soviet Reality. Idealized examples are the sprawling, well-appointed apartments of the movie *Moscow Does Not Believe in Tears,* with *lebensraum* for six generations of New Soviet men, women, and children. The leather-jacketed guy would have proposed to the heroine for the real estate alone; maybe he did.

But the reality with a little r would be Valera's apartment, tucked away on the sixth floor of a ten-story apartment house near the Dinamo stadium. The exterior is *tuf,* a pink sandstone imported from Armenia to catch sunsets long since stolen away by taller projects nearby. The archway of the main entrance is supported by life-size, heroic discus throwers, cast in plaster, and flecked with decaying paint. A complementary line of sports figures runs along the top of the arch, now partially obscured in a fluffy blanket of *pukh.* But a pedestrain in the winter would see that each statue is a tiny athlete, running, launching a javelin, throwing a ball.

The ceilings were high, but the flat was small, and foreshortened by the bulky square furniture shoved against the walls. A *shkaf,* a seven-foot-tall wooden cupboard top-heavy with the aggregata of five lifetimes, dominated Valera's apartment, slouching toward the center of the room like the tired old giant himself.

Valera waited until I crossed the threshold to shake hands. "Bad luck," he mumbled, ushering me toward a bulging green velveteen sofa, and a low-slung table where he had laid out a tea service. He paused in front of a glass-faced display cabinet filled with trophies and medals.

"Here's Stalin." Valera pulled a yellowing photograph from behind a trophy. The mustached dictator was smiling broadly, surrounded by eight young men, each one standing behind a long oar. In another photo, I saw Stalin clasping the hand of a much younger Valera, smiling just faintly, or was the picture obscure? There was a dock decked out with racing pennants, and a huge Soviet flag, hanging next to a portrait of Stalin, in the background.

"The cult of personality," Valera mused, holding out the leader's face embossed on a Stalin Prize medal, 100 grams of pure gold, dated 1937.

"We were young. He was everything." Valera turned a tarnished brass cup engraved with Stalin's picture over in his huge hand. "We raced just like those poor soldiers fought—with his name on our lips. That was how we won this race—" he fumbled under another trophy and pulled out a cutting from an English paper: "Red Eight Wins Challenge Cup." "And against the best rowers in England. Here's Shanley, the great stroke for two British Olympic teams." He passed his fingers over the misty picture of Shanley's face, like a memory and a blessing, then lay the clip back on the shelf. "We beat him.

"Please, I am a bad host. Have some tea." He waved vaguely toward the teacups.

The coincidence seemed incredible. Valera must have rowed on the same team as Pavlovich's brother.

"England." He spoke slowly, clearing his throat. "In those days, of course, you didn't fly. We took the train, five days of it, including the Channel crossing. We were confined to our carriage for most of the trip. Borzov, the trainer, had us doing calisthenics during daylight hours, so we couldn't look out the windows, I suppose. When we left the Russian frontier, he posted security men at each end of the wagon, to make sure we didn't converse with anyone walking through." He lowered himself onto the sofa, and poured tea into the cups. "And there was no pocketful of currency for the tax-free shops, believe me."

His wife Vera, small, birdlike, and gray, jangled inside the front door. Peering into the living room, she could see Valera settling comfortably in his memories. She tiptoed toward us, introduced herself, and sat down next to her husband on the sofa. Valera told her I was from America.

"Oh, yes, America." Vera frowned. She was well over sixty, and remembered the years when entertaining foreigners meant a jail sentence, or worse.

"I am telling him about the rowing."

"Ah yes, the rowing." She frowned, again, more disapprovingly. "The rowing."

"It was after one of the Oxford heats," he recalled. "I felt a pain in my chest, and fainted stepping out of the boat. They laid me down in the sunshine, on a grassy bank next to the river . . . I remember the bright green, the blue of the sky, this English Arcadia, bleeding color in front of my eyes. I thought I was falling asleep . . ." Valera blinked away tears.

He woke up, healthy, in the university hospital. A young English doctor, through a student interpreter, explained he had suffered a heart fibrillation, a spasm. It could happen again, as a coronary. He must stop rowing.

"I told that to Borzov. He laughed. 'The English want us to give you up,' was his response. He told me to keep rowing, until I saw one of 'our' doctors in Moscow . . ."

Valera rose off the sofa like a crane, and swung slowly back to the trophy cabinet.

"They made him keep rowing in England, and like a fool, he did it," Vera scolded.

"In those days, one did what one was told," Valera said, carrying a letter over to my chair.

In the letter, dated 1935, the sports committee medical board decreed him to be in perfect health, and condemned the British "wreckers" for trying to sabotage the health of a loyal Socialist athlete.

Valera leaned back on the sofa, crossing his legs. "Then came the Olympics." He laughed, jerking his thumb out the window. "If you think *this* crowd takes the Olympics seriously, imagine what Stalin wanted for Berlin, in 1936!" His heavy laugh degenerated into a fit of coughing.

The doorbell rang. Vera excused herself, and fell into a whispered conversation on the landing. Valera listened for a moment, then continued to talk. "It's just as well . . . she doesn't enjoy hearing this any more. 1936! Stalin told the sports committee he wanted sixty gold medals, in half the events, twice as many as the Americans! That was the word. . . .

"We trained as we never had before. I had just married, but I didn't see Vera for six months after the wedding. We needed warm weather, so they built us a special rowing pool down in Georgia, draining one of the rivers. Labor was plentiful in those days, as you may know. . . ."

Vera scurried back into the room, picking up the conversation. "He wrote me letters, but they were full of lies." Valera grimaced. "Yes! You wrote that your health was good, the heart problems had disappeared . . ."

"Maybe you've forgotten what it was like, to write letters, then?"

"I haven't forgotten anything!" She turned to me, pleading. "But in fact, he collapsed three times during the spring, after practice. They wouldn't let him leave, because he was the strongest, the . . . what is it?"

"The stroke."

"Yes, so—"

Valera was tiring, and cut her off. "Well, Stalin really was God back then. You lived with him, and you died with him. He decided to let me live. At the last minute, he ordered us not to go to Berlin. The sports committee had told him we might not win." Valera shrugged his shoulders.

Vera leaned forward to talk, but Valera went on. "Yes, Vera is going to add," he rested his hand on her knee affectionately, "that it came too late for me, and she's right. They finally dropped me from the team. They left me for dead." He rested his back on the sofa, panting lightly.

The afterword, told by Vera, was more pathetic. Stalin issued gold prize medals, and ordered up this brand new apartment building for the entire team. "After the war, he even gave them each cars, those tiny Zaporozhets they were handing out to the cripples. He can't fit into it, but I use it now and then."

The tea had chilled. They hadn't invited me to stay.

Vera fidgeted while Valera described his two heart operations, the second more debilitating than the first. I could see he wasn't going to stand up from the sofa. Vera rose, and escorted me to the door, while he raised a hand, waving a feeble farewell. "To next Thursday."

"Now we've tired him," Vera fretted on the landing. "I'm not sure that sauna of yours is doing him any good—" She slammed the door in midsentence.

I trembled down six flights in the cramped, vibrating elevator, and loitered in front of the apartment building to take a second look at the sports statues. I spotted an oarsman, gritting his teeth, and pulling against the tide.

Good God! Valera was the car owner who drank with Pavlovich, and was rewarded with free auto parts in memory of the lost brother.

What had gone going through the brother's mind, when he saw the nineteen-year-old Valera collapsed on the Oxford greensward, wrapping his arms around his wounded heart? "He'll be dead before I will"? He would have been wrong.

When I rang his doorbell two evenings later, Andrei was still outside, under the car, mounting the new brake shoes. "It's his favorite place," Lilya said. "Go out and bring him in for supper."

While he bent over the kitchen sink, scraping chassis grease from his hands, I mentioned my visit to Valera. "Stalin," he grunted, scrubbing the backs of his hands with a floor brush. "We love Stalin."

Lilya, who had been sitting on the refrigerator reading, let her book crash to the floor.

"Not *all* of us love Stalin," Andrei resumed while drying his hands. "Well, starting again, no, no one with either a brain or a memory loves Stalin, but neither one is such a useful commodity in this country."

The jury seemed out on Stalin. Ekaterina Sergeyevna worshiped the old fellow, and claimed several times that she had seen him at the battle of Stalingrad, rallying the soldiers at the front. When I reminded her that Stalin had never left Moscow during the entire war, excluding the first two days after the German invasion, when he tried to escape to Kuybyshev, she flew into a rage.

"You're telling *me*, who was there, who remembers how he pulled his cavalry coat up around his mustache and read the order of the day from the balcony of the Tsentralny Hotel . . ." She sucked in an enormous lungful of air, like a frog blowing up its gullet. "Me, hearing this from *you*, who wasn't even born, whose parents were brewing champagne in bathtubs on Wall Street, while we boiled straw for soup!"

There is an old Russian saying: He lies like an eyewitness.

One day, out of doors, Boris the translator hinted darkly that "the whole Stalin story hasn't been told." Some questioning pried loose a second statement: "He was a greater man than we are allowed to know."

And Valera? Stalin's surgeons tore his heart out, twice. But didn't he cherish his prizes, and the yellowing memento of his handshake with the supreme leader?

Andrei had lost his father to the purges, but he was no Stalin hater. "I'm forty-five years old," he said, rubbing his balding head for emphasis. "It's like weather to me, Stalin, the thaw, this latest idiocy. Sometimes the air is cold, sometimes it's warm. But you breathe it all the same. You have to."

Lilya slipped off the refrigerator. "Russians are funny—I'm speaking as a Georgian now, though heaven knows we're not so different. Our parents used to warn us, 'Don't complain, things could always get worse.' And for a long time, they did."

"Eternal optimists," Andrei chuckled. "There was a slogan that sprang up in the camps, after Khrushchev began the mass rehabilitations. When the news about the general amnesty started to circulate among the prisoners, the guards lined them up for a special announcement. 'Things are going to get better,' they said, taunting the bedraggled men and women. 'But not immediately. And not for everyone.'" Andrei grabbed a handful of silverware and began setting the table. "They were right."

Lilya returned from the living room with two envelopes from Aron. "It dies hard, this Russianness. Listen to this."

In July, Pasha and Rima traveled from Pittsburgh to visit us in our new house. For three long evenings we painted the walls of our suburban subdivide Moscow red. It's hard to believe that he and I studied together in sixth grade, at the special physics school next to the Puppet Theater. (Rima insists there is a *new* Puppet Theater. Is this true?) We were happy little scientists, with minds full of sputniks and the "scientific technical revolution" that was upon us, or always almost upon us. Khrushchev had promised to "overtake the United States by 1980"! Anything seemed possible.

Back then, Rima was the political lecturer of our Young Communist group. Now she throws down her napkin at dinner to switch on the latest American television programs. Is their magic stronger than ours? We drank to you, and to Moscow. In the course of the evening, we drank to everything, to mothers, to camel jokes, even to the Carry-All Mall, which sells Zhivago vodka for five dollars a bottle, open all night. The last toast was for our lives together again.

Pasha had his guitar, and we sang every song we knew. Galich, Vysotsky, Okudjhava, the singers of our serene 1960s, not the cartoon of violence that the Americans cherish as their favorite decade. Pasha's voice has hardened from age and smoking, and suddenly his hair is gray, but he can still purr

> Arbat, Arbat, you're my religion
> My faith, my happiness, my anguish . . .

A song about a street that brings tears to our eyes? Everyone here wants things, but we have only these songs. Perhaps they are enough?

Lilya's eyes had watered, and she dabbed a sleeve against her cheek. "He writes very well, doesn't he?" I nodded assent. She skipped forward a page or two.

Rima brought some children's books of the early 1950s, which she was using to teach her two boys Russian. We laughed hysterically at poem after poem to "the great genius Stalin," "our real father Stalin," or "the good father of the White Kremlin." In one poem, the son of a Chuvash fisherman from the Kamchatka blessed Stalin for "sending the fish jumping into our nets." The book included a woodcut of the small almond-eyed boy bent over his tiny desk in an igloo addressing his verses to "Moscow—The Kremlin."

But our children have no interest in such books, and less in the language. For those three days they huddled in front of the television, showing off their English by acting out scenes from commercial messages. Grisha plays a worried housewife, and little Zaychik is the Man from Glad. Don't worry if you can't understand. It would take too long to explain.

Rima remembered that at their age we wore red scarves, listened to Radio Moscow each morning, and lined up outside our classrooms, facing the papier mâché bust of Lenin to chant:

We're not just Young Octobrists
We're faithful students of Ilyich

All that sewage has drained from our minds, thank the
Lord. But were we so wrong to believe in something?

19 / *Respect*

Spring thunderstorms had long since rinsed the air of poplar spores. We no longer needed the baths, we *wanted* them. Huddled in "heaven," flush under the roof, we discussed strategy, and respect.

As a "contribution" for the new director, Lyonya had brought a jar of cloudberry preserves, made by his wife. "It's just the right touch for an ex-schoolteacher," he insisted, hyperventilating in the 140-degree heat. "Not money, not alcohol, but a real gift, something . . . humane."

Andrei whipped a thick trail of sweat down his chest, flicking a few drops toward the hot coals. He had brought a flask of his home-brewed *spirt,* an offering he viewed as more respectful: "This guy's no schoolteacher any more."

I volunteered a small atomizer of French perfume, quickly rejected as a gift idea. "Too foreign. He'll get spoiled. If we can get him French perfume, why not a Betamax and a home computer?"

Valera had brought the first three volumes of a new edition of Dumas père, a coveted Moscow best-seller. The printing had long ago sold out, but Valera subscribed by agreeing to purchase several tomes of Leonid Brezhnev's memoirs as a tie-in. "Dumas is just the thing!" our linguist piped up. "Intellectual, of course, but with . . . market value." He suggested we pay out the edition, one volume at a time, as we renewed our monthly ticket. The collective approved the measure, slapping wet feet on the hot floorboards.

Just in case, we had plenty of cash.

We ascended single file up a small unlit staircase to the director's enclave. In front of us loomed a padded leather door adorned with a brass nameplate: Director. Between us and the door sat a modishly dressed secretary with a magazine crossword unfolded on her desk. At her left, a battery of phones was ringing, unattended.

She kept her face buried in the crossword, scrubbing out an error with a wet fingertip. "Do you have an appointment?"

"Natalya Andreyevna suggested we come—"

"Who?"

"The woman who looks after the first floor sauna, you know, the—"

"Never heard of her," the secretary drawled, picking at a blemish on her cheek with the tip of her pen. Andrei nudged me, indicating the time had come to show some respect. Edging forward, with the delicacy befitting a grand perfume, I laid the small bottle of Chanel on the corner of her desk, just within range of her crossword vision. She never blinked.

Suddenly, the door flew open, and a boisterous dance began. Shouting gaily, slapping the director on the back, Misha, briefcaseless, bounded out of the inner office, bowling aside our delegation like tenpins. Victor Sergeyich frowned. "Nina, who's this lot? Not the subway people?"

She began to speak, but Misha cut her off. "Victor Sergeyich! These are grand fellows!" He strode over and clapped me on the back. His breath smelled of liquor.

"These boys keep the beer cooler—ha, ha!—I mean the plunge, so cold that—" he glanced at the secretary and hesitated. I noticed the perfume had vanished from her desk. "Well, you know what! Ha ha!" He hopped off down the stairs, whistling the "Internationale."

Victor Sergeyich stared at us. He was still young, with a full head of sandy hair, and eager blue eyes. But he had come a long way from the classroom. A gold-plated Cross pen nudged against reflector sunglasses at the throat of his lime green polo shirt. His designer jeans sported an Italian label. On his feet he wore Moscow's latest status symbol, Puma track shoes, the acme of administrative fashion.

"Friends of Misha's? Come in, please."

We filed sheepishly into his enormous office, bare except for a large desk and a life-size poster of Vladimir Lenin tacked on the wall behind the director's easy chair. He kept no chairs for visitors. Sergeyich mumbled an apology for the office, emphasizing that "it reflects the tastes of my not long departed predecessor." Seeing me eye the Lenin poster, he added coyly: "Naturally I refer to the immodest size of the office, not its furnishings."

Now followed the familiar quadrille, which he had quickly assimilated. We would like to renew? Yes, let's look at next month's schedule. Oh, a minor problem . . . some very old clients need to switch from working hours into the 8:00 A.M. slot. Things are a little hot for them with the New Discipline, you know. . . .

We nodded gravely, paying homage to the New Discipline. The New Discipline was going to cost us some respect.

Andrei stepped forward quietly, and eased the first

Dumas volume onto the director's desk. "We were grateful to you for accommodating us during this first month; we thought. . . ." His trailing voice emphasized the unspoken statement. Sergeyich reached for the book, and ran a finger along the spine approvingly.

"Volume one," he murmured.

"The first of a series," Borya said.

"I will certainly read it. I used to teach literature, as you may know." He carefully laid the book to one side. "It's possible that my friends from the ministry could be persuaded to come on Wednesday. . . ." He shuffled through his subscription papers, clucking his tongue, occasionally flashing his gold pen to make notes. He grabbed a pile of admission tickets and filled them in.

"No problem for friends of Misha's—here you go. Thursday next month, eight A.M. Steam in peace!" He handed over our papers, and herded us towards the door. Leaning against the inside handle, he asked Valera if *The Count of Monte Cristo* was included in volume two.

"I think that's in volume three."

Sergeyich laughed. "So we will be seeing each other again!" He slapped some more backs, and pushed us past the somnolent Nina to the stairs. We felt our way down, one step at a time, and gathered, blinking, in a patch of late spring sunlight on the sidewalk in front of the baths. The air was clear of *pukh*, the morning was a success. We stood a jar of preserves, a bottle of *spirt*, and two volumes of Dumas to the good.

"He's a very impressive young man," Andrei concluded. "Certainly worthy of respect."

There are words in Russian that don't exist in English, and vice versa. Any student of the language can tell you that Russian has no word for "privacy;" draw your own conclusions. As far as I could remember,

Russian also lacked a word for "favor," that word that shows up so often on the lips of New Yorkers: "Hey buddy—do me a favor and drop dead, willya?"

Inside the phone booth, I was racking my brains. My car had expired just down the street, and I was calling Andrei for help. The line buzzed, then connected.

"Andrei, what's the word for 'favor'?"

Andrei remembered some English from the university. "As in 'make me a favor'?"

"Yeah, like that."

"I guess we don't have one. What do you need?"

"A favor."

"Oh. I'll come right away."

When he emerged from the subway, I was still groping for words of thanks. Had I disturbed him? He wiggled the distributor, swabbed some spark plugs, and tickled the engine back to life. What did it matter?

"Friends come first."

Today Andrei needed me to "make him a favor." Zazie was out of order. Could I drive him to Aeroflot's main ticket office, tomorrow at 6:00 A.M.?

"That's some favor."

"We don't use that word, remember?" I felt a nip of shame. "It's important, I want to beat the spring vacation rush."

"Where's the airline ticket office?"

"Inside the Riga train station." Naturally.

We pulled up outside the station just after six. But the rush had beaten us. A line about 100 persons long had already formed outside the padlocked double glass doors, which were to open at nine.

Andrei's reaction: "Oh, good. I'll be one of the first."

He focused his attention on the handwritten list of available tickets hanging in the office window, while I watched the line swell behind us. The morning was dark and cold. The Russians hugged the side of the building like gray sacks of flour stood end to end outside a warehouse. I had forgotten to dress down. In my Adirondack Guide hunting jacket, I stood out like a rosebush in a parking lot.

"How about Kherson?" Andrei asked. "How are the beaches in Kherson?"

"I thought you were going to Estonia this year."

"Too many intellectuals going there. I'm off to the Black Sea to get back in with the proletariat." A genuine-looking labor heroine slouched under a dirty yellow synthetic coat shot him an evil glance from a few paces up the line. Andrei smiled faintly, and eliminated Kherson. "They're building that damned aircraft carrier there, they probably wouldn't let us near the water."

"Maybe Sukhumi?" I had always liked the name.

"Vacation with the fiercely proud Abkhazian minority?" Andrei glanced nervously up and down the line for Abkhazian faces. "If they found out Lilya was a Gerogian, they'd cut our throats. Or else force us to listen to their squeaky folk music. Plus they have those damned cancerous monkeys there, I don't think Lilya could take it." The Academy of Sciences operates a famous oncological center in Sukhumi, using a local macaque species for tests.

"Maybe further up the coast? Pitsunda?" He pointed to a glossy travel poster of six twenty-story resort hotels towering over a seaside pine forest.

"Forget it, chum," a voice croaked from the line behind us. "That's just for foreigners now." I hunched my head deeper into my shoulders, and crossed my arms to damp the éclat of my tartan hunting jacket.

Andrei reflected. "Hmmm, foreigners are everywhere . . . Yalta!" His gaze had reached the end of the list. "Yalta! That's it! We've never been there before.

Lilya can go to the museums, while Anya and I can bronze on the beach."

"Suppose Brezhnev's there?"

"His place is up the coast a little. He won't bother us." This time Andrei lowered his indiscretion to a whisper. "He'll be dead by then anyway."

"Maybe there'll be someone else."

The worker woman in the synthetic coat glared back at us. "They're out of Yalta, my sister was here yesterday. There's a summer bobsledding tournament there in June." She squared back into line, without explanation.

Andrei and I stared at each other, perplexed. "Let's get out of here," he said at last. "We'll skip spring vacation and spend the summer at the dacha."

20 / Kapitsa's Dacha

The illusion that Susan and I could make love to each other and wake up together each morning, living inside a parenthesis separated from our "real lives," was fast eroding. The price of remaining outside the current of each other's lives was meaninglessness. With our parting now just six weeks away, we had to face the questions: What will become of us? What do we mean to each other?

We were more deeply entwined than we might have admitted, even to each other. Ever since she returned from England, without Sam as an emotional fallback position, Susan could fall only forward, toward me. She—we both, really—felt a bit embarrassed by enjoying each other's company more and more, cutting corners off our office hours to linger over coffee, or desserts, or skipping a cocktail party to sip Cognac in my apartment, or make love. We fancied ourselves such tough cookies, and here we were, going soft. It seemed so banal; we were falling in love.

Was this really happening to me? Yes, I was teetering in Susan's direction, without being pushed. Ever since our first chance meeting—or had she been waiting for me to bump her at the embassy cocktail party, so she could woo me with her contrarian charm?—we had been more married than single. We had never dated, nor particularly courted. With our out-of-synch work schedules, our main preoccupations were housekeeping, scribbling phone messages for the absent party, and sex.

But Susan and I were both aware that I had another loyalty, fast becoming a love: Andrei, his friends, and Russia itself. For many months I justified my long sojourns at Kolomenskoye to Susan by explaining that I would probably never see Andrei again. Russia was a fleeting pleasure, I argued to myself. Susan would always be there.

For her part, Susan had taken some steps in my direction. She was trying to enjoy Russia, even if only from the outside, and I appreciated that. But at the same time, she had been reminding me that she *wouldn't* always be here for my convenience, as it were. Michelin guides to Paris materialized on the bedside table. Several times a week she brought *Le Monde* home from the office, and stammered through the headlines in her beginner's French. She even played language tapes on the stereo, and recited inane French phrases during lunch or breakfast.

I didn't need a translator to decipher the message: I am leaving, Nick. I am going to Paris. Are you coming with me, or not?

"Passez-moi la selle, s'il vous plaît."

In this morning's dialogue, we were *dans un restaurant.* Susan had even cooked an omelet aux fines herbes, which she was gobbling across the table from me, her yellow terrycloth bathrobe open to her waist.

"That means 'pass me the saddle,' and there's no saddle here, honey."

"You know damn well what I mean. Pass me the bloody salt."

I decided to stop showing off my French. Bludgeoning her omelet with a fork, her full, pink, breasts trembling inside her robe, Susan looked erotic, beautiful, and upset.

"What are you thinking about?"

"What do you think I'm thinking about?" She threw her fork onto her plate with a crashing, metallic clang.

"About our future."

"That's right."

"Susan, everything's going to be fine. If I don't get Paris, I'll get London, or Bonn, and we'll commute like all the modern couples. There's a future out there. Relax."

Her eyes were glossing with tears. "It won't be like this again. We won't be this close."

"You mean living across the hall? No."

"You know what I mean."

"Susan, just wait until I get to New York. The logistics will fall into place. Let's change the subject."

"Fine." She rubbed the bathrobe sleeve across her eyes. "What shall we do this weekend, Nick?"

"I thought you were working tonight."

"I'm off. Someone's taken my duty."

"Oh. I was planning to go see my friends." I waved my arm, to indicate in the country. "Why don't you join us?"

"Nick, you know why." She pulled a silent zipper across her mouth. "I can't talk to anyone."

"What's to lose? You've got your next job."

Susan grimaced, as though that was just the kind of comment she expected to hear from me. "I can't. Can't you change your plans?"

"No. We're taking my car." I reached across the table, and stroked her arm underneath the bathrobe. "Come with us. You'll have fun."

Susan jerked back her hand. "Damn it, *I* want you

some of the time!" She leapt up from her chair and ran across the hall, banging the door behind her.

I sat alone at the table for a few minutes, waiting for Susan to return. She didn't. Tearful scenes and door slamming; we might as well be married.

Ever the dutiful husband, I carried the dishes into the kitchen, and began to wash them off. Glancing over my shoulder, I noticed something unusual on the wall calendar. Someone had circled today's date in bright red Magic Marker, and drawn a shower of tiny stars leading to a handwritten message at the bottom: "Susan's birthday!!!"

I had written the words myself, several weeks ago, before I started eating most of my dinners with Andrei and Lilya at their dacha. I had never seen the reminder again. I had completely forgotten about Susan's birthday.

A Russian once described heaven as a "small room with the right people," and Andrei's dacha fit the description. The sky blue, one-story walls enclosed one large room for sleeping, eating, and drinking—which usually took place outside—and in one corner, a sink, a range, and a toilet stall. Andrei's crib had stood on a raised platform next to the garden window for the first year and a half of the war.

"Apparently, I used to stand up and talk to the plants, especially the taller tomatoes, during the growing season," Andrei said, rubbing his ankle against the foot-high dais. "I have no recollection of this."

Most of the activities happened outside, at an unsteady wooden table surrounded by two low benches and a jumble of wicker chairs stolen from indoors. Lilya's pride was the twenty-foot-square vegetable garden, which had fed the family for almost five decades.

Each evening before dinner, Lilya would ask Andrei to unearth several ingredients for the pot. Resolute, he and I stalked out to the garden, and quickly lost ourselves in the clutter of leaves, stems, and ankle-high bushes vying for space in the tiny plot. Inevitably we returned to the kitchen empty-handed.

"The rabbits must have eaten them."

"Or else the Colorado beetles."

Sighing, drying her hands, Lilya walked outside to the correct spot in the middle of the garden, plunged her hand above the wrist into the dry earth, and delivered the needed carrot or onion on cue.

While we scrubbed the vegetables clean in the sink, Lilya would press fresh scallions and cucumber and tomato slices into my mouth. "Won't find these in your New York!"

I munched. "We leave farming to the farmers."

Lilya wagged her finger. "Big mistake."

Nibbling at my second handful of baby carrots, I secretly agreed.

These were my sinfully pleasurable weekends, seasoned ever so lightly with guilty thoughts about Susan, and how the time being stolen from her account might never be reimbursed. Aron had written that we Americans are "too purposeful," but I fell into the pace of dacha living as if I were born for it. Even though we slept out of doors on the veranda, we rose late. Each morning, Andrei and I swam in the river before breakfast, then read, played tennis, or visited neighbors, a simple matter of walking a few dozen paces and lifting one's knee across a midget fence, until lunch. The afternoons were "free" time. We reassembled for the vegetable hunt, and dinner, around sunset.

The nights? I was tired by night, and dozed over tea on the porch if Andrei tried to read me Esenin's nature poetry, or initiate a talk about life. Half-asleep,

I stared out into the perfect darkness of the forest, dreaming and content.

One evening, I dreamed that all the protagonists in my still short life had gathered around the dacha's trestle table for dinner. My mother, my brother, some childhood friends, Sharon, of course her mother, Andrei, Lilya, Susan, and all my Russian acquaintances were sitting together sipping vodka, reaching across each other for a taste of pickled garlic or eggplant caviar.

Suddenly, everyone stopped eating. We heard a rustling in the forest, then measured footsteps, crackling branches underfoot. A stranger was approaching, stopping every few moments to find the path. When the figure emerged from the underbrush surrounding our clearing, I saw a dark-uniformed man, his neck slightly bowed by a long day's work, carrying a small souvenir in his hand.

I recognized my father.

He mumbled a few general words of greeting, apologized for being late, and seated himself quietly at the opposite end of the table from me. I was about to climb off the bench and embrace him when Andrei shook me awake.

"It's time for bed. You can't go to sleep in that chair."

For a few moments, I stared at him like a stranger. I was trying to retrieve the dream, which was sinking away from me, like a stone plummeting to the dark ocean floor. Where had my father gone?

Andrei reached under my shoulders, and caught my weight as I stumbled sleepily toward my cot.

"Remember Martinov?" I asked. "This *is* life."

It sounded humorous, and true. Andrei smiled, and lowered me into bed. The shudder of leaves breathing the soft wind between the trees rolled me to sleep.

*   *   *

Where the willows—"weeping elms" in Russian—dip into the narrow river, you can't tell the trailing boughs from the thick, curved rushes stroked down by the running water. The Yauza moves quickly this close to Moscow, especially at the bends, where the reeds sweep backward into tangles that catch at the ankles of careless swimmers.

"There's the minister's bathhouse—" Andrei pointed upstream to a peeling green shack hunched down at the water's edge. "Of course, the minister himself never came, but now no one does, ever since his cook drowned. . . ."

Facing into the sun, he gestured toward a towering willow poised over a crook in the river a hundred yards away. Next to the huge tree, four brown horses, propped delicately on ancient racers' legs, were dipping their noses in the river. "The cook's body lay on the bank by the stud farm all evening until his friends came out to look for him with flashlights. Finally they found him under that tree—bald, where the horses had chewed the hair off his scalp. His face was wriggling with leeches. . . ." Already we were passing the willow on the opposite bank, and the river straightened out in front of us.

"Best not to swim over there—pfoo!" Andrei spat for good luck, waving the summer gnats off his face.

Russia, the old country, has an old landscape. The grassy hills near Moscow, through long experience, lie close to the ground. Mile-square patches of pine and birch forest interrupt the view, politely, and never at great length. Out here dozens of rivers curl toward the city, or toward the Volga in the north.

The landscape is elegant and purposeless. There is little hope for farming; cut down the forests, and the meadows blow away, clogging the rivers with silt. Every few years the underground peat bogs catch fire, driving the dacha owners back to the city, and reminding the villagers that they are now lucky not to live only off the land.

In our time, huts with hand-carved painted window frames still cluster around a pump or well, guarded by howling dogs tearing their necks against their chains, no freer than when Chekhov described them. The churches may be storehouses now, but the golden domes of Orthodoxy still gleam over each village and valley, a reminder that this is Holy Russia.

Russia interrupts its reverie, this time with a huge, stain-shingled three-story house looming above us on the river path. "Kapitsa's dacha," Andrei said, as if I knew. The story of the owner is no less startling than the dark, Lake Champlain-style turrets that hang above this small corner of the riverscape.

Kapitsa, the brilliant young particle physicist studying with Rutherford in England, was summoned back to the Soviet Union in 1934 to work on the Russian Manhattan Project. It's said—and who will sabotage a good story?—that Rutherford, learning of his best pupil's forced departure, loaded Kapitsa down with sophisticated lab instruments, which helped the Russians keep current in the race to build the first atomic bomb. It was a gift the student could not repay. Confined by Stalin to a prison research institute, Kapitsa never saw his mentor again.

Ticking our fingers along the fence staves, we peered inside the compound, looking for signs of life, or eminence. Two huge Ashkhabad carpets hung out to air. Underneath them lay an overturned, rusty wagon and three weathered badminton rackets. Through a huge window casement, did I see a dark figure slip by, or hear the cry of a child?

"He knew my father before the war," Andrei explained. "They used to fish together here. The police came for them at the same time, they were both scientists, practically neighbors. Kapitsa tried to convince them my father was his collaborator—he knew Stalin would need him, and he had no illusions about the fate of a lesser light like my father. I was asleep, but my mother saw it all. Kapitsa thundered and smashed on the hoods of their cars. But the agents had two cars, two sets of orders. . . .

"When I woke up, my mother said papa had been called away to secret work. For years, at the dinner table, she would let me imagine him designing attack blimps that rode on light beams, or dissolver rays that would melt Berlin into a pile of sand. At school, I even painted a picture of my father seated at a workbench piled high with secret gadgets. I remember the teacher scolding me, warning that secret work should remain secret."

Andrei paused to clear his throat. "I could have lived with him forever that way, imagining him happily at work, winning the war for us with his clever machines. But my imagination outlived him by six or seven years. He was shot the same night they took him away."

We circled behind the compound, and set off for our dacha, walking through a field of hay. Andrei's pointed boots moved like scythes, slicing sibilants while he talked.

"Kapitsa visited us once, after Stalin died. Mama sent me to my room. I heard him trying to apologize, saying he could have saved my father. My stepfather was in the room, what could she say? No one really saved anyone back then, and it was so dangerous even to have tried. . . ."

Our talk had led us back to the river, and back to the spreading willow tree. In the sunset, the willow caught fire. Across from it, on our side, a red and blue police launch had run up on shore. An exhausted swimmer lay sprawled on the boat's front deck, while two policemen in their loose gray summer tunics chatted with the last pair of picnickers perched on the bank. "Where's a phone?" one shouted. Andrei signaled with his hand, then scrambled up the bank to show the way.

I continued along the river path toward the launch, dazzled by the glare of the sunset in the square-cut windscreen. On the opposite bank, the same four horses splashed their hooves and shook their heads. Looking toward them, I saw two leeches crawling between the toes of the swimmer on the launch.

"Better kick those things off!" I yelled over. The toes twitched, but the leeches slithered further up the swimmer's foot, undisturbed. Shielding my eyes, I saw a green anklet of reeds wrapped around the silent swimmer's leg. I spat—pfoo!—in the water, turning home.

21 / *Olga*

Olga. Are there any Russian girls *not* named Olga, or Natasha, or Lena? At least three-quarters of the female population answers to one of those names, and Tanya would account for the rest. Because the names are so common, each one evokes wildly contradictory images for me. I knew a buxom translator Tanya, efficient, jellified, and jolly, with a weakness for French perfume. Then Tanya from Tbilisi, the free-lance manicurist, a harsh, wiry husband-hunter. Olga the doctor, Olga the postwoman, then this Olga, Andrei's summer neighbor.

Doors stay open in dacha country, so the front door to Olga's summer cottage stood wide ajar when we snaked through the pines for a morning visit. Andrei led me through the sunny wooden house, throwing open first the bedroom, then the kitchen door, looking for his friend. Barging into a small study, we disturbed a white-haired old man hunched over a desk, sheathed in the morning light of a double casement window overlooking the garden. As the man's shoulders began to turn, Andrei closed the door quickly.

"The father," he whispered.

We found Olga on her knees in the garden, sifting purple weed-killer around the stems of her lettuce plants. She rose quickly when she saw Andrei, slapping her palms clean against faded dungarees, and greeted us with an eager smile. She stood unusually tall for a Russian woman, and self-possessed. Dark-haired, handsome, serious-looking, she pulled the two of us into her kitchen for tea.

Seated at a small oilcloth-covered table underneath the kitchen window, Olga gossiped with Andrei. The furnishings were strictly dacha—only splotches of squashed insects or gray watermarks adorned the yellowing wallpaper; the house was little more than a roof for a life that transpired outside.

"I *still* can't find the right job," Olga said, wringing her hands. "It's papa, of course, I want to be with papa." She was a musicologist between jobs, and wanted a sinecure that would leave her plenty of time at home.

"What does a musicologist do in the Soviet Union?" I asked.

"What does a musicologist do anywhere? Teach, write, work for the state record company," she replied. "There are plenty of jobs. Unfortunately, all of them involve working."

"How is your father?" Andrei asked.

"He's writing in the study," she answered, "He doesn't want to be disturbed."

"I think we've already disturbed him."

"Don't worry, he probably thought you were the wind. When he's behind that desk, staring into the garden, he's in his own world."

Retracing our steps, Andrei and I discussed Olga. I thought her attractive, but settled beyond her age, which I estimated at thirty. I guessed that she had been divorced. No, no, Andrei laughed, and told me about the summers when her city suitors used to travel out to the dacha, to tempt her with swimming parties, or tennis, or lead her on romantic walks through the woods.

"Even the most determined ones eventually gave up. She treated them all like brothers, and looked after them just as she looks after her father. They could never catch her alone, and when they did, she would be rooting in the garden, or tending to some other chore. A few days of latrine duty and a few nights on the veranda was plenty for the Moscow boys. She's very devoted to her father." Andrei shrugged, admitting any possibility. "You should meet him. He's an interesting man."

A few days later, during an exchange of herbs with Lilya, Olga invited me to lunch.

Feeling self-conscious, I poached a small bouquet of wildflowers from the perimeter of Lilya's garden before I took off through the forest. Andrei raised his eyebrows; Lilya wondered out loud when she had last received flowers. But handing the bouquet across the doorway, I felt the same asexual chill that had sent the Moscow boys scurrying back to the train station. She turned aside her bright eyes, and snatched primly at the flowers, offering a peremptory smile and thank you in return. "Please come in, Mr. Perkins."

Olga had set three places for lunch in the study overlooking the garden, by throwing a bright embroidered tablecloth over the desk, and pushing the narrow cot where her father slept against a wall. She left for the kitchen to find a vase, and I inspected the room.

Again, there were hardly any furnishings. Next to the desk stood a narrow, waist-high cabinet, with a few freshly dusted trophies on each shelf. On top, I saw a framed oval photo portrait of a young woman, with Olga's jutting chin, high nose, and dark eyebrows angled in the fashion of the 1920s. Next to the portrait of the woman I presumed to be her mother lay a small white memo pad, and a fountain pen.

Olga entered quietly from behind me, with the fluted vase of wildflowers in one hand, and her father leaning on the opposite arm. He shuffled forward to the table in bedroom slippers, using his daughter for guidance rather than support. He wore an aged gray tweed suit over a freshly cleaned and pressed white shirt, open at the neck. His eyes were locked on the table. Just as he drew even with me, he glanced up and smiled with watery eyes, extending his hand.

I felt a strong arm, and a restrained grip. "How do you do?"

He nodded his head, and continued toward the table. "He hears you, but he can't speak," Olga explained. From the desk, she fetched the small memo pad and fountain pen. "You talk, and he will write." She disappeared into the kitchen. I sat down at the old man's elbow, and stared into his wrinkled blue eyes. He looked benevolent, like an accidental survivor bemused by his fate, and far less serious than his daughter. His face was happy as he gripped the fat pen, wrote a message, and turned the pad in my direction.

"I am Berezhov. Welcome to my home."

Each weekend at the dacha, I kept an eye out for Berezhov, remembering our groping lunch.

"What part of the country is your family from?"

His eyes twinkled. He laid his fork at the side of his plate, and reached for his pad and fountain pen. Then he changed his mind, broke into a grin, and waved his hands in front of his face, apologetically. He pointed through the window, outdoors, toward the flower beds, and Olga's neatly aligned vegetable garden.

"That means later," Olga said. "He will explain later."

Four or five other questions also failed; each time he seemed tempted to scrawl a reply, then chuckled quietly and repeated his gesture: later.

I tried Olga. "What part of the country are *you* from?"

"I am from Moscow," she answered stiffly.

"That's like being from Washington in our country. No one's really from Washington. Were you born in Moscow?"

"No." Her father looked up from his plate.

"Where were you born?"

"In the north, in the city of Norilsk."

"What were you doing there?"

Olga ignored the question, and left the table to prepare tea. Berezhov tapped on his plate to catch my attention. He gestured out the window again: later.

After ten more minutes of halting inquiries and awkward pauses, Olga escorted me to the door. Her father rose an inch off his chair and waved a goodbye. On the porch, Olga shook my hand firmly. "Even simple questions require complicated answers," she said, pointing me on the path back to Andrei's.

I saw them occasionally, always together, the tiptoeing white-haired eighty-year-old, and his coolly handsome daughter. In another country, they might have been taken for something else; a Rothschild and his mistress, a faded Mafia don and his moll. In Russia, they were distinctly father and daughter.

In the mornings, they had a bathing ritual. Olga spread a towel for Berezhov high on the river bank, at a safe distance from the unruly children flinging gravel on the tiny patch of beach. Holding him under the elbow, she led him to a small dock, where she eased her father down the stairs into the water, forbidding him to let go of the projecting float.

One day I saw him push away from the float and shoot to the center of the river in the fast, arching current. Olga was watching; she sprang off the dock, and sprinted fifty yards downstream to the children's beach, where she dove into the middle of the stream. She swam against the current until her father, smiling and flying down the river like a falcon off its chain, collided into her grasp. One arm hooked around his chest, she dragged him to the beach, where they stumbled out of the water, hand in hand, each other's willing misfortune. Back at the towel, she rubbed him dry violently, scolding Berezhov like an angry mother. While his stick-thin shoulders trembled in her grip, he smiled sweetly, spreading his hands in silent apology.

When Andrei and I passed their dacha on the way to the tennis court, we stopped at the short green picket fence and chatted with Olga, digging or planting on her knees in the vegetable garden. Through the lace curtains, I could see the outline of her father, hunched over his desk. I waved, and imagined him waving back.

One morning two weeks after our lunch, Olga reached into her dungarees and handed me a thick envelope. "For you, from my father." I glanced at the curtains, and raised a hand. Now was later.

At Andrei's, I unfolded the eight pages onto the kitchen table. The letter was tightly scripted on lined paper torn from a schoolboy's notebook, covering both sides.

Dear Mr. Perkins,

You asked so many questions, I could not hope to answer them all during one meal, or even one week. And balancing peas with a tired hand, or fingering small cakes, who has time to write? The French philosopher Sartre has said: *il faut vivre ou écrire*. But my choice at lunchtimes is more mundane: *il faut écrire ou manger*. I prefer to eat.

Yes, I am a "writer" too, but not by choice. I am an engineer by training, and never needed words. But now I like them. I am garrulous on paper, which is paradoxical, as I was never much of a talker. Nor am I a great writer, just a pensioner, with much free time.

You like Olga? I hope so. She is a good girl—too attached to her father, I'm afraid, but I don't question my good fortune. When I die, she will be free, or very lonely. We have always been good friends; for many years we have had our own language of gestures, taps, and signs. We can even talk on the phone—I use a coin to tap Morse on the receiver. You know how bad the lines are here, cackling with static. We've had some amusing confusions . . .

You are interesting to her, you have seen countries and places she may never see. I know she would like to be friends with you. She has seen places you could never dream existed.

Yes, you heard correctly, she was born in Norilsk, *the* Norilsk, north of the Arctic Circle on the White Sea. I saw your eyebrows flicker, I read your mind. "The camps!" You were astonished. "This lovely girl born in the camps! And this old man then . . ." But the story is older, and more complicated than you suspect.

Here, and elsewhere in the letter, he switched pens, or began a new sheet of paper, to let me know that he had paused, perhaps for as long as a day or two, before starting to write again. The time invested in the letter paid handsome dividends; he arrived at each new episode fresh, as if telling it for the first time.

To go east, you have to go west . . . I was just a teenager during the Civil War, and I took the occasion to leave. In those days, it was easier to switch countries. I lodged with relatives in Warsaw for seven years, where I learned mine engineering, Polish, and French. I also married, which, were I famous, would be "a little-known fact." I told Olga only last year.

In this country one has no memory, and the histories—it would be tactful to say they are no help. You may not remember, but Poland was still at war with Russia as late as 1928. After some years, Warsaw was the wrong city for a Russian. I was young (younger than you, my friend!), with a good skill, no children. I convinced my wife to move with me to Paris.

Paris in 1928! I won't bore you, but think how it was for me, born in a small town in the Western Ukraine, twenty-six years old, to be walking the Champs-Elysées, to see Notre Dame at night! I couldn't stay, of course. The mining work was in the provinces, and within a few weeks I found a job in the mountains, outside of Clermont-Ferrand.

France made me a petit bourgeois. Just so much milk in the coffee, the Camembert just so soft, drink the wine so far down in the bottle and no farther . . . such simple obsessions, which the French parade as *grande culture.* They exaggerate, but how agreeable (nostalgia herds me towards their language, *que c'est agréable!*) to swallow a flask of red wine with lunch, or to feel their pastry soften your fingertips. So much energy devoted to eating! A world of Frenchmen would be a safer and tastier place!

Suddenly, *la crise.* Three short years, and the world stood on its head. Our mine closed, our company collapsed. For a while, I traded on my skills and transferred to the next company, which respected my qualifications. But as the situation worsened, talent counted for less. Soon many talented engineers were out of work, and I wasn't even French. The bosses couldn't hire a Russian. I began to look for solutions.

One morning in the winter of 1934, I found a Russian language magazine, *Voice of the Motherland,* addressed to me, lying on my doorstep. The Soviet authorities had launched a propaganda drive to bring the emigrés home. I still carried a Russian passport and flattered myself to think I was just the kind of person they needed to help with the industrialization program. A foreign-trained engineer, not even anti-Soviet. Merely indifferent to politics, with a taste for foreign cheeses.

Printed inside the front cover was a letter from Stalin. You know, for many years the Soviet press had been

denouncing the emigrés as "renegades," "bloodsuck-
ers," and "scum." But here the tone was quite different:
The smiling man with the big mustache was inviting us
home to serve Mother Russia in her hour of need. With
color pictures of barrel-chested returnees directing construction at Magnitogorsk, sipping tea in "palaces of
culture," listening to wireless in their new apartments. I
was hungry, Mr. Perkins.

I filled in a form enclosed with the magazine, and a
few weeks later the Soviet Embassy summoned me to
Paris. They had organized a whole repatriation committee, thick with friendly faces. The visas would be no
problem, a Polish wife would be no problem. A mine
engineer? Why, there must have been ten thousand
openings for mine engineers back then! "I wouldn't be
surprised if they give you your own mountain range!"
one of the officials joked. I met other men in the waiting rooms, with good specialties like mine, who had also
applied to return. We spoke Russian, read the newspapers, indulged our nostalgia. Some were wary, but almost all returned. Jobs, the old country, a challenge . . .

We did the rest of the paperwork by mail. My wife
agreed that I should go first, take an assignment, and
send for her. Her visa was ready. One evening shortly
before I left, we walked to a small cafe to sip a brandy.
Where were the children, you wonder? We wanted children but had none. We sat on the sidewalk, sipping Cognac, and talked about Russia.

I remember a candle in a wall mounting, flicking
shadows above my wife's shoulder. The night outside
was pure black, without a moon, and clouds hid the
stars, as if the earth had closed its eyes. I was enthusi-
astic. I admitted life would be harder, but the Depression was crushing France in its grip. Strikes were
becoming violent, the political parties were distributing
guns. I was certain it was time to leave. But my wife had
misgivings. On that blackest of nights, she said, "You
know, I'm frightened of Russia. It's so dark out there."

Forgive me—I left you for a brief nap, and now I

have stayed away from our talk for almost a week. But what I am about to write is merely history. A special train awaited us at the Gare du Nord, each wagon decked with tricolor bunting, and the hammer and sickle. The Soviet consul delivered a welcoming speech, as it were, on departure. And we set off on a very long train ride, all the way to Norilsk.

Questions arise in your mind. When did we know we were prisoners? Where did we expect to go? Why didn't we resist? I think we were prisoners the moment we boarded the train, captured by our childish fantasies of a new life.

The champagne flowed up to the French border; after that, the festive atmosphere vanished. Leather-jacketed political commissars gathered up our passports for the border check, but failed to return them, long after we had crossed into Germany, Poland, and entered Russia. Two days later the commissars returned to search the compartments, with uniformed "customs officials" who had been kept out of sight until we crossed into Russia. They confiscated knives, foreign currency, and any valuables they could find, along with books.

Soon there was unrest on the train, but by then our keepers had sealed the connecting doors between the carriages. The policemen fed us bread from a cart, explaining that our wagon had been "quarantined." A few of the stronger fellows assaulted our friendly jailers, who beat them down with gun butts. Sometimes we stopped briefly at country stations inside Russia to take on coal or water, and old peasants shuffled over to stare in the windows. They saw our foreign belongings, and when they noticed the guards loitering outside the carriage doors, they walked away, shaking their heads.

You know how we Russians are, such good prisoners, so docile in captivity. We lapsed easily into the convict mentality, conversing less and less, watching the slow parade of station signposts in sullen, dazed fear. Waiting for the end of the line. The only remaining question was where they would take us, and for how long.

We inspected each station name, but our geography had aged. Such strange new places—Kaliningrad, Chicheringrad, Molotovgrad—as if some savage tribe had invaded our country, and each chieftain named a town after himself. We soon realized that we had by-passed Moscow, and after a few more days of traveling, the locales assumed a new strangeness—Severny Kray, Severodvinsk, Severosayansk—"north" names of the Siberian wilderness. And the weather outside was turning cold; even in June we wouldn't have opened the windows, had they been left unsealed. After four long weeks in the stinking, contaminated train, we arrived at the newest town of the new society—Norilsk.

I won't tell you about the camps. You've probably read what's already been written; most of it is untrue. Our first view of Norilsk was benign. From the station, they transported us in open trucks, along a mountain ridge that suddenly banked toward the huge lake. First we sniffed the moisture in the air; leaning over the side of the truck, we caught a glimpse of the glowing blue water, and the perfect natural harbor below. Across the lake, we saw the nickel mines torn into the low mountains, and the convicts building the town.

Even in summer, the sun glanced off icebergs as large as houses, floating in the blue waves just a few feet from shore. In winter, there was no view; this basin below us filled with fog, condensed exhaust from the mine works that hung in the freezing air for six dark months, when the sun never shone.

We weren't brought in for manual labor, so our chances of surviving were good. But we had to make it through the first winter, and not everyone did. Month after month passed without sunlight, with the temperature rising to forty below at midday. If a new man took off his glove to unjam some machinery, he was stuck. Three or four of us would tear his hand off the metal, leaving gray red patches of bloody frozen skin.

The worst assignment was driving. There were no roads, and trucks broke down frequently, sometimes all four tires exploding at once on the black ice. Men froze to death just a few hundred meters from town. A lucky one might grab on to a passing vehicle, but no one could risk stopping or even slowing down to help at an accident. Sometimes I wonder how I stayed alive for fifteen years. I was strong, but not brave.

During those fifteen years only two things happened, perhaps three if you include the chess. Yes, I became an official chess grandmaster. There were plenty of brains behind barbed wire during those years, and as Norilsk was teeming with grandmasters, it wasn't hard to accumulate points. I was even city champion for six years—you may have noticed the trophies in my bookcase. And we competed with other camp cities, by mail of course.

I should mention that I did work my own mine, and directed over a thousand workers. So they were applying our talents. And you who are an attentive reader, you ask what became of my wife? The first week, they sat us down, with a soldier peering over our shoulders, and forced us to write home and summon any relatives left behind. "You were right. It's very dark out here," I wrote. Thank God, she never came.

Back to our talk. It is fashionable to complain that writing is difficult, but when writing has taken the place of your tongue, the pen no longer feels heavy. What happened to my voice? I lost it during the war, I think, although dates were never precise up there. We experienced black cold for six months of the year, followed by hot sun in July and August, when the permafrost turned muddy underfoot, and supply ships nosed their way through the icebergs in the harbor. We kept track of the summers, but wishing too much, I think we muddled the years. And being politicals, we weren't given newspapers to read. But I think it was during the war.

One evening in November—of course evening was just a time after work, as the darkness lasted all day—one of the bosses, a colonel, informed me that three of my deputies had escaped. We managers didn't live behind barbed wire, or under guard, because the whole city was an armed camp, with no population except for the prisoners and guards. No one could have survived a winter night in the countryside, and during the summer they could send the dogs across the tundra to tear you apart. We were little ants trapped on top of a huge ice cube. . . .

But to be told your staff had escaped meant you had to find them, or suffer serious consequences. In my case, I would have spent two or three years at manual labor; it might have killed me. But how could I possibly find them?

I had one idea of where to look. During the summer, we sometimes swam in front of a grotto down by the water, hidden by a spit of land. We joked about camping there through the winter, and swimming out to freedom on one of the foreign ships that occasionally called at the harbor—but only as a joke, to preserve the illusion that we could somehow leave of our own accord, which of course we could not. Furthermore, even if this guess was correct, and they had acted on our shared fantasy, I had no interest in finding these fellows—I thought they would kill me if I stumbled on them. And if I reported their whereabouts, they would be shot.

I dressed warmly, and set off down the shore. There was no shore, because there was no margin between the snow-covered ice on land and on the lake. In winter, there was no weather at all, no sky, no landscape, no day or night. Just duration, gray and cold.

For three hours I tramped around this cave, out onto the ice packs, back onto land, screaming their names. I became sleepy. I was thumping my gloves together, but I knew my fingers would be frostbitten in another half hour. I didn't care. I wanted to keep shouting, but my throat hurt. I leaned against a rock to rest. I fell asleep.

I awoke on a sofa, in the camp hospital, under a glaring yellow lightbulb. When they couldn't hear my voice any longer, the three men had emerged from the cave, and found me slouched sideways on the rock, breathing slowly. When they brought me in, the doctor said I was smiling, happy that I was finally going to die.

Awake, I lay still, and flexed the muscles of my fingers and toes. Then I remembered that the brain still registers signals from missing limbs. I slid my hands up slowly from under the blanket, frightened of what I would see. Both small fingers were gone. Not bad, I thought. I didn't need them for much. I tugged the blanket back off my toes. All there.

I fell back asleep, as happy to be alive as I had been to be dead a few hours before. Early in the morning, the doctor came in with the colonel, both smiling.

"Your friends brought you back just in time," the doctor said, patting my feet under the blanket. "But for them, you would have died. They sacrificed their freedom to save your life." Faintly, I nodded gratitude.

The colonel smiled in response. "Yes, instead, it is they who are dead, and you who are on your way to recovery."

I snapped up, screaming. But I felt flesh tear my tongue, and instead of noise, only air rushed out of my throat. I stood paralyzed, enraged, terrified. The colonel walked out. I fell to the floor, weeping, wheezing instead of crying. The doctor sat me down. He explained he had removed a section of my vocal cords, because of frostbite. They would not grow back.

Now I am back. The second event is a fonder memory for me, Olga's birth. My hands and eyes are tiring, there's much I can't tell you now. I was married to another "returnee" for nine years; my second wife died in Norilsk. She arrived tubercular, and had no chance of surviving. She knew that from the beginning. If anything, she overstayed her time. But we were ecstatic to have Olga, a lantern in our darkness, our only joy.

Our comrades regarded childbirth as a tragedy—another mouth to feed, without extra rations. There were hardly any children in Norilsk then; Soviet power had provided them with their own camps, and thus there was no baby food, no children's clothing, not even a nursery school in all of Norilsk. We had to forage materials, sometimes from the morgue, for diapers, dresses, boots. And if the child had any weakness, the climate would exploit it, and extinguish the baby. But for us, Olga was no tragedy. Just the opposite, she was the meaning of our lives.

She was born in 1951. Three years later, the Rehabilitation reached us, in the first newspaper I had read in fifteen years. We returned to Moscow, to relatives who took us in. For Olga, Norilsk is a city name on her passport, a word engraved on my chess trophies, my only "souvenirs." She remembers nothing, thank God.

It could be made to sound dramatic. God knows not everyone lived through those years. But history was so much bigger than we grains of sand, blown here, blown there. I look at my own life: twenty years of bondage, sixty years of "freedom." Not a bad average, if you are prepared to die without regrets. As I am. Perhaps God is playing chess with the universe, what do you think?

Berezhov

22 / Postcards from Home

I had experienced moments of weightlessness, skiing with Martinov, or drained of fluids in the baths, when I completely escaped the gravity of America, and of Nick Perkins, journalist. I had savored sips of true freedom, small moments of flight from a personality assigned, not assumed. To feel like this, I had to be far away, perhaps only in Russia.

But I had passed the apogee, and now gravity, in the form of telexes from Jonas discussing future assignments, was pulling me home. It was early June, and both Susan I were leaving in July. Jonas wanted me to make plans, to think about my next assignment, and about who might best replace me. Someone who knew how to enjoy life, I felt tempted to reply, and did not. I couldn't feel any pull from within. Was I happy to be falling back to earth?

"When you think of America, what do you miss?" Andrei was watching the road while I rested my eyes on the darkening countryside outside the car window.

"I don't know. My mother."

"Is that all?"

"No, there's something there I miss very much, something very good. But it's hard to put my finger on. Energy, maybe."

"What kind?"

"Well some of it's the wrong kind, the energy that made us kill off the Indians, and provoke a war or two. It's hateful, but it's part of the spirit I like. We may not be nice, but we're not dull. People wearing loud shirts and funny shoes, dying to sell you a car, Puerto Ricans with loud radios—it's like a nation of trembling molecules."

"And here?"

"Here it's different. Things are at rest. That's good."

"What will you miss about us?"

"I'll miss you, and Lilya."

"We'll miss you, too."

"But if I hadn't come from America, I wouldn't have enjoyed it as much."

"We enjoy it, from the inside."

I slapped him on the knee. "But the Russians are happy anywhere."

"In Russia."

"Ah, yes. And Americans are unhappy everywhere."

"Except in Russia."

I saw Richard squirming in the back seat, and switched back to English. "Sorry."

"That's OK," he said.

Richard was a messenger, reminding me that it was time to come home.

Richard worked in Aron's accounting firm, and had bought a fifteen-day tour to Russia. When Aron heard, he loaded his colleague down with the amulets of the other world, now piled in the back seat: panty hose, stretch pants, jeans, "Kiss Me, I'm Russian" T-shirts, sticky spiders for the children, and even three Sony Walkmans—a customs officer confiscated the fourth. And addresses, and letters, which Richard felt silly to admit he had slid into the waistband of his underwear.

While Lilya and Andrei stage-managed dinner, I escorted Richard, fresh off the plane and looking very young in his madras sports jacket and red alligator shirt, down to the Yauza. I found myself pressing him for news of New York. Hearing him talk reminded me of Martinov describing the breathless poop from Moscow: This fad on, this fad off. This play wins the approval of the bosses . . .

Richard raved about three fabulous new Australian films, which he hadn't seen. Shakespeare in the Park was offering its best repertory ever, but it was a long trip from Queens. He confessed that he missed his exercise machine. Richard rubbed the backs of his calves anxiously. "On the plane, I could actually *feel* my quadriceps flattening out."

He turned the questioning on me. "Who are these people?"

"They're Aron's relatives, friends of mine."

He glanced behind us on the path. "Can we trust them?"

"For what?"

"I don't know, not to report on us."

"Is there anything to report?"

Richard pondered for a moment. "I guess not." We stopped at the river bank, and looked across to the horse farm. I put myself in Richard's shoes. A few hours ago he hadn't dreamed of being whisked away to the countryside, beyond the protective ring of souvenir shops and tourist hotels, to meet our Common Enemy. He'd have his own stories to tell.

"How long have you been here?"

"Ten months."

"Do you like it?"

"I didn't expect to."

"But you do, don't you?"

"Is it that obvious?"

Yes, it was that obvious, and Richard wasn't sure it was a good thing. "Isn't it strange, living here for so long?"

"I'll be leaving in July." I started us back toward the dacha. "I'm just a visitor, too."

We sat down to eat at the long trestle table underneath the huge pines. A standup lamp, joined to the cottage with a ten yard extension cord, flickered in the dark night. For half an hour, Andrei had been jamming thin sticks of kindling down the throat of a crackling samovar, trying to bring the water to a boil. When the time came for tea, Lilya brought a steaming kettle from the gas range in the kitchen, and poured the first glass for our visitor from New York.

Andrei turned to me as the translator. "Ask him how Aron is doing."

Rosa, Aron's former secretary who had driven over from the farm to hear news of her ex-boss, froze when she heard Andrei ask after his cousin. The table, heavy with hospitality—fruits, vegetables, bottles, and thick slices of dark bread—lay still. In the silence, Andrei crunched a cucumber, punctuating his question. Lilya stared distractedly into the hidden forest, zebra-striped with an occasional birch trunk. This was the forest where I dreamt I had seen my father.

Richard folded his hands in front of him, and surveyed the expectant faces. "Yes, Aron . . ." he smiled. While we were assembling the dinner in the kitchen, he had passed around color snapshots of Aron and his family, sitting on a shiny yellow Mazda parked outside a row house in Queens. Is the car his? Yes. Is the house his? No.

Also Aron and Lena on the trail at Smugglers' Notch, 4000 feet above the Vermont-Canada border, their first vacation after two and a half years in the United States. Where are the borderguards? Where are the watchtowers? The company examined each photo at length, intently, trying to stare through the little windows of colored paper to the unknown world beyond. What is it *really* like? Are they *really* happy? But the scenes and expressions were noncommittal, frozen in smiles and sunshine.

"Well, Queens is—" As he began, each face strained forward. They saw he was choosing his words too carefully, too hesitant to offend. "Well, Queens is not like Moscow." He laughed, alone. "We work very hard, as I guess Aron has written you. You see, neither of us is a licensed CPA, that is, we're not licensed accountants, so we work long hours, and we don't get as much pay as a CPA." He smiled sheepishly. "The truth is, we're kind of exploited. . . ."

Rosa and Lilya smiled politely. He stumbled on. "But Aron, and actually I too, we're both studying for the license so we can get better jobs later on. And, well, you've seen the picture of the inside of his apartment, so you have an idea how they live."

Jamaica. What a strange resonance, especially in translation. Is it near the United Nations? Near the Statue of Liberty? For them, Aron had vanished into a dream, imperfectly remembered, never understood. Is it near Harlem? If the exploited drive Mazdas, what do the exploiters drive? Helicopters?

"So the apartment is nice, and he can take the subway to work. Lena walks Samuel to school, and then she might go shopping. She still takes in some odd sewing jobs, you know, and she's sold some of those nice embroidered handkerchiefs you have. But now they have a bit more money, so she only does it for fun. Let's see . . . Aron bought a videotape recorder ('*Videomagnetofon*', Andrei quickly translated) so we trade tapes, and stuff . . ."

Rosa cleared her throat. "Lena writes that crime is bad."

Richard squirmed in his chair, and lifted his eyes to stare into the night outside the lamplight, a complete darkness with no shadows, imposed by the trees.

"The crime is bad. It's awful. I mean, I guess there's some crime everywhere, but in New York, all kinds of things can happen." He paused.

"Like what?"

"Like, for instance, your apartment can be broken into, that happened to Lena and Aron just after they arrived . . . and then, well, there are purse-snatchings, and muggings, and holdups, and—"

"—and rapes?" Rosa asked. "Lena writes that the papers are full of rapes."

"Yes, there are rapes. Last year, though, I think I read that statistic—"

"It's the Negroes, isn't it?" Rosa interrupted. In part, she was curious about this world of idle violence, and in part she wanted to assure herself that Aron was wrong to have left Russia.

Richard stared out into the darkness again, for help. "Well, we don't . . . I mean, there are lots of people other than blacks who commit crimes in America . . ."

The Russians nodded knowingly. Lena had described them in a letter: Muscular young basketball players in tight T-shirts cut off at the shoulders, carrying knives on the street in full daylight, ready for a fight. "In Russia I was unhappy. Here I am frightened," she wrote. "I cry when I see our door, with three padlocks, stacked one on top of the other. Thank heavens we cannot return. Sometimes it is so tempting."

Lilya set a second round of tea glasses in front of us, hot cylinders of steam rising into the night. Andrei touched his lips to the edge of the boiling glass, withdrew, then tentatively began to drink again. Each person sat silently with his or her own thoughts, traveling to the United States and back again. For them, America was an imagined nation: fast, violent, powerful, absurd. Colored, colorful like a kaleidoscope; each half turn you see a different picture. You keep turning, but the first image never returns.

For me? From this end of the telescope, I too was looking at those trembling molecules through different eyes. America. The frosty land where I was born.

"Do you think they are happy?" Andrei asked. I translated.

Richard caught my eyes, pleading. "What a question. . . ." I shrugged my shoulders: I can't help you.

He adjusted his jacket lapel, casting his eyes down at the table. "Well, sure he's happy. We're all happy, aren't we?" He looked at me again. "I mean, that's why he left, wasn't it? Because he couldn't stand it here?"

Now it was the hosts' turn to stare down at their tea. Lilya exhaled deeply, sighing. "Yes."

Rosa coiled her shoulders, then relaxed. "Yes." She drummed her fingers on the wooden table, and walked inside the dacha.

"We bought some presents for Samuel." She carried out a small pile of children's books and stacked them in front of Richard. "Some of them are too silly for him, we know, but perhaps he will have children who will want to know Russian."

She leafed through the brightly colored picture books, like a lament. "And my mother sends this—" she handled a small antique book, still tightly bound in gold-embossed leather. "It's for Samuel, too. It's only Pushkin, but she thought it might be difficult to find in America . . ."

"And please," Rosa continued, clearing her throat of a sob. "Tell them we miss them terribly, and want them to be happy. And that wherever they live, they will always be living here, in our hearts, with us. We will never forget—" She burst into tears.

254

Andrei pulled her sobbing shoulders under his arm, and addressed Richard. "Just tell them that we miss them very much, and that with us everything is all right. Everything is all right."

The village generator switched off at midnight. The lamp faded, and died. Andrei walked off to start the car for the drive back to Moscow.

23 / *Going Back*

Back in Moscow, I telephoned Olga for lunch. She had found the right job, organizing children's song contests for *Pioneers' Pravda,* the "organ" of the Young Pioneers. Her schedule was light, but I had invited her on Wednesday, one of her three work days.

We met in the ground floor cafe of the Hotel Belgrade, just around the corner from Olga's office. The meal was rushed. I happened to have her father's letter in my briefcase. We both laughed at his choice of schoolboy's ruled paper, and his heavy, orthodox penmanship, while Olga read quickly through the manuscript.

"It's quite a story."

"He's some editor," she remarked, laying the pages down beside me. "He makes Norilsk sound like a real holiday."

"Maybe there were difficult memories."

"Not for him alone."

"What do you mean?"

She fidgeted, and called for coffee. Her father had written more than she wanted to say.

"What do you mean?"

"Well, here's an example." She rested her fingertips against her closed eyes. "He writes that Norilsk is just a memory for me—" she waved indifferently towards his letter —"a place name in my passport. But I remember Norilsk quite well. I remember sitting in a clearing halfway up a hillside on my eighth birthday in July, swatting flies off my little pound cake with candles. I pointed across the city to a set of parallel three-story buildings near the shore, and told my friends: 'That's where mama and papa used to be in jail.'"

Some red had gushed into her face, underneath her gardening suntan. "That's a detail that escaped his 'testament.' Or what about Christmas, 1960? We went ice fishing in the river. One of the fishermen lent us his shed, and we built a fire right on the ice, dipping the trout in vinegar and slapping them into the pan as quickly as we caught them. That was the first time I saw John Kennedy, on a tiny convex television screen at the director's home, during the children's Christmas party. I was nine. We all thought he was so handsome. . . ."

Her voice was tense, near breaking. She saw I didn't understand why her story differed from her father's, and she didn't care. We drank our coffees in embarrassed silence. She looked out the window, she shuffled her hair, she locked hands in a tight double fist on the table until I had paid the bill. At the exit, she shook my hand, definitively. "I enjoyed meeting you," she said. "I always like to meet Andrei's friends. I apologize for my father's letter. Please don't think you know everything about us."

I tripped across her father unexpectedly, at a wedding party later in the month. Tanya, the grimly determined manicurist, had netted a Moscow husband, and her family had rented out the back room of the capital's finest Georgian restaurant for a village-style hoedown. I arrived late, and stood at the back of the oak-paneled hall, craning my head to catch the complicated toasts and watch the frenzied dancing next to the head table. In the opposite corner, also behind the action, I saw a small man in a gray tweed suit watching the wedding party, clapping his hands to the bouncy Caucasus music. Berezhov.

Between outbursts, I caught his attention, and waved. He waved back, grinning, motioning toward the rows of bottles arrayed on a table along the back wall. I squeezed through to his side of the room, and he handed me a full glass of Kinsmarauli, Stalin's favorite wine. While I drank, he laid his finger above his lip, and pointed to his glass. Mustache, Stalin, wine. Yes, yes, I know. He laughed, and now waved in the direction of the plump bride, rubbing his hands, raising an approving thumb. "A lovely wedding," I said. He nodded his head vigorously along with the music.

After a few more songs, he pulled out his pen and pad, and scrawled me a note: Olga should marry.

"I'm sure she's had many proposals, she's pretty and intelligent . . ."

He nodded agreement, then frowned, and shrugged his shoulders helplessly. Another note. "She doesn't want to leave home."

I shrugged my shoulders in turn. "What can you do?"

He raised his pen to catch my eye, then tore off another message. "She was very upset by my letter. For the first time, she threatened to leave."

I was surprised. "I'm sure she doesn't mean it," I shouted above the din. "She cares for you very much." I hoped I was telling the truth. Had he heard me? He didn't respond. The music had surged again, family members were pulling guests into the dancing. Berezhov stared at the dance floor, smiling and clapping his hands to the beat.

I stayed with him during the song, then gestured my intention to go greet other friends across the room. He smiled broadly, and grabbed my hand to say goodbye. Winking, he pulled out his pad for the last time, and handed me a scrap of paper. *"Il faut vivre la vie."* He smiled again, and urged me toward my friends. When I reached the other side of the room, he had disappeared.

At the dacha, I saw Olga and her father only at a distance. Andrei took a new route to the tennis courts, skirting their property. Olga must have spoken to him.

Down by the river Olga and her father had changed their schedule, to finish bathing when we arrived. Once I saw them on the opposite bank. How did they get there? There was no bridge. In his white bathrobe, the sun blazing at his back, Berezhov lifted his arms to wave feebly across the stream. Backlit, and in the blazing terrycloth, he shone like an angel.

Olga spotted us, and turned her father inland, toward the horse farm. Later in June, I found their dacha prematurely boarded up for the summer, and the garden plowed under.

In my apartment mailbox I received a second letter, again on pulpy, lined paper, from Berezhov.

Dear Mr. Perkins,

Now I am embarrassed, thinking that we may never meet again, and of the opinion you must have of me, a muddleheaded, eccentric old fool. Well, I resume my "testament" where I left off, pleading a sore arm and failing eyesight, as I recall. But I tell you at the outset, I don't think you will understand.

We did return to Moscow, we did live with relatives, and we applied for an apartment. I worked, while a cousin took care of Olga, for a bit of money. After a year, I became impatient. We were sharing a flat with virtual strangers, causing problems for everyone, and there was no sign of a new apartment. First in line were the war veterans, the nearer death the better. Then the Hero Mothers, then the shock workers—I think you know how this works. We would have to wait. I decided to return to Norilsk.

Why? Because I wanted to. They offered me an important job, with a good salary. Some of my colleagues had stayed, though not many, I'll admit. But young people were arriving, engineers like ourselves twenty years before, who wanted hard work, important work, of their own accord. I sound like a "case," unable to live outside the camp. But we didn't return to a camp, we returned to small huts and apartment buildings to do the same job as free men.

The Polar North had become familiar. The climate had long ceased to bother me, and of course the years in Norilsk had given me Olga, more of a dream than I could ever fulfill in Moscow, or Paris. A few people had stayed behind: some of my chess-playing friends, and some of the former guards, who were afraid of going back to the "mainland." Now, one drove the office car, one was a bulldozer operator, one was the gym instructor in the school. Things had indeed gotten better, as the old camp saying went. Though not immediately, and not for everyone.

But things were better for us. Olga was happy, far happier than sleeping in a tiny bedroom with four other children, next to a smoking kitchen. We had space, and walks, our own sled and even reindeer, which we kept for three winters . . . I was more of a mother than a father. We slept together in a huge down bed, I listened to her school stories, followed her entanglements. She grew up strong; she's still strong.

After eight years, our Moscow apartment was ready, and we moved back. Olga fell into Moscow life, and within just a few weeks her classmates had forgotten that she came from somewhere else. In university she first learned about the camps, the slavery, and about her mother. As a child, she loved the North, but today she never speaks of it, and will never forgive me for having returned there.

One evening, she screamed at me: "I can't believe what your generation sat through, just *sat through*!" She says she wouldn't have endured it. If true, more power to her. No one wants each generation to be the same.

Why didn't I write this before? Did I fear your scorn? I think not. My own daughter understands little, but you understand less. We had a choice only of prisons, and I chose the one I knew best.

Berezhov

On my last Monday morning, I was a commuter like everyone else on the train platform, waiting for the forest green *elektrichka* that linked the dacha country to Moscow. The weekenders were laden with loot. Entire families were burdened like packhorses, grandmother groaning under a full knapsack of new potatoes, the parents hauling bags of fruit, the children clasping gallon jugs of berry juice against their chests. I was a co-conspirator; Lilya had emptied my bag of clothes, stuffing it with freshly cleaned tomatoes, cucumbers, and carrots. "Come back later for the clothes," she tutted, patting the bulging green stencil on the thick canvas: Save a Tree.

Just as I heard the train sputtering a half mile away through the forest, I felt a tug on my arm. Turning, I saw one of the dozens of squat, kerchiefed babushki, stooped under a heavy load: Ekaterina Sergeyevna.

"Nikolai Pavlovich! What are *you* doing here?" She seemed genuinely concerned, as if I had been kidnaped from the foreigners' compound, and forced at gunpoint to spend a weekend in the country.

"Working the land, of course." I showed off my vegetable trove, which she inspected with a probing hand.

"Cucumbers too soft, but the tomatoes look decent. . . ." She turned suspicious. "Do you have friends out here?"

I avoided the question, and she didn't pursue it. She perceived that I was devious enough to let slip back in Moscow that I had been visiting *her,* which she would have trouble explaining.

"Well . . . here, meet Vanyushka." From behind her huge back, she produced a plump little grandson, dressed in white cotton shorts and a T-shirt with a picture of a volleyball. She pressed tightly down on his shoulders with both hands, as if he would float away. "Vanya, meet Nikolai Pavlovich. Vanyushka's coming with me to Children's World, we're going to buy a pair of the new East German sneakers for kindergarten."

Vanya was holding his own plastic bag filled with yellow apricots. He stared up at me, and leaned over the edge of my canvas bag to peer inside. Unprompted, he grabbed a small handful of his apricots, and dropped them in my bag.

I thanked him, and patted his head. Sergeyevna smiled, and scolded the boy at the same time. "Vanya, don't give fruit to strangers!"

The little boy whined back at her. "But grandmother, this is your comrade from work!"

Ekaterina Sergeyevna and I stared blankly at each other. "Well, of course. But he doesn't enjoy fruit. See you soon, Nikolai Pavlovich." She laughed nervously, and hustled Vanya through the crowd, closer to the arriving train.

The boy's remark stayed with me as I crammed my way into the packed commuter carriage. We did work together, I suppose, in the tawdry symbiosis of mistrust that assigns some people to monitor the movements of others. How pleasant to put off context, and be waiting for a train.

24 / Last Things

In the thin soil of work and official contacts, I had planted shallow roots. Leaving was no struggle; indeed, the Soviet system worked more smoothly in reverse. While it took four weeks to open a bank account, it took just a few minutes to close one. The Korpus V "commandant" who made me wait two months before issuing my residence permit, rescinded it with just a phone call. I was on my way to becoming a nonperson.

The question of my next assignment was to be resolved by Jonas and me, as planned, in New York the following month. My furniture and personal effects would remain in storage until my successor arrived to send them onward.

The flurry of "succession" telexes confused Boris, whose masters must have asked him to psych out our plans for the Moscow correspondency. Would we leave the job open, he asked tentatively? Had my year gone well? What did New York *really* think? Our organization was as opaque to him as his was to me.

During my last week at the office, Boris shuffled dolefully from room to room. Too late, I think we both regretted not having become friends. We had approached each other with too much mistrust, the officially assigned interpreter wary of the bourgeois slanderer, and vice versa.

But there had been moments of thaw, even warmth, between us. Boris told me my favorite joke: A Frenchman, an American, and a Russian are stranded on a desert island, playing cards and drinking beer from a crate washed up on shore. A genie escapes from an empty beer bottle, and grants each man one wish. The Frenchman asks to return to his mistress, the American to his business. The Russian? He ponders a moment, forlorn. "The company was so good . . . we had cards . . . beer. Bring my friends back!"

Boris knew I was enjoying Russia. His censorious side disapproved. Rather like Susan, he felt I *shouldn't* be having a good time, on principle. Moscow wasn't meant to be *fun,* least of all for the ideological adversary. Unlike Susan, Boris may have viewed my unexpectedly happy stay as a dereliction of his duty. Perhaps he should have made life miserable for me, and hadn't. If pressed, he could always argue that I hadn't shown up in the office much, to be hectored. But I think the Russian squelched down inside this New Soviet Man welcomed my acceptance of the Russian way.

In the office I kept a peel-off calendar, which offered some new homily for each day of the year. One morning in June, he dropped that day's saying on my desk: "Everybody is lying, but no one is listening."

He raised his eyebrows.

I nodded my head. I agree.

Inevitably, we botched our farewell. Boris had decided to take vacation for the last week in June, and warned me repeatedly that he would be absent the preceding Friday as well. I spent Thursday afternoon gift-shopping, and took a Friday morning train to the dacha without phoning the office. When I arrived at my desk on Monday, I found a small package, with a note from Boris: "Wanted to give you this in person. Good health and happiness in your future career."

The present was a palm-size brass medallion, with a profile of Yuri Dolgoruky, founder of Moscow, on one face, and the Kremlin towers on the other. It was too late to send it home, and it promised to weigh down my hand luggage for the airplane. It was a nuisance. It was ugly. I was touched.

Ekaterina Sergeyevna had successfully repressed our humanizing moment on the train platform, at least in front of me. On one of my last mornings, I asked after her grandson. "Fine, he's fine," she answered brusquely, craning her head for eavesdroppers. She changed the subject; no more personal business.

Sergeyevna viewed my departure not as a loss but an opportunity. Watching the movers haul my furniture and clothing boxes down the stairwell, she was unable to suppress her feverish greed.

"Mr. Perkins! You always said you owned nothing valuable! . . . Ooh, that lamp! You're taking that lamp? And those Ashkhabad rugs, they are such treasures, those rugs!" She scrutinized each load carefully, checking if I "really" wanted to send such items back to America, or to my next assignment. She proposed a better home for them—her own. Sergeyevna supplemented her small pension by purchasing household goods from departing foreigners, and then selling them on the black market.

"I have plenty to offer—" One afternoon, as the last parade of boxes was marched down the stairs, she turned the hem of her dress inside out, and pulled a fist-thick wad of 100-ruble notes from a pocket sewn deep inside her smock.

"Maybe you would prefer gold instead?" she whispered.

Against my better judgment, I sold her an armload of fraying clothes in return for cash to pay some customs fees. "Perfectly legal, perfectly legal," she chattered, counting out hundred-ruble notes into my palm inside her pork larder. "Just some private business between friends."

As I slid the last of her bills into my wallet, she seized my arm. I froze. Was she making a citizen's arrest? She squeezed harder.

"Give your Americans warm greetings from the Russian people," she said, staring deeply into my eyes. "Tell them we want peace."

"Fine. I'll tell them." I tried to release myself from her clamplike grip. She held on.

"I mean it. We've seen war. We don't want it. Tell them that."

"I will. I promise."

"Good." She relaxed her grip, and escorted me into the afternoon sunlight. "And next time you come, take one of our nice Russian girls away with you."

After sleeping late on our last full day in Moscow, Susan and I sortied onto the Arbat to photograph each other, "for the memory," as the Russians say. As I posed Susan in the middle of Kropotkin Square, I noticed a kerchiefed old country woman crossing herself fervently, mechanically, on a parapet overlooking the city's main swimming pool. Why? Susan knew the answer from her reading. The pool lay in the foundation of what had been the largest cathedral in Moscow, Christ Savior, built in the nineteenth century and razed by Soviet power. We were in the presence of one of Moscow's holy shrines: the central swimming pool.

"You're going to miss it, aren't you?" Susan had caught me daydreaming in front of the statue of Kropotkin, wondering how the old anarchist would feel, having been resurrected as a subway stop. I also remembered that this was one of the last places I had seen Natasha before her trip to the North.

"Me?" I recovered quickly. "Yes. By all means, yes." I thought for a moment. "Best time of my life, really."

Susan thrust her hands down the front pockets of my jeans. "For me too."

"Here, in awful Russia?"

"Here, in awful Russia."

"Forgotten birthday and all?"

"Forgotten birthday and all." She stood on my toes. "You should be flattered."

"I am. I am." I kissed her nose. "We can come back."

"Maybe some day." Susan locked her wrists behind my back, and squeezed the breath out of me. "Russian bear hug." She smiled. "Let's go to dinner."

My last evening in Russia, Andrei still couldn't light the samovar. We started jamming the kindling down its thin pewter throat in the late afternoon, but now at sunset the water hadn't yet boiled.

"What kind of Russian are you?" I asked, as he knelt on the ground, trying to blow life into the gray embers. "You probably can't even dance on your heels."

Andrei and I had been swimming, and I was flapping our wet towels above the samovar's stovepipe, lifting shapeless blobs of smoke up to the roof of pines. I was practicing smoke signals learned in Boy Scouts—two long puffs for "enemy," two longs and a short for "friend." Even with no wind, my unformed smoke clouds blotched and disappeared.

Andrei laughed at my failure. "What kind of an American are you?" he asked. "I'll bet you can't even rob a bank."

I walked inside the dacha to change out of my swimsuit, and caught sight of Susan helping Lilya and grandmother Aya in the kitchen, ferrying plate after plate of my favorite appetizers outside to the jiggly trestle table. I heard Aya practicing the few words of

English she had gleaned from her years of movie idolatry, to Susan's giggling delight.

I was standing alone in front of the window where Andrei's crib had been mounted during the war, watching the garden darken, and the plants turn to shadows in the night. I watched the women through the dusty pane, turning opaque in the fading light. Were they working, or walking, more slowly than usual? I wanted the moments to stretch out, and time to slow down.

From the front of the house, I heard the broken sputter of a Zaporozhets. Vera and Valera had arrived from the city, with Andrei's mother Liza.

As I stepped outside, Susan ambushed me from behind the door, and pinned me against the flimsy dacha wall while Andrei and Lilya greeted the guests. "This place is *gorgeous*! I can see why you forgot my birthday." She bumped her forehead against my chest for emphasis. "Let's stay!"

"You're moving in the wrong direction, Susan. We're leaving, remember?" I stared again at the shadowy forest, and the ramshackle dacha with its walls akimbo, and its hastily patched roof. "It's funny, we don't have places like this in America. We're too dignified, or something. How are the people treating you?"

"They're fun. That old woman's positively bonkers! She's very high on the royal family, especially Charles and Diana. She thinks I should convince them to visit Russia!"

"Maybe you should."

"Your other friend's quite nice, too. What's her name?"

"Lilya."

"Right. She said I was very thin, which I took as a compliment."

"It's not. It means they want to feed you, to fatten you up."

268

Susan cupped her hands under her ample backside. "Do you think I'm thin?"

"I think you're just right."

"Do you love me?"

"I do."

Susan squeezed herself up against me.

"Is that another Russian bear hug?"

She nodded her head. She was crying, quietly, wiping her eyes against my shirtsleeve. "I hope this isn't all over tonight."

I kissed her head, and kneaded my fingers along the nape of her neck. "I don't think it will be."

A few moments later, I led Susan over to the dinner table, and introduced her to Liza, Valera, and Vera.

Ever the romantic, Aya disdained my characterization of Susan as a "friend." "She's not your 'friend,' as you call it," she corrected. "Andrei is a friend. This beautiful girl is your sweetheart, your . . . fiancée."

I glared at Susan, who shrugged her shoulders helplessly: I told you the woman was bonkers.

"And what is Susan doing here, in Moscow?" Vera asked.

"She works at the British Embassy," I replied, trying to tack on an unthreatening job description. "She's a clerk."

Vera gazed coolly at Susan, and raised her eyebrows ever so slightly. Her skepticism was palpable, if unvoiced. While she didn't exactly look like Mata Hari, Susan certainly didn't resemble a clerk.

Andrei directed us to our places, and, fueled by the appetizers and healthy doses of wine and vodka, the dinner party found its momentum. For the first half hour, conversation was quick and tangential. The grandmothers were still complaining, or had begun a new cycle of complaining, that foreigners had snapped up all the season tickets to the Conservatory.

"You didn't miss many concerts last season," Andrei observed drily.

"Well, of course we had some help from Nina Semyonovna in the ticket office," Liza retorted. "But Lord knows she won't be there forever."

Between courses, Andrei presented me with a small bottle of *spirt* that Martinov had sent through the mails, with a farewell note. "In memory of our days at Z——. Please don't forget us."

"I don't think there's much danger of that," Andrei said, filling my shot glass with the village alcohol.

Susan nudged me. "What was that all about?"

I was on the verge of telling her about our ski trip in the wilderness, when I remembered that I had lied to her about my plans. Best to unpack that baggage in a different setting. "Oh, it's a present from some guy we met." Quick thinking, Nick, and under the influence of alcohol to boot. It occurred to me that I held my liquor considerably better than I had when I arrived. Would I need this skill outside the USSR?

Next, Valera stood up slowly from his low bench, until his head and shoulders rose into the dark above the standup lamp. His shirt buttons gleamed in the light.

"The bath men have authorized me to present this farewell gift, to the only American who's been to heaven and back." He leaned across the table, and gave me a floppy gray felt bath hat, the head covering of Russia's professional leisure class. I had officially joined the ranks of the men who knew how to enjoy life.

I laughed. "I was expecting Dumas, volume three."

"We save Dumas for our high-level contacts," Valera said. "Besides, Dumas you can get in your Woolworth's or Sears. You'll never find a hat like this." A rush of laughter and conversation broke over the table.

Under cover of the general exchange, I asked Valera if he remembered Pavlovich, the samovar who had sold him spare parts?

"Good God! How do you know *him*?"

Andrei grinned. "We showed this guy everything."

Valera shook his head. "I remember his brother. A nice boy, younger than I. He was cocky, you know. Always showing off things, always standing up to people. He talked about his older brother. He had wanted to row, too, but their sports club had only one boat, there weren't enough seats for everyone."

I told him the story of Berezhov, who had returned to Norilsk. He shook his head again. "The most improbable live, the rest die," he mused. "There's no explaining who's doing the choosing." He breathed deeply, swelling his chest, then coughed. "I don't know why I'm here." His wife glared from the far end of the table.

Aya too was eavesdropping, and chided us for being so glum. "Come on, you two, cheer up! Nick is taking his sweetheart home! Be happy!" She spoke in the spirit of a Russian funeral, a celebration for those left behind.

Aya was still bubbly, and inquisitive. She leaned across the table, training her immobile wall eye on me like a camera lens. "So tell me—first you will arrive at Kennedy Airport, once called La Guardia. Then— how, by helicopter?—to Lincoln Center, next to the Empire State Building, right? *Ooooooh!* I would *love* to see New York! Then, of course, take the train to Hollywood."

"That's in California, and the cross-country trains hardly run anymore." Somehow I couldn't see Aya taking the red-eye from Los Angeles with the movie crowd. . . .

"Oh, forget it then." Aya switched to English, and turned to Susan. "You go to London?"

"Paris."

"Paris! You see airport where Lindbergh landed!

Champs-Elysées! Bebbies! Good city for bebbies!" she leaned across the table to poke my arm.

Susan lowered her voice. "Should I tell her you're thinking of not joining me, Nick?"

I kicked Susan under the table. "Now might not be the time."

Grandmother Liza had been scowling throughout the meal, and had especially bristled at the mention of things American. She had built a bridge to Vera, anchored on their shared distrust of foreigners. After the first course, I smiled at Liza. She frowned back, and resumed whispering in Vera's ear. I had imagined a surprise reconciliation between us, perhaps a sneak attack to make her admit not *all* Americans were awful. It wasn't going to happen. I let Aya take my first plate off to the kitchen.

Lilya carried out the main course, steaming in a deep tureen—spearmint chicken, Georgian style. "Better than the Hotel Peking," Andrei said.

I chewed agreement. "How did it all begin? How did you end up at my table?"

"The place was full. Also, Lilya whispered to me that you looked Polish. She thought you might be interesting." Through the steam of the serving dish, Lilya winked.

"I must have been a disappointment."

"Not to me," Andrei replied. "I don't like Poles."

"You asked me some silly question . . ."

"I inquired as to why you weren't drinking vodka with us."

"That's right . . . You were having attitude problems, I remember. Something about the scientific review board . . ."

"So were you, as I recall. Something about Moscow, and the Russians . . ."

"All solved, I hope?" We both smiled.

"You turned down my vodka then."

"I was much younger."

He filled my glass. "To a short year." We touched glasses.

"To a good year," I answered. "Let's hope for another one."

"With pleasure. We'll always be here." He smiled and we drank.

Valera told some jokes, which Andrei tried to translate for Susan. I tore my fork across the wet chicken, intermittently, and occasionally rubbed my fingers against the soft felt of the bath hat, "in the desultory spirit of my abandonment"—words I had used to describe Sharon almost a year ago. But I wasn't the one being abandoned. Yet again, I was doing the abandoning.

Andrei proposed several traditional toasts: to our parents, to our children (Susan and I got a big wink from Aya on that one), to our next meeting. It didn't seem likely. The Russians had been treating me preciously, certain that I would never reappear. I suddenly felt very American, spoiled by the instant replay, very wrong in my assumption that experience can be repeated at will. My hosts knew what Susan had divined many weeks ago, when she first began reaching out to keep hold of me—we would never be here again.

Lilya had been observing me for a year now, and tonight. During a silence, she leaned toward me and said, loud enough for everyone to hear: "So now what do you think of us? What will you tell your friends about us Russians?"

Vera and Liza broke off talking. I saw Valera, sad and interested, raise his eyes. Aya's eyelid was flapping involuntarily.

"I'm just a tourist," I pleaded. I didn't want to tell the truth.

"We're all just tourists," Andrei said. "But answer the question."

I hesitated between the long answer and the short answer. "I think you're wonderful. I love you—" I couldn't finish the sentence. I burst into tears.

"There, there . . ." Aya stroked my hair.

Andrei put his arm around me. "These Americans— so emotional!" I smiled, and wiped my cheeks. No one made me feel ashamed. I had answered the question.

Some things happen of themselves. The generator switched off at midnight. Lilya mustered a few candles, but the guests from Moscow were already preparing to leave. I remember shaking Valera's hand, twice as large as mine, and all the others. I was worn out, and drunk. Susan was woozy, enraptured with both the novelty and the finality of her first evening among Russians. Andrei and Lilya escorted us to the cot on the veranda, and said goodnight.

"Tomorrow night you'll be waking up where?" Lilya asked.

"We're flying to Germany, and then traveling to different places."

"Is that our Germany, or your Germany?" she asked.

"It's ours," I replied.

"Ah, of course." She stroked my forehead, and kissed Susan on the cheek. "Sleep tight." Andrei waved good night from the door of the living room.

Susan and I slipped out of our clothes, and bumped hips for several minutes in the tiny cot, warring for territory.

"Move over."

"*You* move over!"

"You're twice as big as me."

"Here." I lifted Susan by the hips, and set her down lengthwise, with her back perpendicular to the wall. She flopped down on top of me, laughing hysterically.

"*Susan.* I want to go to sleep."

"So do I." She began nibbling my neck, and running her hands up my thighs. I wish I could remember what happened next, but I don't. I passed out.

We breakfasted at seven, to be at the airport by ten. Lilya seemed cool working the toaster. We were all dulled from the night before. Aya had stayed the night to help clean up, and now was snoring loudly, a heavy bundled heap lying across the room. Whispering, Lilya asked me if I had the "necessary things." She had no idea what they might be, and stared for over a minute at my blue and yellow Lufthansa ticket folder, my United States passport, and my olive green exit visa.

"You look younger," was her comment on my passport photo. She turned the exit visa over in her fingers, gingerly. "Aron's was pink."

"Aron couldn't come back," Andrei said. "Nick is in a different category."

"Oh." She slipped the papers back in my passport. "If we left, we'd have to come back. Still another category."

I gathered up the documents and worked my arms into my jacket.

"Ahhh, you're going . . ." she draped her arms around our necks, embracing Susan and me together. "Good health to you both. Happiness. Bring your children to visit."

Andrei pulled us apart. "Let them get married first."

Lilya kissed us each one last time, then sat us down on the dacha steps. The four of us sat in silence, listening to Aya's wheezy breathing inside. By custom, we were sitting for the road.

"Now you can go." Lilya touched our backs, pushing

us toward the car. She waved goodbye once, and then walked inside the house.

The drive took us through the flat countryside back toward Moscow's beltway, a quarter turn around, then out to the international airport. I asked to be remembered to Andrei's children, to Martinov, and to Olga and Natasha, when he saw them again. He nodded at each name. "Find Aron," he said. "I think you'd both like to meet each other."

I gazed at the last of the landscape gliding by. We snaked between satellite cities of apartment complexes planted at the side of a duck pond, or at the edge of a pine forest. More than once, just behind the box towers of modern living, I saw a brown *izba* huddled low to the ground, and old women in white kerchiefs sowing feed for pigs. We drove past a line of ten men scything hay on the roadside, rocking their shoulders with the thick blades, swinging slowly through time. Andrei had always told me about the city encroaching on the country. But the city invaded impotently. The country prevailed.

Zazie was incongruous, stuttering up the swooping concrete entrance ramp of Sheremetyevo International Airport, designed by West Germans for Mercedeses, BMWs, or the fat Chaikas of the Soviet elite. Andrei had never been here before. He parked the car, and escorted us into the gleaming terminal, an angular panorama of plate glass set in a frame of dark brown steel. Inside, he stared at the automated departure board, also purchased from the Germans.

He broke off his gaze, and handed me my flight bag. "Frankfurt. I'd like to go to Frankfurt."

"Well, we're going to Frankfurt. . . ."

"Oh, then you go instead." He smiled. "As long as some of us get to go."

We embraced, and I wept a second time.

"Good luck. Good health." Andrei embraced Susan, and pointed us in the direction of the customs area. He left the terminal.

The gray-suited customs inspector idly poked at my personal effects, mumbling some questions about gold, silver, and icons. I had none. In my canvas bag, he found my address book, where I had camouflaged the names and addresses of my Russian friends in a code long since forgotten. He thumbed a few of the pages.

"Have many friends in Moscow?"

"Not really."

"Too bad." He tossed the address book back in the bag, and marked my bags with a piece of chalk. "Russians are very friendly people. You missed a good opportunity."

25 / Home

The Frankfurt Airport shopping arcade was a cathedral devoted to the worship of things. Susan and I walked agog past store after store jammed with jewelry, crystal, liquors, television sets, records, new books, exotic foods, and of course sex videos, sex manuals, and sex aids. How had we survived the year without things? The culture shock was acute; after eleven months of access to almost nothing, suddenly I had access to almost everything. Should I buy a digital watch with a calendar memory function, or a scientific calculating chip? Or Bob Dylan's new double album—on compact disc, tape, or record? Or a dress for Susan—Dior, Cardin, or Marimekko? They all had stores here, competing for our trade. My Moscow instincts raged inside me; where was the watch store, with ten-ruble movements imported from India? Where was the dress store, which seldom stocked anything worth wearing? Where were the lines? Where was a salesclerk to bribe? I had no idea where to begin.

In the end, it didn't matter. As I wandered groggily through the most plentifully stocked delicatessen I had ever seen—I was on the verge of buying some jellied quail's eggs—Susan heard my flight being announced over the loudspeaker.

"It's boarding!" she shrieked, pressing herself against me in a farewell kiss. Her arms were loaded with Hungarian pepper sausage. The bitter, spicy fragrance clinging to my tie was my only souvenir of our ten months together.

The New York flight repatriated me, fast. My seat was on the cusp of two sections, so I could watch two different movies at once, without sound. In the near parlor, Clint Eastwood pressed his .38 Magnum to victims' heads with the predictability of a glockenspiel hammering out the quarter hour. I imagined the script: "One move and this room'll look like Jackson Pollock's studio."

Thirty rows forward in the bulging belly of the 747, I discerned the key ingredients of an English romance: full-breasted Empire gowns, sword fights, Michael York. After fifteen minutes of musketeering, a small phalanx of passengers, carrying their headsets like catheters, migrated to the back of the plane to watch the gun movie. A fat man in a swollen polo shirt settled in the empty seat next to me. On the screen, Clint was waving his Magnum again, threatening to turn the room into an early de Kooning. My seatmate sighed contentedly. "Go Clint, go. This is more like it." I was watching our magic at work.

On the ground at Kennedy, the customs officer was berating the Yankees. "What's Steinbrenner's prahblum?" he asked me, glancing at my declaration. "All that dough, and no team. Whereya bin, mistah? Ruh-sha! Ruh-sha? Say! Don't tell me yah're bringin' back those Cyuban cihgahzz?"

"I don't smoke."

"That doesn't mattah, everybody brings 'em back. Say—open this wahn, willya—whatzit like ovah theyah?"

I thought for a moment, but by the time I had an

answer for him, he had zipped up my bag, thrust my declaration back in my hand, and plunged into the next passenger's luggage. "Yah hid those cihgahzz too good for me, pal. Have a nice day."

What looked new in America? Nothing much. Some advertising campaigns had changed, some new products had appeared, mostly to save time on one operation that could be wasted on another. The trend seemed propitious—soon we wouldn't be doing anything at all. Driving from Kennedy to Manhattan, I saw the graveyard Aron had mentioned in one of his first letters. To me, it looked spacious, not confining as he had described it. Maybe he didn't appreciate the convenience of being near the highway.

The magazine lodged me in the Hotel Renwick, a few blocks north of our Rockefeller Center offices. I wished some of the new owners' wealth had been applied to my lodging account. The Renwick's management must have reclaimed my room from the auxiliary elevator shaft, and subdivided the space two more times to maximize revenues per square foot. The building's only functioning elevator roared past the headboard of my foldout bed all night. I dreamed I had been assigned to cover 1300 successive Thor-Delta rocket blast-offs, from a front-row seat on the launching pad. Escape was futile—I couldn't open the door to the corridor while the bed was extended. I suffered, wallowed in self-pity, and occasionally slept.

At the office, Jonas greeted me heartily as "Parkinson," and promised to schedule a "sit down" to discuss my fate. My former cubicle had been interior-decorated out of existence—maybe they had finally found a computer to edit letters and write captions—so I sat at the far end of the writers' corridor, in a bare office reserved for the recently hired, or the recently fired.

While I waited for Jonas's schedule to "free up," I had nothing to do, other than hold court for the steady procession of staffers who slouched against my doorjamb to inquire about Russia. Fully half of them treated me like a kidnap victim released from a year-long ordeal, asking questions in a hushed tone of voice, lest the memories prove painful. Did they feed you? Did they let you go to the bathroom? Could you write letters home?

Friends who knew me better repeated the customs officer's question: "What's it like over there?" I tried to describe the open-ended hospitality of Andrei and his circle, and explain my affection for Boris and Ekaterina Sergeyevna, the watchers whom I secretly missed. But my message never got through. Eyes wandered, hands fidgeted, my workmates passed up a second cup of coffee to go back to work. I felt as if I had just returned from an interesting vacation. No one cares where you've been.

One of my first days back, I telephoned Sharon at her office. She was in a meeting, a secretary informed me; could I call back? Fifteen minutes later, I caught her.

"Nick! What a surprise!"

"I'm back."

"Great! I hope we can get together." Her voice had new bounce, like a hairdo.

"Well, I'm free."

"This week is bad for me. Jimmy's parents are in town. . . ."

"Oh, I see."

"Did I tell you we're engaged? Isn't that great?"

"Sure. When are you getting married?"

"Maybe next spring. Jimmy wants to wait."

Still no satisfaction for Mrs. Sherwin, I thought. Everyone wants to wait.

Sharon took pity on me, and let herself be cajoled into lunch.

We met halfway between our offices, near Grand Central. I hardly recognized her, she blended so well with the hurtling crowd of noontime New Yorkers, fleetly gliding from the best jobs to the best stores, in the best company. But Sharon had barely changed— she still dressed artfully, draping clothes around her dark, slender beauty, and her perfectly styled hair still fell like a slash of black curtain across her forehead and face. But until she detached herself from the self-directed stream of midtown Manhattanites, and pecked me coolly on the cheek, I didn't recognize her at all.

I was the one who had changed. I must have been like her once, and shared her brisk sense of dutiful socializing sandwiched between a morning and afternoon of telephone conversations. In Moscow, I had been sandwiching dutiful work binges in between mornings and afternoons of visiting with friends.

We walked to a newly opened fast-soup restaurant, which had taken the "fast" concept about as far as it could go. After ten minutes of wetting our lips on overpriced and under-apportioned bowls of chowder, our allotted time was up. The owners needed six or seven seatings to "make the nut," as the waitress explained when she urged us for the third time to get the hell out.

We had frittered away most of our meeting discussing Sharon and Jimmy, who were advancing nicely, thank you. They were living together, in an East Side co-op financed by his father's bank. Sharon boasted of a good "phone relationship" with Jimmy's mother, who invited her would-be daughter-in-law to lunch when she visited the city. To plot wedding dates, I imagined. I pitied Jimmy. There but for the grace of God go I.

Sharon was faring well, and wanted me to know it.

What better revenge, than to prove how skillfully she had turned my departure to her benefit? Over coffee, she turned her attention to me. Unlike my colleagues, she didn't ask what Moscow was like. She wanted to know what it was *really* like. Was that a different question? I treated it differently, scratching my head for effect.

"It's hard to describe. I felt more *intimate* with people there . . ."

"Nick, this isn't some kind of come-on, is it?"

"No, really." I realized how rarely she and I had serious talks. "Friends are more important there, I think."

She straightened her hair, and looked at her watch. "Of course, they don't have anything else, do they?"

"But—" involuntarily, I was eavesdropping on four conversations at neighboring tables, none more than a foot and a half away. Real estate, orgasm, bracket creep, and orgasm, moving counterclockwise. But—what else matters?

"Did you meet someone?"

"Sure, I met a lot of people."

"I mean, someone, you know . . ."

"Well, maybe. I'm not sure yet. You should have come to visit."

She wrinkled her nose, and stole a second glance at her watch. "I don't think so. It doesn't sound like my kind of place."

This time the dark-suited restaurant manager approached us, with two famished clients in tow. Just as he flexed his tarantula smile, we rose to leave.

Out on the street, we walked a few blocks in the comforting din of car horns and jackhammers. We half-pursued our restaurant conversation, though each time one of us tried to finish a sentence, it was lost in the gong of a sidewalk elevator, or the first flashing of "Don't Walk."

In front of her skyscraper, I kissed her on the cheek. "I'm happy to see you." I waved my hands, to disperse the noise. "The whole Russia thing—it's hard to explain."

She smiled and walked toward the revolving doors. "Good luck with Jimmy!" I shouted. Had she heard me? She was gone.

But was it *really* hard to explain? I don't think so. Like a good book, my memories were hard to put down. One morning I stared out my hotel window to see the sun hanging low in the gray smog over Brooklyn, and I thought of Z——, where the sun pushed, but never broke through, hinted but never shone. The old widows were probably still gossiping about Natasha's dark, foreign beauty, which shot across their lives like a black comet. While she slopped plaster in the Solovki, the village women were making her a saint.

My mother's Washington apartment was dimly lit with low-watt bulbs. Thick velvet lampshades colluded with the dusky rugs and wall hangings to smother the light. The furnishings reminded me of the faint illumination of Andrei's kitchen, or the screened veranda in the country, where his voice, and the hum of nature, lulled me to sleep. I was staring into the unlit fireplace, ignoring my mother and the evening news.

"You've become so serious," my mother said, and it wasn't a compliment.

I started. "Sorry, I was just daydreaming."

"Maybe it's something in their water. You seem so heavy, like those awful novels of theirs." I patted my waistline. "Not there, stupid. *Here.*" She pressed a finger against her head.

"Are you happy to be back, at least?"

I twisted in my chair. "I guess."

"Sounds like you turned into a regular Commie over there."

I noticed a small pamphlet on the cocktail table next to my chair, *The Brahmacharya and You*.

"What's this?" Inside, I found pictures of Gandhi, and a miniature reproduction of a *Playboy* centerfold.

"It's the Way of Chastity. Gandhi did it."

"You mean when he diddled those little girls?"

"They were big girls and he didn't diddle them, to use your disgusting and disrespectful phrase." No one could say my mother didn't have a perfect sense of timing: "Have you seen your friend Sharon?"

"Mom—what's the point of this?" I was still flapping the pamphlet.

"It teaches you to live without desire."

"Do you have desire?"

"Nick, there are some questions you don't ask even your mother. So how's Sharon?"

"Practicing chastity with somebody else. Have you seen Dad lately?"

"Nick, what do you mean?"

"When I phoned you last year you were seeing him on video from outer space, or something."

"Oh, that. No, I resigned from the group."

"I see."

She walked to the kitchen to remove our frozen pizzas from the oven. "Didn't you meet any nice girls in Russia?" Her voice clanged off the shiny cabinets and appliances. "I thought they all wanted to marry Americans to get out."

In her next life, I told her, she could work as a stool pigeon in the foreigners' compound on Kutuzov Prospect.

Back in New York, his schedule clear, Jonas was ebullient. Like a politician shilling for votes, he charged across his enlarged office to pump my hands as I stepped through his door.

"Hel-*lo*! Superb! Fantastic! I'm so glad you've come!" As a mate for his new desk—a gull-winged power model that resembled the flight deck of an aircraft carrier—he had added a small meeting area, with two gleaming Eames chairs and an overstuffed black leather sofa, to his empire. He plopped me into the sofa, and lowered himself into one of the chairs, pulling his half-frames down his nose to size me up.

"You look great, just great!"

"Thank you, thank you." It seemed appropriate to say everything twice.

"Things are just hopping here!" He surveyed his refurbished quarters with a self-satisfied grin. "Wonderful! The new magazine is sensational! The owners couldn't be more pleased."

Jonas had been shaking the money tree. Not only had his personal preserve expanded, but I noticed that the pins stuck in the map over his desk had multiplied several times since my last visit. The magazine now had enough correspondents in place to cover stories from Alaska to Zanzibar. Respectability was creeping up on us like a skin disease.

"So, what can I do for you?" In the flush of success, Jonas had become a true executive, armed with a one-size-fits-all set of pleasantries for any occasion. For a brief moment, I panicked—doesn't he even know why I'm here? Then I saw him pull a small index card from his breast pocket, and run his thumb down a series of typewritten entries. Simultaneously, he glanced at his watch.

"Perkins! Aha! Yes, indeed. Our man in Moscow . . .

how are *you*?" He focused his attention on me with renewed interest.

Someone had to take charge of this conversation, or
we'd end up introducing ourselves for the next half
hour.

"Jonas, I'm fine. And by the way, you look good, too.
And I'm glad the magazine is thriving."

Jonas beamed.

"We're here to talk about my next assignment. I've
just spent a year in Moscow, at the end of which you
promised me a job in Western Europe. I'd like to go to
Paris."

Jonas hoisted his eyebrows up his leathery forehead.
"Paris. Hmm. Lovely city." He clasped his hands
around his knee, and leaned forward. "What's Moscow
like?"

"It's big, sort of nondescript. It's the capital of Russia."

"Yes, Perkins, even editors know things like that. I've
always been curious, what are the people like? Do they
walk around with their faces all scrunched up like cab-
bages, waiting for World War Three, or are they having a good time of it?"

"Well, they're very friendly, really. They know how
to enjoy life."

"Hmm. I loved your work, by the way. We always
gave it good play, as you can tell. Good stuff, nice on
the street feel." I blushed and shuffled my feet, promising myself to either buy or write a book called *How to
Take a Compliment.*

Jonas glanced out his window, grinning. "I especially
liked the New Discipline, with everyone having to come
to work on time. Sounds awful . . . like New York. Tell
me, one thing I never really understood—what was the
Old Discipline?"

I explained as best I could, about the bathhouses,

and the lackadaisical work habits, and the drunks screaming up at God, hurling empty bottles into the Moscow River. I told him about long lunches, not just on Friday, but every day, and people who traveled into the city from their dachas twice a month, to collect their paychecks.

"Dachas! Yes! That was a great story you wrote." I had sent in a sort of photo essay on dacha life, illustrated with pictures of Lilya tending her vegetable garden, of the tiny beach next to the river, and of the train platform on Monday morning, jammed with Muscovites lugging their produce back into the city.

Jonas had indeed given the story good "play." After reading the article, my mother had written me a letter: "Why in heaven's name don't they buy their food in stores, like normal people?"

"Does everyone have a dacha?" Jonas asked.

"Does everyone have a house in the Hamptons?"

He laughed. "Jesus, I hope not, or mine'll be worth a lot less."

I tried to explain who had dachas, and who didn't. We concluded that more Russians had dachas than New Yorkers had places in the Hamptons, but there was no cause for envy, as the dachas were smaller, by a factor of about ten. Land was cheaper by a factor of about ten, but I left that part out, lest Jonas start a migration from East Hampton to the USSR.

"Could you have friends? I mean, with all the guards around, watching where you went?"

"Yes, I could. They really had to want to be your friends, though." I remembered the words of the customs woman when I first arrived in Moscow: There could be unpleasantness.

"Did you make friends?"

"Yes."

"That's great. What an unusual opportunity. It

showed up in your stuff. Reading your articles, I almost thought that you were—dare I say it?—happy."

I laughed, and avoided his eyes. "Dare I say it, I think I was."

"And you went kicking and screaming, as I recall."

"True enough." The memory of Berezhov, who so enjoyed life in Norilsk, flashed across my mind. Was Jonas setting me up to go back? Would I go?

"And now you want to go to Paris?"

"That's right."

"Back to civilization—punko-video sex, snuff movies, television running like a sewer through your living room—"

"—I want it all. Quiet evenings next to the Seine, onion soup at Les Halles, a studio apartment in Montmartre."

"You're in the wrong century, Nick. I was in Paris last month. The Seine stinks, Les Halles was torn down about ten years ago, and with the salary we're paying you, you'll be living out by the airport."

Was this the double cross Susan and I had feared? "Jonas, this is no kidding. I want to go."

He waved his index finger over me like a wand. "Done. Congratulations. We're adding a slot there, and it's yours. You deserve it." He mulled for a moment. "Maybe you can light a fire under those guys. They haven't produced much, short of restaurant reviews. They seem to be into the *old* discipline over there."

We stared at each other blankly, realizing the conversation was over, with neither of us anxious to leave.

Jonas rose slowly from his chair. "If you ever want to go back . . ."

I glided through the deep pile carpet towards the door. "Maybe some day." I shook his hand. "Right now I have some unfinished business in Paris."

*　*　*

The next day, Friday, I arrived at work to find a postcard on my desk. As a staffer in limbo, I assumed the mail room had made one of its routine mistakes, until I saw the picture—ten Frou-Frou girls hiding behind yellow ostrich feathers at the Crazy Horse Saloon. Flipping the card over, I recognized the neatly manicured handwriting that had graced many a note left on my Moscow doorstep. Susan had not fallen through the ice.

Dearest Nick,

Paris is as advertised: divine. I've found a charming little flat in the 19th, right next to the Gare de Lyon. No militiamen, no old hens squatting in my stairwell, and no *odeur de* salted pork fat smelling up the entryway. I'm turning down visas at the slightest whiff of anything Communist—such as a fondness for dacha living—and having a whale of a time. Capitalism is indeed rotting, but the fragrance is most sweet indeed. Keeping the frogs' legs warm—

Love, Susan

She and Jonas had apparently visited different cities. Maybe Paris wouldn't be so hellish after all.

26 / *Epilogue*

Aron's increasing affluence was moving him farther
from New York City. Four years after his arrival, he
had landed in New Paltz, as half-owner of an entryway
in a row of brown brick houses, chocolate-colored, but
not chocolate-smelling like Andrei's childhood.

What was I expecting when I crossed the threshold
of his apartment that Saturday morning? All my fantasies were at work. I searched for signs of Russia in
exile—the eight-foot-tall blue oven, the closet-sized
kitchen, the fresh smell of foliage blowing through the
screen from the veranda. Or worse, would I find a gas
fire flickering between cast-iron logs, and "Dallas" re-
runs blaring on the videotape machine? Real symbols
are so much smaller, the size of the tiny aspirin bottle
full of dusty soil, his farewell gift from his coworkers,
set on the center of the mantelpiece.

"Come in." Aron ignored my hand until I had
passed through the door. He pointed to the threshold.
"Bad luck."

"Nick Perkins. I've heard a lot about you."

He laughed and turned away to lead me into his sitting room. Except for the tiny icon of soil—and you
had to have entered pretty early in his story to recognize that—he had arranged the room, and his person,

to give no clues. The furniture set was fresh out of a discount showroom, perhaps with the paintings on the wall thrown in. And Aron dressed neutrally, this Saturday in gray polyester slacks and a stiff-collared white shirt, left over from work.

Broad-shouldered and flat-stomached, he still looked as healthy as a collective-farm manager. His jet black hair was combed, not styled. He had even brushed the waves out of his Russian accent. Aron had become an American fast.

"Can I get you a beer? Lena and Samuel should be back shortly."

I followed him into his kitchen, and unpacked a small plastic bag of gifts from Andrei and Lilya: some jars of honey from the dacha market, an enamel tray, and a few children's books. Aron chuckled as I laid the presents down on the Formica counter.

"They're too embarrassed to send anything more, because they think we have it all, here in America."

As we sank back into facing easy chairs in the living room, Aron asked about the gifts he had sent with Richard. Anya had reaped a harvest of demerits after planting a sticky spider in her school's "Lenin Corner." Lilya thanked him for the panty hose, and Natalya was the belle of Liebknecht Street, preening in her "Kiss Me, I'm Russian" T-shirt.

"Good, good. From here we never know what to send because we assume they have nothing. How absurd it all is."

He drained half his beer glass in a swallow. "So, Nick. How does it feel to be back?"

"Good and bad. I'm happy to be home, I guess."

"Yes. I imagine that feels nice."

We paused. I asked a question in Russian. "How's your life?"

Aron switched back to English. "It's OK. We have a

new apartment"—he spread his hands—"with all the amenities, as they say in Moscow. Electricity, hot and cold running water."

"Did you pass the CPA exam?"

"Oh, sure. I had to study nights, it was hard on Lena and Samuel. No going out, not much fun. But it got me a raise." He poured himself a new glass. "That was a problem for me in Russia. I was a hard worker. But there was nothing for me to do."

"Is that why you left?"

Aron stared at me sharply. He exuded power, and will—the power to have summoned his wife and son back from the supermarket at just this moment in the conversation.

Aron leapt to the door to relieve Lena of her two shopping bags. Thirteen-year-old Samuel was dangling a box of animal crackers in one hand and a six-pack of diet soda in the other. Lena was short, dark, and pretty, older-looking than Lilya, though she was younger by ten years.

"You must be Nick." Her hand trembled in my grip. "This is Samuel, you can speak Russian to him. He's forgetting it fast."

While the parents prepared lunch in the kitchen, I tried to converse with Samuel, who stuck with monosyllabic English. School was OK, America was OK, mom was OK. I switched back into Russian for a last question.

"What do you remember best about Moscow?"

He glared. "I don't remember anything." This family sidestepped tough questions like a professional chorus line. Lena and Aron entered the living room, carrying trays of beer, cold cuts, and sandwich fixings.

"Have you been practicing your Russian?" Lena asked too sweetly of Samuel, who ran away to his room.

We settled in over the trays, piling up fat sandwiches. "So how is Moscow now?" Lena asked as if I had just come from the funeral of an unlamented relative. How did he look?

"Well, you know . . ."

"Yes, I'm sure little has changed." Was this the woman who wept twelve hours a day in the Ostia transit camp? Somewhere she had picked up a lacquer finish, hard enough to knock on. "Any butter in the stores?"

"No."

She grunted, glancing sideways at Aron. "We eat butter here, every day."

Aron winced. "Lena, Nick is an American. He knows about butter." She continued eating, unperturbed.

Aron inquired about Andrei and Lilya, who hadn't written in six months. I talked about our trip to Martinov, the summer at the dacha, the baths.

"It sounds like he took you under his wing."

"Yes, very much so."

"You're lucky."

Lena rejoined the conversation, gulping down a mouthful of roast beef. "I'm surprised they can entertain at all, in that tiny apartment of theirs."

"Honey, we ate there ourselves."

"But it was always so cramped. We could fit an army in here." She gestured toward the high ceilings, and a corridor full of unused bedrooms.

I tried to change the subject. Was Lena still working? "Not really. Aron makes enough for the two of us now. I—we—are thinking of having another child. To have a real American in the family."

"I thought Samuel was becoming an American."

"He doesn't know what he is," Aron said. "He won't speak Russian with us, but his teachers say he bursts into Russian sometimes at school. He makes good friends, then demands they speak Russian with him. If they don't, he runs home and cries."

"He pretends not to be interested, but he's already made off with those books you left on the kitchen counter," Lena added. "As if we wouldn't notice."

I had brought a few snapshots of Andrei and Lilya, taken during a shopping expedition on the Arbat. Aron hunched over the coffee table, while Lena watched coolly from her chair.

"There's the Gogol statue, and the boulevards . . . he's lost some hair, hasn't he?" Aron was pointing to a picture of Andrei and me, taken by Lilya, in front of the Hunter store near the Garden Ring. "What were you buying there? Night crawlers?"

"Actually, we were next door, at the Prague restaurant, buying some roast beef at the delivery entrance. Lilya knows one of the cooks . . ."

"No meat in the stores, of course," Lena mumbled.

Aron squinted closer. "What are those bulldozers in the background? Is there some construction going on?"

I explained that the defense ministry was excavating the Arbat to lay communications lines for their new staff building across from the Kremlin. Once that was finished, there was a plan to straighten the loping S-curve of the Arbat into a pedestrian shopping mall.

"Good God! That's just like here! It'll be hard to sing poignant ballads about a shopping mall, won't it?"

He grinned, and pointed his fingernail to a narrow sliver of storefront at the edge of the photograph. "There's the Knowledge Society cinema, where Andrei and I used to go as children to watch documentaries about Africa, and see the naked women. Next door, right here—" he sighted along his fingernail again—"is the army bookstore. They sold back issues of *Life* magazine, for some reason . . ."

Lena left the room. "She won't be back," Aron explained. "It's hard for her, seeing Russia again."

"And for you?"

He paused to gaze out the window at the lines of apartment houses filing down the street. In front of the buildings, a few trees stood in yellow dirt, where there had once been grass. "For me? When I left, the choice was concrete, you know, freedom versus oppression, opportunity versus, I don't know, going so far and no farther." He stared hard into my face. No, I wouldn't really know.

"Now, it's just abstractions, a question of preferences. The past compared with the present, old friends compared with . . . new acquaintances. Your former self versus your present self. Nostalgia is submission, but living is submissive. I know that's a very un-American thing to say—"

Aron flipped through the Moscow snapshots a second time, and tossed them back on the table.

"There's no difference, you know—you must have seen that in Andrei. He's a Russian. He doesn't care where he is. Out here, we cherish our two favorite illusions, that the future will be better, and the past was always best. You can tear your life apart that way, if you want to."

"But you're a Russian, aren't you?"

"There aren't any Russians outside Russia."

He breathed deeply. Was his message coming across? Again, he searched my face. He wasn't sure. "They're living for the present, that's why we miss them." Aron tossed up his hands, and stood up to see me out.

Behind the building, he walked me past his new white Camaro. On the rear fender, he had pasted a bumper sticker: "Honk If You Want to Go Home with Me".

"My little joke," he laughed. We shook hands, and I walked away toward the train station.